DOWNRIVER

Poison River Series, Book 1

Jennifer M. Lane

DEDICATION

To the bay. To the river. And to the creeks.

CHAPTER ONE

Three generations of the Morris family have worn quite a path on this floor. I never noticed before, even when we pulled the rugs up to beat them, but now that the house is nearly empty, the path stands out. Through the keeping room, past the spot where Father's old chair used to be, and through the dining room, past little scrapes dug into the floor where table legs sat.

One last glance in the kitchen. The calendar is still pinned to the side of the cupboard, stuck in January of 1900. I lost the will to turn the pages as four months of sickness fell on the house and people streamed through to offer up their pity. Neighbors. Friends. The doctor with his lies and excuses. Our aunt and uncle and a stream of cousins, and then all the men who sat around our table with Father, plotting those uprisings. The speeches I wrote are nothing but ashes now. Burned in the stove just like Father asked.

It's like life decomposed here, and all that's left is bones.

The people. The chairs. Tables. Beds and the wardrobes. Almost everything in my life is gone, except Emmett and the grandfather clock. It chimes one last time, ten minutes past the hour, ticking out of time on its way to the end. There's no sense winding it now. I bite back the urge to topple it to the floor and stomp it to smithereens just to keep that stupid bank from taking one more thing.

"Charlotte?" Emmett calls me from outside. "Sophie's here."

"One minute." I take one last glance around the kitchen where Mother should be. A fine layer of coal dust has settled on everything since she died. I've been doing my best to keep up with it to impress the people from the state, but I gave up on it when they gave up on me. It's a good thing the house is the farthest from the mine or absolutely everything would be black, and we might be sicker. The distance may be what spared me.

I take in my last breath of home and step out the door onto the porch. The sun warms the wood. It smells like endless summer days that belong to a different version of me.

Emmett clings to the pigsty fence with one hand, doubled over with a coughing fit while our cousin Sophie looks on in horror. They're just months apart, both of them fifteen. Emmett's too young to be falling apart like this, and Sophie's too young to be losing so many people.

Emmett shivers despite the heat, dabbing the cuff of his sleeve against his bleeding gums.

"He's getting worse," Sophie whispers, joining us at the fence.

"Yeah." The shaking started a few weeks before. "It's just like our parents."

His cheeks are still pink though, not splotchy and red yet. That comes just before the poison really sets in, before teeth start bleeding and falling out. Before the body falls apart.

I tug a handkerchief from my pocket and hand it to him. He glares at me and swats me away until something makes him change his mind, and he sighs and snatches it from my hand. He's been like this since he started getting sick, grumpy and bitter all the time. Resentful about needing help, I suppose. I can't blame him for being angry. Being shipped off to God knows where, far from his friends, but he won't talk about it. The thought of losing him is more than I can bear. The only silver lining to leaving Stoke is the chance that Emmett might put some weight back on, stop coughing and bleeding from the gums so much, when we put some distance between us and this awful place. That's what they say, anyway.

The wind picks up. Emmett wads up the handkerchief and brushes his hair from his eyes.

"I'm sorry your father will never know for sure what causes that smell." Sophie wrinkles her nose and winces at the horizon.

"He thought it was some kind of sulfur, maybe, coming out of the mine and the coal plant." I shrug. Pritchard says it's harmless. The man is a liar and a monster.

Some days that smell wraps around the house, keeping us inside. On days like that, we shut the windows and play games until the wind changes again. We make up stories and dream about hiring a fancy carriage or hopping on a train and going west to become silent film stars. At least, we used to. Before life got too heavy to carry.

I'm too numb, too consumed with all the goodbyes to feel much of anything, but I hate Pritchard so much that a hot bile still rises in me at the thought of him.

"How long is—" Emmett coughs, a deep rattling that worsens every day. He wheezes and ratchets his breath back to a voice close to being steady but not quite. "Is it gonna take that orphan court man to show up?"

"He should be here soon." I kick at a fence post, and dirt falls from my shoe.

"I wish you could live with us." Sophie's eyes grow red again.

"Don't," I plead. We've both been crying off and on for days. My pendulum swings between tears and a strange numbness. In between, there are people. So many people who want to buy our things, tell me how sorry they are, how angry that nothing could be done. People from the bank who won't let us stay because Father took out a mortgage to pay the bills, and they say I'm not capable of paying it back. People from the state who wouldn't let Emmett and me go together until I sent so many letters, they nearly drowned in them. It's all too much. "Your mother hasn't room for us with ten children in the house. She can barely feed all of you. Besides, this won't last forever. We'll be back. I promise."

"You can't promise that," she says.

"Yes, I can."

"What do you want to… Why do you…" Emmett's breath hitches with a cough. "Why come back?"

"Because it's home."

"You'd be better off running and never looking back," Sophie says. "Get Emmett through school like you promised your father. Make some new friends. Get as far from this place as you can. And you can write me a million letters now that you aren't writing speeches."

I shoot daggers at her with my eyes, because Emmett never knew. She mouths the word *sorry* at me. I doubt Emmett heard, though, over his hacking.

Looking back at the house, at all I've lost, hurts in a way I never knew possible. My grandfather made the rocking chairs that were on the porch until the Blakes bought them for a pittance. Father used to sit here and whittle animals from coal. The smell of the boards warming in the sun and the damp from snow and summer rains. The gentle, rhythmic *swish, swash* as Mother swept it free. Not a speck of coal dust could rest. The broom became poetry, the floor my foundation. In and out, through the screen door. A billion times. I took it all for granted.

"I want my home back," I say. "This place is all I've ever known, and I don't want to be anywhere but here." I can't explain it, and I shouldn't have to. This home should have been ours forever. It's home.

Sophie pushes out her bottom lip. She understands. "Maybe you'll find a dandy fisherman who'll sweep you off your feet. Just like the ones in those silent films. You'll move into a grand house ten times as nice as Pritchard's."

The idea makes my skin crawl. "I wouldn't marry some bachelor miner just to stay in Stoke, and I won't marry some random fisherman just to stay away. Marrying at seventeen? That man from the state should be lashed for suggesting it."

"You never know, Charlie." Sophie gave me a doubtful look. "People fall in love all the time."

Sometimes the two years that separate us seem like a lifetime. The real world doesn't work that way. Handsome men don't just show up and treat you like a princess. The day you marry, you leave all your dreams behind to tend house for a man who will work his fingers to the bone, die young, and leave you with a dozen mouths to feed. Not all women think that's a dream come true.

"No, thanks." I try to keep the coldness from my voice but fail. "But I will make the most of it. I'll find some sewing work and put money away to buy this place back one day. A piece of it anyway.

The poison wasn't always here, and it can't last forever."

The unmistakable sound of a horseless carriage turning onto our lane makes Sophie wrinkle her nose and raise her shoulders to her ears.

"Duryea," Emmett says.

The odd beast grumbles like a metal dragon, flying along in a cloud of dust.

"Those God-awful things are so loud." I shove my hands deep into the pockets I'd sewn into my skirt.

Sophie grabs me by the shoulders, growing serious and looking an awful lot like her mother. "I guess we're not stealing that automobile and running off to make silent films, then, huh?"

"Doesn't seem like it."

The air between us thickens, and a knot forms in my throat. I blink up at the clouds, hoping Sophie won't get too sappy and make me sob. I am not leaving this place in tears. I will leave with my chin up.

"Are they driving you all the way there?" Sophie presses her hand against her stomach as if the goodbye makes her sick.

"Just to the station." I hold in my breath. I don't want to remember home this way, the smell of rotten eggs and the salty taste of tears.

"I wish they could find someplace closer." Sophie pulls me in, squeezing me so tight my ribs might break. "Maryland seems so far."

Far, but our only option. The alternative was being shipped to opposite ends of the universe. The state said they had no choice but to separate us, that no one wanted two teenage orphans, and I used every piece of paper in the house writing letters to urge them otherwise. Lucky for us, someone either took pity on us or got tired of hearing from me and found a place sixty miles away in Maryland.

Emmett leans across the fence and spits a wad of pink on the dry ground.

I peel myself away from Sophie. "It's not far. Just across the border. There was no place in this part of Pennsylvania that would take us both."

"I could have worked," he says. "In the mine."

The horseless carriage gets closer and it'll drown me out soon, but I'm done with this conversation, anyway.

"Em, we've been over this. You'd never make enough money. Father took out that mortgage because he couldn't keep all this going on a miner's salary. It has to be sold to pay the debt. There's no sense fighting it. It's over."

My determination doesn't amount to anything when it comes to the state or the bank. It seems none of us can put a price tag on my resolve, and grief wouldn't buy me any time.

I reach down for the handle of my suitcase, and sun glints off a shiny black coal lump nestled in the dirt. One of Father's carvings. My little coal lion. Father would sit at night on the porch and whittle, carving away at spare clumps of coal. He made a whole circus for me over the years. It must have fallen out of a crate when they took everything away.

Fighting back tears, again, I dust him off and trace the little chisel marks in his mane.

"I haven't thought about those in years." Sophie smiles.

He won't be safe in my pocket. My skirt puddles beneath me when I crouch and fling open the case, and I tuck the lion among my things.

Back straight and knuckles white, gripping the suitcase for dear life, I refuse to look back at my home again. I won't glance at that porch floor where I played as a little girl or the door I slammed a thousand times. Though I keep telling myself I'll hear my parents' voices in my head forever, that they aren't tied to this place, I know if I look back, I'll hear them call me to dinner, and I can't bear it. I won't say goodbye.

The Duryea pulls to a stop and Emmett hops down off the fence. He chats with the driver, a portly man with a wiry white beard who looks like he belongs behind a desk, squinting at an account book, not driving a spine-crunching horseless carriage.

"Write to me," I say. "I'll send you a letter as soon as we arrive, so you have our address."

"I wrote you this." Sophie reaches into her pocket and pulls out a wrinkled letter. "Don't read it until you're settled."

I nod and cross the hard-packed dirt path that leads from the porch to the car, climb in next to Emmett, the suitcase on my lap. The three of us press together on the seat with Emmett in the middle. It smells like oil and leather and hot metal.

If I blink enough and stare at the floor, my tears will dry up before they fall, and Emmett won't call me a sissy. And if I just face forward, I won't have to see Cousin Sophie fade into the distance. I won't have to watch the only home I've ever known, stripped to the bone yet packed full of memories, fade into the cloud of exhaust and coal dust. For now.

CHAPTER TWO

The train ride takes half a day, stopping here and there to let people on and off. Over and over. So many people for a Friday. It grinds itself to a halt, howling and letting off steam, then heaves itself back up to speed. The landscape flattens the further south we go, and Pennsylvania's rolling hills dissolve into forest and fields of young corn and wheat. I fog the window with my breath, watching the pink redbuds blur and the fiery nodding heads of columbine as we pass. We soar over creeks and streams on wooden bridges, and I wonder what it will be like to live so close to water that isn't stained blue and devoid of life. Maybe the Ryans will have a fishing boat.

I'm determined for this not to be terrible if for no other reason than its terribleness could be all-consuming. I could make a terrible first impression if I fall apart, and the only way to get back home is to work hard and save some money. Wallowing will only make it harder.

As the miles chug past, I tell myself that Emmett will get better now that we're no longer under that poisoned sky. That I'll find work sewing for money, and I can save it up so we can leave as soon as he's out of school like we promised Father. The man from the state said the school there was new, so surely it must be good. Emmett has always been smart with numbers. He can learn to be an accountant or a chemist. Maybe Father's friends will win against Pritchard, and the poison will be gone in two years, and we can go home and have nothing to do with that awful man and his coal plant.

With an acre or two of land, I could run a farm. Even if I can't afford to buy our house back, a small piece of land closer to home would make a good start.

Beside me, Emmett breaks into a fit of giggles. It starts as a sputter, his shoulders quaking as he tries to hold it in. I glance around but see no cause for it. No woman in a silly hat. He loses his battle with his wits, and heads turn as he doubles over, roaring with laughter.

"Emmett, whatever is the matter with you?" His laughter is contagious, and I find myself fighting against a smile as a man in front of us twists in his seat and glares at me. "I'm truly sorry, sir."

The man huffs and faces forward.

"I just remembered…" Emmett's laughs devolve into coughing. "The cemetery…"

"What about it?" I ask.

"When I walked away."

I'd forgotten about that. Just as the minister began to talk about Father's service to the church, all eyes pinned on the plain wood box with our father inside, Emmett had covered his face with his hands, turned and walked away. Our uncle went after him, and all anyone could talk about afterward was how absolutely devastated Emmett must have been.

"How is that funny?" I ask.

"I wasn't sad," he says, clearing the last few coughs from his throat. He leans close and whispers. "I mean, I was sad, of course, but that's not why I walked away. I had to fart. Then Uncle followed me so I had to keep walking, and I farted on half the cemetery."

"No. Emmett! Uncle thought you were beside yourself. He walked with you for an easy mile trying to get you to talk." The laughs nearly escape me, and I press my fist to my mouth to hold them in.

"Promise you'll never tell a soul," he pleads.

"Of course. I pinky swear." I hold up a pinky finger and he locks his with mine.

"What's the name of this town, again?" he asks.

"North East. Two words."

He wrinkles his nose. "But that's a direction."

"And a town in Maryland."

"Why'd they call it that?" he asks then dabs at his gums with his sleeve.

I point at the handkerchief on his lap, and he rolls his eyes as he picks it up. "Because apparently the man who named it was on a boat heading right for land. His compass said it was due north east of him, so that's when he named it when he got there."

"Whatever. It's still a dumb name for a town. What happens next?" he asks.

I spread out the map the driver gave us and press it flat on my lap. A house is circled in ink, not far from the train station.

"We find Finn and Regina Ryan."

On the map, the town is small, with a main road that runs south, lined with little shops to explore. Streets shoot off to the east and west. Creeks and little rivers wind among the small houses and flow south, until they meet at a park and form a large body of water that, as far as I can tell, is the top of the Chesapeake Bay.

The road seems to keep going south, along a peninsula, until it ends at a lighthouse.

Quaint, I think.

I study the street names until we approach the station.

It teems with people. Most wait for the train, but some dash in and out of the station. A woman sells fruit and vegetables from a cart, and a dog waits at her heels for a treat. It's vibrant, colorful for the lack of coal dust, and perhaps this place holds promise.

"Let's go." I nudge Emmett.

He grabs our bags. When the train rocks to a stop, we wait in the short line to hop off. I thank the conductor for offering me a hand as I reach the ground, and I step over a puddle of last night's rain and out of the way to wait for Em.

I spin the map to orient myself, putting the station in front of me and a bridge to the left, and I step directly into the path of a man in motion. It sends me scrambling to stay on my feet, and I lose the map. It flutters from my hand and tumbles up the street.

"Well, hello, Blondie." His voice is a little nasally, and his hand squeezes my arm. The man smells like sweat and dead fish. "Look where you're going."

"Let go of me, please." I twist myself free and face him, but he isn't a man. He's about my age. He has dark hair slicked in a severe part, and an even more severe brow that hangs over his muddy brown eyes. His suit is nice and well-tailored, which makes the dust on his pants and shirt stand out.

A dozen people stack up behind him, but they aren't travelers trying to get around. It's his horde. The pack of young men seems made from the same earth, coated in it to varying degrees, and angry. They look as if they sprouted out of the ground with something to prove, still covered in soil. Tight suspenders dig into the shoulders of their well-worn shirts. Some wear jaunty hats, vests, and jackets. Others wear pants that are soggy at the hems, a bit too baggy in the knees, slouchy, past due for a washing. I can tell by the way they plant their feet they think they own this town.

Beyond them, Emmett lunges and stomps up the sidewalk after the map, trying to pin it down.

"It looks like we have a special delivery." The boy's voice drips with ridicule. He steps closer, inching me backwards, toward the station.

He reaches out and takes the end of my braid.

I snatch my hair out of his grip. "You may not touch me."

A growing realization lifts his cheeks and brightens his eyes. There's a chilling cruelty in it. He's discovered a path for malice, and it shows in the curl of his lip.

"I know who you are," he says. "You're that stray animal from up north come to live with Finn Ryan."

"Get off my sister." Emmett returns with the map, rasping back a coughing fit.

"Emmett, don't." Grief and sickness eat at his patience, and he isn't any match for these boys.

"Or what? What'll you do?" The boy steps up to Emmett, eyes blazing.

"Leave her alone, Pine." A hand reaches through the small crowd and grabs his shoulder. I follow the arm back to a tall boy my age or a little older with the jaw of a Greek statue and the eyes of a poet, dark hair, and a chin nearly cleft. There's a light to his eyes that makes him seem unlike the others. His rebuke seems to soften the boy named Pine, but only for the smallest of instants.

Pine? He's named for a tree?

"It was just an accident," I say.

"There are no accidents." Pine straightens his spine. "You're a waif. Flotsam. Litter. Trash. We don't need you here, but I can find a use."

Now I'm even more motivated to leave this place.

He looks at me the way a cat looks at an injured mouse. He thinks I'm an easy meal, but he wants to play with me first.

Emmett lifts his chin. "Come on, Charlie. Let's go. We have things to do."

"Yeah." That hand lands on Pine's shoulder again. "Us too."

I brush the sweat from my palms onto my skirt. Em and I head in one direction, and I cast a glance back over my shoulder as they walk in the other.

"I hope the rest of the town is nicer than they are," I say.

"They are, dear." The woman tending the fruit and vegetable cart makes change for a man in an oversized suit who stuffs his purchase in his pocket. "Pine's bark is worse than his bite."

She places the coins in her apron. I hope she's right. It looks as if she might say more, but a woman with her hair in a neat chignon declares herself late to board the train and asks about the price of pickled herring.

"What's that smell?" Emmett covers his nose with his hand. The smell hits me again too. Dead fish.

"Don't ask me," I say. "You're the one with the farting problem."

"It's not me. I swear."

"I thought it was that Pine boy, but it's everywhere." I take the map from Emmett. It's soaking wet. I can't decipher a thing.

"Where are you headed?" The woman at the market table digs jars from a crate.

"Russell Street." I look to Emmett for confirmation, but he shrugs, bags hanging limply at his sides. "I think that's what it was called."

"That way." She points up the sidewalk. "Cross the tracks. The first road you come to is Main Street. Make a left there. Russell Street is on the right, this side of the river. Are you staying with the Ryans?"

"Yes, ma'am."

"Four houses down. Can't miss it," she says. The tuck of the woman's lower lip is the type of sympathy I've been avoiding the last few weeks. Either I look pitiable or the Ryans take in enough orphans to be known for it.

I thank her and take my suitcase from Emmett. We trudge up the gentle hill with Em coughing like mad and dabbing his bleeding gums, and we pause for him to catch his breath. He masks it well enough, but I know he's struggling.

A narrow bridge goes over the train tracks here, and it curves down a hill where trees and gas lamp posts line the road, and a steeple on the horizon hints at the shops and stores beyond.

I walk to the bridge and peer down and find the source of that fishy smell. Thousands of little dead herring slap against the rocks, their silver bodies shining in the sun. They form a dam, an island of death clogging the stream.

Em makes a derisive little rattle in the back of his throat and wipes at his brow with the back of his hand. A breeze washes over us, bathing us in the sour stench of dead fish.

"What do you think they'll be like?" he asks. "The Ryans?"

"Nice, probably. They don't have any children of their own. The lady from the state said we're the first teenagers they've had, but they've had orphans before. The house is probably tidy and clean."

"What if I get sicker, Charlie?" He kicks at a rock, and it tumbles to the water below.

"You won't. Now that you're not breathing in that air, you'll get better."

"None of this feels real," he says. "Doesn't it seem like we could get back on the train and go home, and everything would be normal?"

I grip the wall and stare down at the fish. "It does feel like that, except we can't. I promise, though, things will be okay. We'll look out for each other, and someday we will go home again." Maybe it won't be our house or the same land, but I'm going to try damn hard to get back there.

The sight of all those dead fish brings the familiar lump back into my throat, and sorrow wells in my eyes. Such a sad scene. Whatever happened to them was out of their control. They'd been helpless, just floating along, living their fish lives until someone or something came along and slaughtered them all. Why? And why doesn't anyone seem to care?

"What happened to them?" Emmett asks.

My nose tingles as my eyes start to well and turn away. "I don't know."

Behind us the train lets out another howl.

"Come on," Emmett says, his voice muffled by his sleeve. "Stinks."

We stick to the edge of the bridge, avoiding horse droppings and a passing carriage.

I have to admit, North East is nicer than Stoke, despite the smell. The houses are small, made of brick or wood. There are little stone walls and whitewashed fences. Tidy shrubs and kitchen gardens. I wonder if the Ryans will have a nice little plot, maybe a chicken coop.

We turn onto Russell Street, and I count four houses and pause in front of the home of Finn and Regina Ryan.

Paint peels from the wood siding, and the window trim is bare and gray with age. Half the shutters are missing. One leans against the house, waiting for someone to care, dark with damp and rotting at the corners. The porch roof bows in the middle, and it's heavy with moss and pine needles. An old wooden bench is the only sign of comfort, the last shards of dark green paint hanging on for dear life. It is the opposite of poetry. Brittle shards pressed together without any hope or form.

My heart sinks to my shoes.

The woman from the state had walked through our home and criticized every fleck of dust that clung to the curtains. She'd called me unfit for not wearing black, as if mourning clothes were a sign of being able to take care of myself and Em. And this is a better alternative?

Emmett makes a gurgling sound and ratchets back a cough. "This looks dreadful."

"It's just a porch. They're probably wonderful people. I bet the inside is nice."

Besides, it's better than being poisoned.

The suitcase handle slips in my sweaty hand. I tighten my grip and straighten my shoulders.

"Are you sure this is right?" he asks.

"It's just a place to sleep, Em. I'm sure it's all right. And it's good of them to welcome us."

I check the mailbox anyway. *The Ryan's* is painted on the side in chipping white paint. I can't take my eyes off the misplaced apostrophe. It's the right house, but everything about it feels wrong.

CHAPTER THREE

A woman in a blue gingham dress and a stained apron answers the door. With a squarish jaw and deep-set eyes, she looks as stern as any teacher I've ever known. Her brown shoes are scuffed and worn. Her graying brown hair is swept back into a bun. Coarse strands wave in the breeze, and dirt stains her clothes. Glancing past her, I can see it also clings to the windows, the floors, and the walls.

The man who must be Finn wobbles next to her. He's a gaunt, angular thing, with a crooked nose, pockmarks and scars. Even his bones seem contentious. His eyes dart between us, beyond us, as if he can't focus. Thin lips twist beneath a handlebar mustache. His hair is greasy, and his clothes are so dark they're either stained or soot-soaked.

"You must be the Morris children. Charlotte and Emmett? I'm Regina." The woman sticks out a hand to shake mine. She glances at Finn as if she needs permission. Her smile is far too wide, her hand clammy.

"Get in," Finn huffs.

It's less an invitation than an order.

The front sitting room has no chairs, and the raw wood floor hasn't seen polish in thirty years or more. There's no grandfather clock like the one Mother wound each Sunday. No wingback chair where Finn might sit to read the way Father had. No drum table, no embroidered pictures on the wall. It's just worn floors and scuffed walls.

Finn reaches behind us and slams the door, and Emmett jumps.

Despite the smell of rotting fish carcasses blasting through the open window, I can smell stale beer on him yards away. He opens his mouth. His teeth are blackened stubs.

"We each got jobs here. Yours is to keep this place clean. I don't tell people to do things twice," he says.

Regina wrings her hands.

"No running or yelling in the house," Finn says. "And do not get underfoot. Last children we had in here were useless." He slurs his words and tries to fix his eyes on Emmett, but they drift between my brother and the wall beyond. "You will go down to that water every evening to set the nets, and you will go back down there at dawn every day to haul in your dinner. And you will keep your mouth shut. Both of you."

"Yes, sir." I swallow hard. As angsty and impatient as Emmett's become in his grief, I pray he keeps his mouth shut.

Everything about the house seems dark. I don't want to step one foot further, in case its sticky dank attaches itself to me, but there's no place else to go.

It's not a home, I tell myself. It doesn't need to be. I just need a place to sleep until I can put the pieces of life back in order.

Another gust of dead fish air comes in the window, and I do my best to hide the revulsion that helixes from my nose to my stomach and back again, but Emmett doesn't bother. He makes a guttural burbling sound, covering his nose and mouth with his sleeve.

Finn doesn't seem to notice. He staggers back, through the wide doorway, and into a room that must be the kitchen, using the wall for balance.

Maybe he isn't always like this.

"What is that stench?" Emmett mashes his nose flat with the back of his hand.

"You'll get used to it," Regina says. "We just had a fish kill."

His eyes narrow, confused. "Why would you do that?"

Regina tucks in her chin. "We don't do it on purpose."

"They wash up like that," Finn grumbles over his shoulder. "Catch the live ones. Don't bring no dead fish in this house."

"What kills them?" I glance over my shoulder, out the window.

"Beats me," Finn growls from the kitchen. "Could be algae, they say. Happens all up and down this river."

"And we're supposed to catch them?" Emmett asks.

"Don't ask stupid questions," Finn says.

Regina claps her hands together, eyes wide and far too bright. Something in the sharp contrast between her stern countenance and this over-compensation for Finn's gruffness makes my blood run cold.

"Let's get you two settled in. Then we can talk about chores. The kitchen's back there, near our room. You each got your own room upstairs."

Regina's monumental smile never wavers. She hikes her skirt over her shoes and climbs, motioning us to follow.

"You think there's light up there?" Emmett isn't scared of the dark, not in the usual way. Night terrors grip him, making him panic and gasp for air.

"I saw gas street lamps. If there's no light, we'll explain." My suitcase is somehow a hundred pounds heavier than it was when we left Stoke. "We'll get some extra candles."

The stairs are narrow and missing a few balusters, and a few of them bow beneath my feet. I want to be grateful for a roof over my head, and room to myself is a luxury compared to what most people in Stoke have. I try to tell myself it's better than being crammed in a room with eight of my cousins, but I'd much rather be there than in this place.

At the top of the steps, Regina nudges a door. It opens and creeps shut again. Inside is a narrow bed with a suitable mattress and a worn but good blanket. A small wardrobe sits in the corner, barely large enough for my few clothes. A cracked mirror hangs crooked on the wall and a little table I can use as a desk sits beneath the window. One leg is too short, and it wobbles when I put the suitcase on it. Everything's covered in cobwebs and a layer of filth, as if the bed and furniture and walls all just grew here organically like fungus from the forest floor, but I can clean it. I can make it shine.

"This should be good enough for you," Regina says.

I muster a smile and thank her, but it isn't good enough. Nothing short of having our parents back and healthy, living in my own home with my family, will ever be good enough. It's a solid roof and place to put my head, though.

I catch Regina's expectant stare and swallow the wave of resentment hard. Am I expected to gush about a bed and a wardrobe, tucked in a dark and dismal house with a man who can't bother to be sober to meet us?

"Well?" Regina asks.

For a week, I've been managing my expectations, doing my best to hang onto the past, clinging to the shredded remains of my life. I don't know who I am without my family. Emmett is all I have left, and what am I supposed to say?

"It's lovely. Thank you." Suddenly I realize that being an orphan will mean spending the rest of my days here paying homage. Am I expected to be overly gracious while diminishing everything I've lost?

I peer out the back window to the tall grasses and woods beyond. I just have to get through this hurdle of newness. Once I get settled, there will be plenty of pleasant diversions here.

"You each got chores to do." Regina's voice echoes off the bare walls. "Charlotte, you'll be cleaning, doing laundry and helping with the cooking."

"Of course." Having something to do will keep my hands busy. Laundry and cooking can't possibly take up all my time. I'll still have some for school work and maybe even enough time to make some friends and take on some sewing jobs because I have plenty of work ahead of me if I'm going to get back to Stoke sooner rather than later.

"You'll be pulling up the nets in the morning, Emmett." Regina turns to him, but her words are drowned out by a coughing fit as he doubles over. "Are you contagious?"

"I'm…" He sputters, tucking his bloody sleeve in his fist, tongue raking over his teeth.

"He isn't." I sit on the bed and sink four inches. "It has something to do with the coal. He'll get better now that he's not around it."

"I can answer for myself." Emmett glares at me.

Regina glances over her shoulder, wary. "Finn hates noise. If you want to get by, earn your keep and don't make a racket. Be careful when you set those nets and haul them in. It's illegal to fish unless you pay a tax, and Finn won't. We fish to feed ourselves. Charlotte, be in the kitchen at three to get started on dinner."

Regina turns to leave.

"Ma'am. Can I work?" I avoid Emmett's worried gaze. "I hope to make a few extra dollars sewing."

There are thirty dollars sewn into the hem of my skirt, my mother's idea in her dying days. She knew the state would take every penny, either giving it to debtors or handing it to a foster family to pay for our care, but Father had suffered and saved for us, and I have no intention of handing it over to anyone. It's for me and Em. For our future. If I add to it, with luck, I might have enough to get home one day. And if I make enough, Emmett won't have to work until he finishes school.

"What kind of sewing are you talking about?" Regina asks.

The bed groans and creaks when I stand. I fling open my suitcase and pull out a skirt, holding it out and kicking it as if I'm testing it for size. It's cream colored, almost tan, and the most vibrant garden blooms from the hem. Flowers reach toward the waist on tender stems in every shade of green. There are lilies and lavender, poppies and peonies, all hand-embroidered. I saved my pennies for any color I could find. And I filled in the gaps with threads pilfered from Mother's scrap pile, my aunt's laundry, old clothes, and rags, and I dyed them in a thousand colors.

"You made this?" Regina holds the skirt up and spins it slowly. She blinks at me, her eyes narrowed in a gaze that sizes me up. "You sewed pockets in."

"I did." I spread the skirt out on the bed and pull out a yellow bodice embroidered with little pink and blue flowers, but Regina isn't impressed.

She clicks her tongue. "These clothes won't help you here. You'll need something plainer for work and school. It's good enough sewing, though." Regina lowers her voice. "What do you need money for?"

"I'm seventeen." The lid to my suitcase falls closed. "I graduate from high school in just a few months, and I'll need to make a life for myself."

Regina mulls it over, and whether it's her sensibilities or her sense of my plight, she slumps a little with a sigh and nods. She glances into the hall and whispers as if she's doing me a favor. She whispers a lot, I notice.

"If you make money outside this house, keep it to yourself. Finn doesn't like flashy, showy things. My best advice to you is not to draw attention. Be in the kitchen at three." She steps into the hall. "Emmett. Come."

At least Regina hasn't said no. Whether she'll make a good buffer for whatever kind of man Finn is, only time will tell.

In the next room, Regina shows Emmett how to unstick the window, how to wiggle it just right so it opens.

I can't panic about Finn. Surely the state wouldn't put us in a house with a man who's more bite than bark. It's probably just a bad day. Regina's compensating for him an awful lot, but time spent worrying about that man will be wasted. I need to make the most of this, and if that means making a new skirt or two to fit in around here, that's not the worst that can happen.

I hang my clothes in the wardrobe, then sit on the edge of the bed with the little coal lion in the palm of my hand. The little girl my father carved it for had been brave, he'd said, just like this lion. I wonder what became of the rest of them, the little giraffe and the disproportionate elephant with a really long tail and a too-short trunk. I should have taken better care of them. At least I have the little lion. It's the only thing of my father's I have left.

That familiar lump returns to my throat again. I put the lion on the windowsill next to the bed where he'll be safe and dig in my pocket for Sophie's letter.

Dearest Cousin,

Please write as soon as you arrive so I know how to reach you. Father is quieter about Pritchard and the protests than ever, and the few things I have overheard were whispers. All eyes are on him, of course, rumors swirling that he'll take over your father's role, and with so many children in the house who repeat everything they hear, I can't blame him for keeping mum. I wouldn't dare put anything notable in a letter, not with Pritchard being so heavy-handed, but I will do my best to relay any news I can. Of course, after a time, you may find being away from Stoke diverting. Pleasurable, even. Should your curiosity wane or thoughts of the place become too painful, I do hope you'll let me know. I hope to hear from you soon.

Much love, Sophie

I pull paper and a pencil from my suitcase and settle at the wobbly table.

My Dear Sophie,

I can't fathom ever being bored of news from Stoke, and I do hope you write often. I've been here for mere moments and have yet to form a full impression of the place, but it bears the promise of being far from Pritchard. Though you are wise to safeguard your words, I crave the relief mine could bring. He knows he's making people sick. All he does is lie. The way he traps entire families in debt to him is a shade above slavery. Oh, that someone might finally make him pay.

As for North East, my impressions of this place are fair so far. It smells like dead fish, and…

I stop my hand before I mention Finn and Regina. If I pour my impressions onto the page, Sophie will only worry, and with the way my luck has been going lately, Finn could get his hands on it.

Other than that, the town seems quiet and quaint. It may be just what Emmett needs. He's been so angry. You saw him at Mother's funeral. I can't blame him for being so angry, close as they were. Now he's stuck with me, and I don't know how to be his sister while keeping my promise to Father to keep Emmett in school. But he only has three years left. Once he gets into schoolwork and makes some friends, maybe he'll feel better. I sure will.

In the meantime, I shall make some friends. With any luck, I'll find sewing work soon.

Yours forever, Charlotte

I seal the letter in an envelope, take some money from my stash, and peek in on Emmett. He must find the room satisfactory enough because he's fast asleep in his bed. With so much anguish and change lately, so much disappointment, it's nice to see him relaxed, even if it is on a questionable blanket. He looks young, like the sweet little brother who nursed an orphaned baby squirrel back to health.

Emmett deserves a chance to sleep off the poison, so I creep down the stairs with my letter to find Regina lost in a stream of thought over a sink full of dirty dishes, staring blankly out the kitchen window, across the grassy field.

"Excuse me?" I interrupt, clutching my missive. "I hope I didn't startle you. Where can I mail a letter?"

Without looking back at me, Regina mumbles. "You can take it to the train station. The post office is inside. Do what you want, but be back by three."

"Are you saying it's all right to go out? We don't have to ask permission, as long as we get our work done?"

Regina plunges her hands back into the sink and scrubs at a pan. "I'm saying it's all right until Finn says it's not."

CHAPTER FOUR

I intend to find a seamstress, a dressmaker, or milliner who needs some help, and I won't return to the Ryans' until I've at least made a good attempt.

Main Street is a wide dusty road with a clean sidewalk and storefronts that stretch into the narrow horizon over a gentle hill crest. It's quiet and empty but for horses twitching their skin to throw off flies, shuffling their feet, hitched to wagons that groan and creak. Men's voices waft out of a tavern.

I pass a bank with a regal columned entrance, too grand, it seems, for a town of such simple wants. Two women step from a bookstore onto the street, their arms heavy with purchases. They talk in serious tones and cut between buildings, down a small alley. There's a pharmacy offering tinctures and salves, bandages, and ointments, and a man inside catches my eye. He offers a friendly wave, which I return. It gives me hope that there's warmth in this town, after all.

A small sewing shop occupies a narrow strip of building between a second-hand store and a barber. Inside, dust from cut fabric dances in the light when I close the door behind me. Shelves full of fabric bolts, spools of thread, and baskets with trailing vines of satin ribbons make me homesick for Mother's old sewing machine.

"Can I help you?" A slim, bald man with wide eyes and wiry white eyebrows blinks at me from behind the counter. His words are muffled, a pin is pressed between his lips.

"Yes, sir. I'm looking for sewing work, and I can do embroidery too. I wondered if you needed a set of hands."

He pulls the pin from his mouth. "We have little in that way of work. Most people here do their own sewing. Are you new here?"

"I am. Staying with Finn and Regina Ryan. On Russell Street."

Something less than pleasant flashes in his eyes before he glances back down at his work. It isn't pity, but I can't put my finger on it.

"Do you know them?" I ask.

He raises a shoulder ever so slightly, and there's no mistaking the shifting in his countenance as he considers his words. "Finn is… Well, everyone knows of them. No one knows them well, I'm afraid. And you're staying with them because your family—"

"Is gone? Dead? The ones who are left can't take me in? Yes. Unfortunately."

The door swings open, and I step out of the way. A much older woman dressed all in black, with a carpetbag half her height, drags herself over the threshold. The shopkeeper greets her with gentleness, and she runs her skeletal hand along the fabrics. Her wool dress is far too heavy for the weather. Hints of soft white eyelet feather from her cuffs, and she clutches the carpetbag to her chest, muttering words I can't discern. There's a gentle distance to her eyes as she lifts a bowed finger.

"How is your mother, dear?" The woman shakes her finger at my chest, but her eyes are fixed on some spot in the distance.

I give her a smile. "You must have me mistaken for someone else. I'm so sorry."

"No, no." The woman shakes her head, strands of wiry white hair unaffected. "I have something for her."

She digs through the bag, extracting a hairbrush and a trinket box, her bewilderment growing satisfied when she grasps something small and shiny. She beams and places it in my hand. It's hard and black, like a horse's hoof, but puffy like a seed pod. It's pouch-like, but with barbs at each corner, as if it has hooks or little claws. There's a threateningly animal nature to it, and I fear an insect could burst from it at any moment and try to suck out my eyes.

"No, thank you," I say. "It's kind of you to offer, but my mother…" I place the oddity back into her hand. "Please. Keep it."

"It's a mermaid's purse. It's painted." She flips it over to a painted scene of a beach, tan sand and blue water that meet at a light blue sky. "It's a good luck charm. For your mother."

"What's a mermaid's purse?"

"From the waters. It's a skate egg." She looks perplexed, as if I've just fallen out of the sky.

I glance at the man behind the counter. He gives me a look as if to say it's best to humor her.

"Everyone needs a good luck charm." She curls my fingers around the egg. "Mermaids carry their treasures in here, along with a bit of magic. If you find one, it's yours to keep. It gives you new life. Rebirth. Renewal. Give it to your mother and tell her the bleeding will end soon. The kidney trouble will pass."

Shuffling to the door, she steps outside and pulls it closed behind her with great care.

"She means well," he says. "Been through a lot, poor dear. Did you embroider those flowers on your skirt?"

I glance down and stick out a foot, lifting a corner of my skirt to display it better. There was never a reason to count all the poppies and larkspurs, the hollyhocks and sunflowers, but there could be a hundred of them blooming from the hem.

"I did. I used what I had, sir."

He pushes out his bottom lip and nods. "I don't have work right now, but I sometimes do. My hands aren't what they used to be, and there are times I could use the help. I'll send a note if work comes in. It's nice meeting you, though. Call me Sidney. Name's Sidney Barber, but folks just call me Sidney. You can see why." He aims his thumb at the barbershop.

"I can see how that might be confusing. Thank you, sir. Sidney. Of course." I thank him and step back onto the street.

I have no need for a mermaid's purse, for magic or fairy tales, but I can't let it go. A good luck charm never hurt anyone. It sure wouldn't hurt Emmett, who could use all the luck he can get. And I could use a bit of renewal, even if I didn't want a new life. I examine the little black pod as I walk back to the post office tucked inside the train station. Rebirth and renewal, indeed.

A train shudders on the tracks, bellows and lets off a rush of steam. I envy that kind of catharsis. Once my ears stop ringing, a clatter of industry fills the void, coming from a brickyard back by the tree line where little clusters of buildings are scattered. I can't see much of the workers' toiling through the steam, but a thick black plume rises from the site and mounds of clay tower next to giant heaps of lumber. No doubt it's dirty out there, and heat ripples up, warbling my view of the houses and woods.

But it doesn't obscure my view of Pine.

He leans against the station wall, chewing and spitting a wad of tobacco two feet in front of him. To avoid him, I'd have to retrace my steps and make a wide berth around the station to approach from the other side. My pride is wounded but still intact, so I straighten my spine and keep going.

"Where's your brother?" he asks as I pass.

"Where are your friends?"

I take two more steps toward the station before Pine is in front of me, his hat in his hands, twisting it like he's wringing water from a rag.

"You got a boy back home?"

"It's none of your business." I step around him. "Excuse me, please."

"I want to make it my business." He falls into step beside me. "You could do worse than me."

I don't see how that's possible, I think.

"What's in your hand?" he asks.

He's in front of me again, blocking my path. Something untrustworthy and sinister comes off him like the smoke from that brickyard, wrapping around me and unsettling the air. I tuck the mermaid's purse in my pocket.

"Show it to me," he says. "Did you steal it?"

"No, I didn't steal it. What an appalling accusation. It's mine." I take a step around him; he takes a step back. It's an awkward dance.

In an instant he lunges at me, shoving his hand into my pocket. Twisting away, I slap at his hand, but he's quick on his feet and maneuvers with me. When his friends tumble out of the station and spot us, a hot wave of panic rushes over me. But fear makes me strong. I spread my fingers and bend my wrist back, smashing the heel of my hand to his nose, pressing upward on his nostrils as hard as I can. His nose crunches, and he falls back, clutching his face.

I feel in my pocket for my letter and the mermaid's purse.

Pine gurgles and squeezes his eyes shut, his face laced with pain. His cheeks and ears redden. He looks mad enough to pummel me, and his growl threatens it. Blood oozes from between his fingers. Tears stream down Pine's face, the involuntary reaction of his sinuses to the blow.

His friends pile in around him. There are no smiles among them this time, and the Greek poet who was so helpful before is noticeably absent.

I turn to run into the station before his pack of feral hyenas sets on me, but a large hand grabs my arm and spins me around.

"What's going on here?"

A large constable looks between Pine and me, maintaining his grip on my arm.

"She hit him," a red-haired boy answers.

My spirits sink.

"It was self-defense," I explain. "He tried to get into my pocket to steal from me."

"Quiet down." The cop throws a hand in my face.

He examines Pine's nose while the crowd feigns innocence.

"What is your name?" the officer demands of me.

"Charlotte Morris."

Recognition lines his brow. "Finn Ryan's new charge. You got a brother with you."

"Yes." I nod and lift my chin. "We haven't been here long enough to deserve to be assaulted in the street."

"What's in your pocket?" he demands.

I hold up the letter and set my jaw. He's not getting that mermaid's purse.

He studies me. "I'll be keeping an eye on you. Get on now. Finish your business."

A strange mix of shame and anger swirls within me, making my cheeks burn. The crowd of boys parts for me, mocking me. He didn't even listen to what I had to say. He just blindly believed that ogre without asking questions at all.

A boy six inches shorter than me with hair the color of milky tea shoves my shoulder as I pass, but I ignore it and plow on to the station. I can't let them know they get to me.

I pull open the station's heavy door and step inside.

It looks a lot like a church, with benches in rows facing the wood-paneled ticket windows. A few people glance up from their tickets and papers like they're praying to the arrivals board. They follow along as the station worker scribbles departure times on the board in chalk. A small sign above the far window declares it the place to deposit mail, so I pay my two pennies and hand over my letter, returning the man's polite smile.

The boys are gone when I step back outside. Even so, I walk swiftly back to the Ryans' house, and I'm out of breath when I turn onto their street. There's a man in a wrinkled suit on the porch, gaping at the door with two stacks of books at his feet. He startles at the sight of me and introduces himself as Mr. Benner from the school.

"It's unconventional, having a school like this. We're fortunate to have one just for our older students," he says. "It's quite progressive. I hope you'll consider joining us."

I tell him about the promise I made to our father to keep Emmett in school, about how good he is at math and my excitement to learn as much as I can. Mr. Benner hands me the books and says I should bring Emmett early on Monday, that we both must take placement tests first thing in the morning. It gives me something to anticipate, even if he can't promise I'll get to take economics or learn how to run a business or a farm of my own.

When he says there's a dance a week from Monday night, my panic must be palpable.

"A dance? On a Monday?" I ask. Emmett is a coughing mess, hardly up to making a good impression, and I don't know if I can handle any more people like Pine.

"It used to be a hayride, but it got in the way of harvest. Then we held it at the church. But with the new school, we have plenty of room. It's part of learning how to live in a civilized society." Mr. Benner lifts a shoulder, as if he finds the idea a waste of time.

I have no idea how to dance and no interest in making a fool of myself in front of the entire school. I do want to meet people, though. Surely not everyone here will be like Pine. Some friends would brighten the place and make the next few months go by much faster.

"But on a Monday?" I ask again.

"So it doesn't interfere with work on family farms on the weekends." Mr. Benner leans in with a secret.

Arranging my face into a grin that sits somewhere between sympathy and understanding, I nod. He must sense my apprehension because he tucks in his lower lip, considering me for a moment.

"There is a really lovely girl in your class who I think you'll like," Mr. Benner says. "If your school records are correct, you share an aptitude for writing."

"I do, but it's not necessary—"

He raises a hand, determined. "Speak nothing of it. Bea is a wonderful young lady. Her father owns the market in town, and she knows everyone. She'll be thrilled to make a new friend and show you around. Tomorrow morning, then." Mr. Benner bows his head and steps off the porch.

I thank him and carry the books inside. I'm such a mess lately with my mood constantly changing, crying at the drop of a hat, that I worry I won't be tolerable company, but a friend will be a great diversion and make my time here more cheerful. Besides, Mother always said that happiness was a habit. I'm not quite ready to be joyful yet, but my sorrow can't last forever.

Regina pokes her head out from the kitchen. "Just in time. You best not be squeamish. There are fish to gut."

I've never gutted herring before, but it turns out to be fairly easy. Slimy, but uncomplicated. The hardest part is standing in the kitchen in silence with Regina. Something about her isn't right, like a wireless radio not quite in tune, like she's on the verge of saying something but won't. Or can't. I don't know the waters well enough yet to make waves, but I have questions. What does Finn do for a living? Why are we eating fish when so many of them wash up dead? Torn between wanting to know and needing to start off on the right foot with her, I say nothing. Her severe expression and cold eyes make her seem wound tight, likely to snap at interruption.

Eventually, Emmett comes down, rubbing sleep from his eyes. Then Finn stumbles in from the bedroom off the kitchen, running his hand over his thin hair and mumbling incoherently to himself.

Finn neither speaks nor breathes between bites of boiled potato and chunks of fish. Food seems to rouse him. Once he's stuffed, and his fork lands on his plate, he leans, one arm draping over the back of the chair, as he picks food from his teeth with a long pinky nail.

"There's a meeting downtown." He flicks a white gob from his thumb to the floor. "We all got to go."

Regina shifts in her chair, unease coming off her like smoke from that brickyard. There's a hint of fear in her eyes. "What kind of meeting this time? What happened?"

"I ain't been yet, woman. How'm I supposed to know?"

"I'm sorry. Of course." Regina gives him a grin, but it trembles ever so slightly.

"Boy?" Finn throws his spindly forearms on the table and laces his fingers. "You fish? With a net?"

Emmett sips his water. "No, sir. Never tried. Just a pole."

"You're gonna learn."

I set my fork down gently. It doesn't make a sound. "If the fish keep washing up dead, why catch and eat them? It seems like something's wrong with the fish."

"Yeah. Why go fishing at all?" Emmett's plate has barely been touched. He's only helped himself to a few bites of potato, and he's already pushing his plate away. I kick him under the table. He doesn't flinch, squaring off against Finn instead, leaning into the conflict with his eyes narrowed and his mop of dark curly hair tumbling into his eyes. "Don't you get paid to feed us?"

Finn's arm snaps across the table. In a blur, the back of his hand strikes Emmett's face, leaving him stunned, licking a split lip.

I launch to my feet, but Emmett beats me to it.

He slams his hands flat on the table and leans across, nose to nose with Finn.

I've never seen a grin as sinister as the one on Finn's face. And I've never seen my brother raise his hackles like this before.

All the anger inside me shifts, shoves to the side, balls up small, and tucks away. In its place is an ice-cold hard rock of fear.

The world around me seems to slow down as Emmett raises his hand.

CHAPTER FIVE

I squeeze Emmett's arm so tight it could pop. "Don't you dare."

"I won't put up with gruff in this house," Finn says through gritted teeth.

Emmett licks blood from his lip, his eyes spitting fire across the table. I've never seen him like this before. He wouldn't hurt a fly. Yet he's coiled tight, a viper ready to strike, and he's no match for Finn.

I reach between them, pushing Emmett back, afraid Finn will strike again and Emmett will urge him to do it, but Regina grabs the back of my shirt and yanks me onto my chair where I fall hard with a thud.

"Go," Finn barks, extending his arm toward the stairs. "Get out of my sight."

Emmett shoves away from the table and takes the stairs two at a time. Coughs rumble from his chest before he reaches the landing. He's always been a bit defiant, but not like this. Judging by the steam coming off Finn, there's no way he'll let this go.

A voice in my head says to run after him, calm him, beg him not to talk back. I should tell Finn I'll talk to him, that he doesn't need to discipline Emmett, but Finn's outrage swells, and I'm pinned to the chair by my defiance. Damn, I would stand in a fire just to watch my shadow grow sometimes. But leaving will mean I go to bed hungry, and if I stay, I might be able to hide some potatoes for Emmett.

Scooting my chair closer to my plate, I cut through a soggy potato, shove it in my mouth and chew, my eyes locked on the bland dinner while this inferno rages inside me.

Regina shifts in her seat, patting her hair into place as if nothing ever happened. "Finn. The meeting? Any word on why?"

"No idea, but I'm not leaving that boy alone in this house." He flicks a hand at me. "You make sure he goes and acts right."

For the first time, Finn and I see eye to eye. With dinner cleaned up and the dishes put away, I climb the stairs and tap on Emmett's door.

"You can't fight with him. You do understand that, right?" I lean in the doorway to his room and toss him a bundle of boiled potatoes tied in a napkin. "Come on. We have to go to this meeting."

He's reclining on his narrow bed, arms folded behind his head, feet crossed, his tongue probing his split lip. "Seems it's best I don't go."

I cross the room, nudge his legs out of the way, and sit. The bed sinks with me. "Listen, Finn could be dangerous. We have to make the best of this. We can't change it, Em. Just maybe try to get along." Getting along seems to be harder than I'd hoped it would be, but given Em's mood, it isn't in either of our best interests to tell him about the boys or the officer I encountered.

"He hit me, Charlie." He licks the slit in his lip.

"Finn never should have touched you, but we're under his roof for now. It's not forever. We can live by his rules for a little while. Just until I can get us out of here. I'll find a place where you can finish school, and we'll go there. If you fight back, this could get ugly fast. Please. Just control your anger, all right? Count to ten or something."

He unlaces his fingers and cracks his knuckles. "I'm not interested in living one year at a time, Charlie. The best I can promise you is one day at a time."

"That's more than fair." I slap his knee. "Get up. We have to go to some big hoopla down at some park."

He swings his legs over the edge of the bed and pushes to his feet. Without a sound to seal our agreement, we walk down the stairs, onto the porch. We follow Finn and Regina down Main Street, passing the town jail and a quaint tavern, past McCullough's Furniture Store with its window full of picture frames and dressers. Johnson's Store sells jeans, tweeds, and flannels. There's a livestock dealer, a pharmacist, and a lumber store, and an alley next to it leading to a livery stable with horses and carriages to rent at all hours. Little brick and wood-clad shops scatter among charming houses. It's like a shiny, sweet glaze on the slab of moldy bread that is the Ryans' home.

There are millers who sell flour, grains, and feed. A general store with everything under the sun, its large glass windows full of household oddities and furnishings. Two little churches sit nearly across from each other, one Episcopal and one Methodist. I ask, and Regina confirms she and Finn belong to neither. It's no surprise. I'm not big on church myself, not because it tells me how to live but because the congregation in Stoke did a better job of showing me how not to.

The closer we get to the park, the thicker the stream of people becomes. Men wear work shirts caked with clay and pants wrinkled up to the knees from a day in the water. A few wear simple suits that fit their trades while the women wear simple dark dresses and skirts cinched at the waist. I stand out in my bold colors and embroidered bodice, and I smile back at the attention I draw, but I avoid eye contact. I don't want to read any criticism into their stares.

The crowd turns right and strolls past small but charming homes. Emmett coughs at my side. He needs a rest, but Finn pays him no mind. Em rolls his eyes at me, clearly frustrated by his own commotion, and pulls away when I pat his arm in an offer of sympathy.

We go with the flow of people, down a side street and toward a sprawling park littered with greenish clumps of goose droppings people skip and skitter around. A man in a dark suit stands in a gazebo, clutching his suspenders and peering out over the crowd. His hair's white, and his suit's dark velvet. His face is deeply lined and skeletal, and he has a condescending air about him. Judging from the murmurs in the crowd, Mayor Whitaker isn't well-liked and demands allegiance, and the town stands in rapt attention while his booming voice stretches over the people.

"Crime has gripped this town for far too long." He grasps his velvet lapels. "We will not tolerate the thievery and trespassing that happens under cover of night. There shall be a curfew among all people, from six each night until seven in the morning. And lest you forget, fishing restrictions remain. There have been too many fish kills to let healthy ones go to waste. Only commercial fishing is allowed. They all must be weighed and taxed each morning. Anyone caught doing otherwise will be jailed on sight. Every herring pulled from these waters is to be weighed, put in the town ledger, and all tax paid immediately."

The indignant crowd of barely a hundred roars its response. The tax and all the restrictions are unfair, they cry, putting undue hardship on families that hunt and fish for food.

"I'm eighteen years old," screams a man just behind them. "I got a wife and a son. How do I get to work at six if I can't leave the house 'til seven?"

"Get a new job," yells a man in the front.

"Damn town can't feed itself." A man next to me spits chew on the ground and asks how he's supposed to set his nets at night. "Can't set a herring net in the day. Everybody knows that. Whitaker's a moron."

A gaggle of teen boys at the front, some of whom I met earlier in the day, laugh, sending prickles down my arms.

"Move," one of them roars. The mayor nods along. "Quit your job. Get another one."

A woman behind them clicks her tongue. "Telling grown folks when they can leave the house? It's another kick in the ribs for the women. How am I supposed to cram all my washing and work in? I have to take care of my mother. Most days, I don't leave there until well after ten."

I nudge Emmett. "He sounds like Nels Pritchard screaming at the coal workers."

A woman on my right cranes her neck and yells, "When can women gather again? Girls should have clubs in school."

I can't be hearing this right. There are precious few places in this country where a woman gets to keep the rights she had in the womb, but even in Stoke, women can sit in the same room together.

A young man at the front breaks away from the crowd. The woman with the baby reaches out for him. He takes a swing at one of the boys. Police are on him in an instant, beating him with a billy club. The woman wails, but no one steps in to help. I wince and refuse to look away. If this town is brutal, I want to know *how* brutal.

Emmett nudges me. "What's with the iron fist around here?"

I shrug. "If you don't straighten up, you could be the one on the ground."

All around us, outrage erupts. Men pump their fists and yell, their words all swarming together like frantic bees. Women step back, clutching their children and each other.

Finn leans back, his eyes like daggers. "This don't apply to you, you hear. Don't think you get out of hauling in those nets."

Nothing about living under Finn's roof is safe. Not only can I not count on this man for safety, there is plenty about him that would make it hard for me to protect myself.

"I'll do it." I step on Emmett's foot to keep him quiet. "He'll make too much noise coughing. I'll fish."

"You do his chores for him, and he'll be sorry," Finn says.

I don't doubt him for an instant. Finn seems the kind of man who dishes out punishments when there aren't even crimes.

The rabble fades, and the skirmishes settle. We slip into a silent stream of people leaving the park, sticking to Finn and Regina like glue. All around us, people shuffle, their heads down, whispering in little groups. When a man rages against the curfew, the woman with him shakes his arm and silences him.

I tug on Emmett's sleeve. "Slow down a second."

When a gap grows between us and Finn, I say, "I don't think we should eat the fish. They have to be sick."

"I was thinking the same thing." Emmett's eyes are fixed on the back of Finn's head.

"We can't just refuse to eat them. Finn will have a fit. There's an old Mason jar in the kitchen, covered in dust. I bet Regina won't miss it. I'll take it, hide it in my room. We can put our fish in there and bury them somewhere when we get a chance. Back by that tree line behind the house."

Emmett nods. His voice is barely above a whisper. "I don't want you to fish in the mornings. These people get money to feed us."

"It's not worth fighting over. I don't want to defend you against Finn."

"Who asked you to?" Emmett steps around an older couple who have stopped to chat, becoming boulders in the stream of people. "I don't need your protection."

"You will if you keep pushing him. Just… try to get along. Focus on school. Learn as much as you can."

"Stop trying to control me all the time." Emmett stomps ahead.

I don't recognize his gait anymore, the way he flexes his shoulders when he walks and the fight in his step. He became a man when I wasn't looking, while I was busy caring for our father and then our mother. When did he get so stubborn, so sure of his place in the world? It seems like just yesterday his best friend was a chicken and he was playing in mud puddles.

He's always been the one I could trust the most. He'd protected me a thousand times. Every time I climbed a tree too high and got stuck, he diverted Mother's attention while I figured it out. Every time I left the gate open and the chickens got out, he'd help me gather them up before anyone noticed. And I'd always repaid the favor when he fell off a horse or nearly ruined his clothes playing with the pigs and running in the woods. Now I'm not so sure I can trust him to make choices that'll keep either of us out of harm's way. In this new world, Em could cause us big trouble, throwing us into the wrath of Finn. And with this fishing ban, if I'm not careful, we could both land in prison. Mayor Whitaker doesn't seem very forgiving.

I lag, letting the distance between Em and me grow.

It takes most of the evening before I find a chance to get the Mason jar from the kitchen, find a weak seam in my mattress and slip the stitches to make an opening. The jar fits right in among the cotton, down by my feet. If someone had told me when I was ten and Emmett put a fish in my bed as a joke that I'd someday sleep with fish in my mattress on purpose, I'd never have believed it.

As I settle in and the moon's shadows creep along the wall, I remember the mermaid's purse in my skirt pocket, hop from bed and tiptoe to my closet, then hold it up in the thin moonlight.

Rebirth, I think. *I could use some of that.*

I need to take my own advice. Get to school early, take my placement test, and prove to that school and the world that I can do this. I can take care of myself and Emmett, and I don't need anyone's help. I didn't ask for this new life, but I have it now, and I have no choice.

The mermaid's purse fits on the windowsill next to my coal lion. And I fit back under the covers again, blanket tight under my chin, where I wait for sleep to sweep me away.

* * *

I'm up before the sun, dressed in the plainest clothes I own, a dark blue skirt and simple white shirt. I tie a stained apron around my waist and sneak down to the creek with the pail Finn left by the door.

The creek reeks of dead fish, their little bodies caking the rocks. Birds of prey peck at the herring and catfish carcasses, taking flight into the trees and showering me with morning dew. A few small live fish scuttle in the water, in a little pool between a fallen branch and some weathered rocks. The morning mist has yet to lift, and the creekside's slick, my shoes unsuitable, but I find the net where Regina said it would be and fuss with the ends, pulling in the morning haul.

Beside me, a black snake slithers onto a rock, waiting for the morning sun to warm his bed. Plucking apart a knot in the net, I remember a time when we were younger. Emmett was four, perhaps. He'd been terrified of a black snake on our porch. I'd picked it up and carried it off to the woods, and it let me. It stuck out its head and hung limp in my hand while I carried it off to a safer home. I'd hated snakes, slithery and unpredictable, but I'd been surprised at how brave I could be when I had to. How easy it was to trust my instincts, to step into the fear and let it evaporate around me while I got more confident.

I can do it again, for just a while. Stand in the Ryans' house and take whatever they throw my way. I can play by the rules in this backwards town until it's time to leave with my head held high, and it'll only cost me a price I'm willing to pay. It doesn't have to wound my pride or dim my spirit, not if I don't let it.

Back at the house, I leave the full pail of fish under the bench where Finn said to. If that doesn't satisfy him, nothing will. Dressed for breakfast in my favorite cream-colored skirt with its field of flowers reaching toward the sun, I bound down the stairs. Our first full day. It had to be better than the one before.

Pausing at the bottom of the steps, however, I hear the

unmistakable brusqueness of Finn's voice come from the kitchen.

"Got some nice fish," Finn grumbles. "I trust you didn't let nobody see you."

Emmett clears his throat. "Not a soul out there this morning."

Gentle knocking at the front door rattles the window in its frame, and I jump two feet in the air. My heart in my throat, certain I was seen and they were coming to collect me, I rush to the door and fling it open to find a startled young woman about my age, forcing a smile and squinting into the darkness. Sunlight picks up light flecks in her brown hair, freckles spatter her cheeks and nose. She's taller than me by about two inches, clothed in a simple blue skirt and matching shirt. She taps the tips of her fingers together, looking more nervous than a pig on slaughter day.

"I think I'm supposed to help you," she says. "I'm Beatrice, but everybody calls me Bea."

CHAPTER SIX

Bea's smile fades as she cranes her neck to scan the room, and I can't blame her. The house isn't even my home, and heat creeps up my cheeks and burns my ears. The shame can only burn hotter if Finn pops out from somewhere, so I spare both Bea and myself the discomfort, step onto the porch, and pull the door shut.

I fumble through my greeting, and Bea does the same, gracious and dainty as she is. As she asks where I'm from and says how sorry she is about my parents, she swats a mosquito and glances around the porch. Her eyes scan the decaying windows and crumbling siding with a smile that never falters. The only place to sit is the dried wooden bench covered in lichen and moss, and it's no place for a young lady.

Her eyes land on the flowers embroidered up my skirt. "That's stunning. Did you do all that?"

"I did. Though I have to admit, I felt out of place last night at that meeting."

Bea waves a hand. "Don't let people bother you."

"I would like to get a few yards of fabric," I say. "To make something plainer for every day."

"Then we must go shopping," she declares. "Besides, you probably need paper and supplies for school."

Emmett declines the invitation, so I promise to bring him something back. With permission from Regina and a few dollars in my pocket, I launch off the porch, and the further down Main Street we get, the more I'm aware of the attention I draw. Two women step out of the pharmacy and do a doubletake, staring me down as they pass. One of them mentions the larkspur sprigs that tower up my skirt. She whispers it to her friend, but I hear her anyway, and warmth creeps up my cheeks. Bea becomes more animated, as if her kindness can soothe the sting.

"I've always loved larkspur. Here's the Five and Dime." Bea says it as if she were discovering a long-lost treasure. "We must go in. They have everything."

Two stories high with a mansard roof, the general store has broad windows and deep-set doors. A welcoming bell rings out when we step inside. It smells like wood and lady's perfume. There's a large, deep table full of candy just inside the door, stuffed with Necco Wafers, taffies, and hard candies. There are captivating aisles of wooden bins and shelves running to the far wall and back again. Toys and games and pots and pans, dolls and shoe polish and household cleaners. I've never seen so many colorful packages in one place. The company store in Stoke had necessities and could order anything special, but I've never seen so many things under one roof, none of it covered in coal dust.

Bea drags me to the back of the store.

"Here are the paper and pencils." She pats some pages on a shelf. "I bet we have most of our classes together. We have the world's worst math teacher. Not that she's bad at math. She's just strict and has no sense of humor."

I cradle two bundles of paper in my arms and stack pencils on top.

"Why do you need so much paper?" she asks.

I glance at the heavy stack in my arms. "There's two of us, me and my brother, and I'll be writing a lot of letters home. Don't I need paper to take notes and do classwork?"

"You won't need to take notes." Bea cocks her head to the side. "You'll take easy classes like boring math, civics, and home economics. You already know how to sew. What else is there to learn?"

I carry my stash to the front register. The woman presses keys on the giant machine. It pings and chimes, and I hand over my dollar.

"History. *Real* economics. I want to go back home and run my own business one day." I accept my change from the woman but reject the raised eyebrow.

As we step outside, Bea gives me one of those appeasing sort of smiles that says she thinks she's in on a joke, but I'm deadly serious.

"Why would you want to run your own business?" Bea asks as we pause to let a lady with a baby carriage pass before crossing the street.

The answer's hard to put into words because girls like Bea don't need to understand. They have parents and friends who can offer support in ways that Emmett and I do not.

"I don't have a choice, Bea. Even if I did, I suppose I'd think it lovely to support myself."

Bea makes a face like she's trying to drag the truth from a child. "Well, I consider it my personal challenge to make you feel right at home here."

My emotions are such a soupy mess that the kindness brings tears to my eyes. I blink them away and try to laugh. "You've been more welcoming than you can imagine."

We step into Sidney's store, and the bell rings out. Bea snags a bolt of blue fabric and carries it to the counter. "Two yards, please. On Mother's account."

"And four yards for me, please. For a new skirt."

"It's nice to see you again so soon." Sidney nods his greeting and unfurls the fabric with a clawed hand, favoring his thumb as he stretches the fabric along the ruler. "I do have a sewing job for you if you're interested. Young lady in town is getting married. I can't pay much."

"I'll do it," I say. No matter how little it pays. I can't resist the urge to touch the shiny yellow ribbon that flutters from a spool on the counter like spun gold. "What kind of stitching do you need?"

"White tulips embroidered on the bodice. I don't have room for you to sew here, though. You would have to take it with you." Once he gets the scissors under control, they slide through the fabric like a hot knife through butter. He shakes his hand when he sets them down. "Arthritis. It's not bad every day, but it's enough I can't keep up with some things. It's not steady work, and I can't pay much, but if you're willing, I will pay something."

"Oh, yes, sir. I promise. I'm very reliable, and I'll even sew the sleeves on if you'd like. Thank you so much for the chance." I catch myself smiling and for the first time in weeks, I don't feel guilty about it. Finally, something I can do that gives me a little hope.

"No need to sew the sleeves. I can give you the materials, and I'll pay half when you start and half when you finish. Four now and five later."

"Nine whole dollars?" That's almost a third of my savings, and much more than I expected.

"It doesn't pay much, I'm afraid. Not as wedding dresses go."

"It's more than generous," I say. "Nine dollars is wonderful. Thank you. I promise I won't let you down."

Sidney shuffles into the back and adds the thread and bodice fabric to my bag of purchases. I promise to have it back in three weeks. All the while, Bea scans bobbins of candy-colored thread before joining me on the sidewalk.

"You're serious about leaving?" Bea asks. She steers us to the left, past the consignment shop, toward her home. "Where will you go? Have you family you plan to stay with?"

"No, but I'll be out of school soon." And with luck, Emmett will be better by then. "I plan to save as much as I can. I know it would take a miracle to buy back our home, but we must be closer to Stoke."

Bea's nose wrinkles when she laughs. "You're going to buy a house with nine dollars?"

"Well..." My cheeks burn. "It sounds ridiculous, doesn't it? But I'm going to work hard and save up and someday, I will."

"That could take *years*," Bea says. "Women can't even buy property here. The town won't allow it. Do you have a beau at home you're planning to marry?"

"That would ruin the plan," I say with a smile.

"If your plan does fail, you can always stay here. I think once you give it a chance, you'll find it's quite nice."

As much as I want to believe her and wish it were true, my gut tells me something different. Between Pine and his pack of roving boys, the officer who lets them run feral, Finn, a town that wants women under its thumb, and an entire generation locked indoors, there's clearly more to this place than meets the eye. Bea's enthusiasm and willingness to look past the oppression make me want to get my home back even more. I don't want to end like that, excusing tyranny as it presses down on me, bending merrily to its will.

"I bet you could use a good lunch and some lemonade." Bea lifts her chin, pointing across the street, toward the market. "My father runs it. He's a butcher, too, and he smokes meat. My mother makes a great stew, and she made me promise I'd bring you by. What do you say?"

"Lunch and lemonade sound wonderful." My stomach is already growling, and I've been aching for a warm meal that doesn't involve fish.

We cross the street, and Bea pauses outside the market. If not for the benches on the porch and the older men huddled there, the store could be mistaken for being part of the house. The left door is plain, white-painted wood. A small sign above it, shaded by the awning, declares it to be Mitchell's Market. The door on the right has a simple brass knocker and a mail slot. Bea greets the cluster of men, half of whom look up at her with grandfatherly affection, the other half engaged in impassioned conversation.

"All I know is I'm not paying no more taxes on no fish." A lean man whose legs are all knees sits ramrod straight, an unlit pipe clenched in his teeth. He fiddles with a book of matches. "God put them fish there, and he didn't do it for Mayor Whitaker."

His friend with a shining bald skull and a rim of white hair framing his face, shakes his head. "You have to pay Caesar what's his. You saw them haul off Vickery. Don't break those rules."

"Shame. Gettin' arrested for fishing out of turn." A man in a brown ivy cap tugs on its brim. "Went down to the water an hour too early 'cause his wife didn't wind the clock. That's what he said, anyway. Counting on the sun instead. Those early hours are for commercial fishing now. They change the rules so much to keep you confused, then nab you when you break 'em. Haul in a net an hour too early, and you're snagged for the pen." He snaps his fingers.

"There's no fish in the afternoon. Everybody knows that." With the flick of a match, a flame sizzles and flares. A thin wisp of sulfur reaches for the sky.

Bea grimaces. "Vickery's not out of jail yet?"

All eyes turn to us. They stroke their beards and rub at their wiry eyebrows. No one's heard a peep from the man, they say. Though rumors run wild.

"Keep his seat warm," Bea says. "They can't hold him forever."

Inside the market, an older man with puppy-dog eyes, hair white as snow, and Bea's chin beams from behind the counter. He raises a cleaver and waves it. His introduction is cut short by a man asking after turkey livers, but the man who must be Bea's father waves a hand at the end of the counter and tells Bea to take as much egg salad and maple fudge as she wants.

Bea grabs a package from the end of the counter and pushes out the back screen door. It slams behind us with a comforting snap of a hinge and a thud. The gravel lot behind the house spans several buildings and stretches out to a tree line where a grassy patch beneath the canopy begs to be sprawled out upon, but Bea steers us through her back door.

"I don't know about you, but I'm starving," Bea says.

The kitchen is tidy, cluttered in the way a warm and useful kitchen should be. The floor is tiled with various shades of reddish brown in a diamond pattern. There isn't a grain of dirt in the grout. Pots, pans, and colanders cling to the walls from nails. A sink sits beneath the window with an enameled wash pan just like Mother's, and a cold wave of grief washes over me, pushing me back, as I recall all the times I snagged that wash pan to play in the yard, filling it with water and washing rocks like potatoes. A table rests in the corner, with dough rising in a bowl, and the whole place smells of a real home, like yeast and wood smoke. A piece of my heart breaks, yearning for my mother's kitchen, for a place where food is there for the taking and where bread is a comfort as much as a necessity.

Someday the memories won't hit me so hard, and these waves of grief will be smaller, farther apart. That's what people say. Until then, all I can do is choke them back.

"I love your kitchen," I say.

Bea throws open a door of the monstrous stove and stokes a fire. "This stove is so old, but it gets the job done. Mother wants a gas one, but father says it makes the food taste bad. I say it's not bad, just different."

"I've heard that," I say, clasping my hands. "Speaking of different, can I ask you a question? Do you know anything about the Ryans?"

Bea pulls the lid off a pot of stew, gives it a stir, and steam mushrooms over the stove. Beef with barley and big chunks of potato swirl in a thick sauce. "They stay to themselves, mostly. Mr. Ryan does odd jobs for people, fixing up porches and things like that. He's not very good at it, if you ask me. Rumor is he's a bit of a stumblebum and drinks on the job. I heard Father say he spends more on the drink than he makes in a day."

That explains the lack of furniture and general care about the upkeep of the place. No wonder Regina gave up.

Bea ladles stew into bowls and sets them aside, leaning this way and that to gather bread and plates and cups and refusing my offer to help. Instead, I savor the energy. Regina's kitchen is bare by comparison, too few pots and not enough room to make such graceful choreography. I haven't ever thought about it before, but in all the best kitchens, cooking is a dance.

"Let's eat in the dining room," Bea says. "Right through here."

I take a bowl from Bea before she drops it.

A small pantry divides the kitchen from the rest of the house, cabinets and shelves of dishes on one side, cans and jars on the other. The small but pleasant dining room is papered with floral wallpaper and there are windows looking out to the alley where birds rustle in a shrub. Narrow stairs in the corner coil up to the second floor. The table is made of the glossiest, shiniest wood I've ever seen, and I lower myself onto an embroidered chair, feeling out of place among all this tidiness.

Bea nods to the front room. "It's a mess in there. We were playing games last night, and there are still cards strewn everywhere."

"No, please don't apologize. It's…" The first piece of permanence I've felt in two days. The Ryans' house is so stark that it's almost like life stopped when we left Stoke. I missed these little signs of living. A clock on the wall. A calendar counting down the days. Games and books.

Bea must notice the mist of memories settling on me, because she talks a mile a minute about school and the dance as she slathers butter on some bread.

"You are coming to the dance, aren't you?" Bea asks, her knife poised in the air.

I take a sip of stew broth and nearly crumble at how delicious it is. "Mr. Benner mentioned it, but I don't want to go, to be honest."

"Oh, you must." Bea's eyes widen. "There's a whole week before then, and you'll meet so many people. You'll love Ruthie and Hazel. I'm sure I can introduce your brother to some new friends too. There are some very nice boys here."

I would have to take Bea's word for it. "I've met the not-so-nice ones. Twice, actually. Some boy named Pine?"

Bea groans and rolls her eyes. "He's the biggest bully we have. Were they hard on you?"

"Somewhat. I suppose I wasn't so kind to him, either. I did break his nose after he tried to dig his hands in my skirt pocket."

Bea winces. "He deserved it, then, for acting like that. He's in our grade, but he's not a great student. Illiterate. It's not a secret, I guess, but no one talks about it. Just mentioning it will unhinge him. Wouldn't recommend it."

"That's not much of a scandal." Most of Stoke was illiterate, and the ability to read certainly doesn't contribute to anyone's character.

"But *he* feels bad about it. He's terrible at school, not just his grades. He lashes out at everyone who studies hard, and he hates the girls. *All* of us. I think it's because his mother left when he was so young. She packed her bags and ran off."

My fork slips and clatters to my plate. "She abandoned her family?"

Bea tilts her head and gives a sympathetic glance at the ceiling. "People say she wasn't the marrying type."

"I can't imagine. To abandon your family? That's ghastly."

Bea straightens her back and stabs her fork into her stew. "Not to gossip, but I think that's why he's like this. He acts feral, girls reject him, and he gets mad. It's a vicious loop. He thinks we're his enemy. And what did you mean before, in the store, when you said you don't want to get married? Are you a sworn spinster? I've never met a sworn spinster before."

"No! Well, I don't think so. I haven't thought about it, but perhaps I am." It seems fitting. I can't imagine what being a wife and having children would be like. "All I know is I have plans. Marriage is a taxing institution, and if I never enter into it, I won't have to pay the price."

Bea looks at me as if I have six heads. "But who would take care of you?"

"Me. I would take care of myself."

There's a flash of admiration in Bea's eyes. "Good for you. It's very brave to go your own way. I'd love to have a family, grow old in the town where I grew up."

"And a long and happy life you shall have," I say. "How *do* people deal with Pine, then?"

"Don't let him get to you. Those boys are all bark, no bite." Bea dabs at her mouth with her napkin. "What about the net tying tomorrow with the suffragists? Are you coming?"

If my mouth weren't full, I'd drop my jaw.

I'd heard about women who want the vote. A lady in Stoke had a copy of *The Woman's Bible.* I'd begged and pleaded, and Father finally borrowed a copy. He said suffragists have a way of bringing issues to light, like temperance and workers' rights, but there's no such movement among the women in Stoke. If there are suffragists here, I want to join them.

"Net tying? Suffragists?" I ask. "Yes, indeed!"

The back door slams, and a woman's voice bellows out from the kitchen. "Yoo-hoo! Beatrice? Are you in there? Is your new friend with you?"

I recognize Bea's mother from the market stall at the train station. I start to thank her for the directions and kindness after we lost our map to the puddle, but she recognizes me too, putting both hands up.

"Oh, we meet again," she says. "I'm Leta, and you must be our Charlotte. That young man with you must have been your brother."

"Yes, ma'am. That was Emmett. And thank you for the directions and lunch. It's wonderful."

Leta settles into a chair, tugging her sleeves smooth. "I'm right glad to hear it. Eat up. No one visits this house and leaves hungry."

Bea pokes at her stew. "Mother, I was telling Charlotte about the net tying. She's never heard of it before."

"We all meet down at the creek to tie nets before church," Leta says. "The fishermen abuse their nets on these rocks, so we do what we can, but we must keep that quiet. Women aren't supposed to gather, but we still get together at times to make new ones."

"Tell her about the suffragists," Bea says, wide-eyed.

Leta purses her lips and gives Bea a look that could kill. "We don't talk about that either. It's not much of an effort, to be truthful. Just some women with opinions. Keep that under lock and seal."

"I won't say a word." I have a million questions. Suffragists! Here? Leta seemed eager not to talk about it, so there must be more to it than some women with ideas.

Leta jumps to her feet. "I have an extra netting needle, I'm sure of it."

She climbs the stairs, and the floor creaks overhead as she

rummages, and when she returns, she places a tool before me. It's about as long as my hand and shaped like a boat, but flat. Smooth, and made of deer antler. Pointy like an arrowhead on one end with a notch cut in the other. Bone has been carved from the middle, leaving a void with a central spear, and judging by the shape of it, I assume twine is wrapped around the spear somehow and the pointy end used as a needle.

It sits heavy in my hand, comfortable. It fits.

"You can keep this one." Leta smiles and pats my hand. "I have so many. I'm happy to see it go to a good home. Regina doesn't participate, and I'd hate to see you miss out."

"It's called a shuttle," says Bea. "Or a netting needle. Now that you have one, you must come."

"That's kind of you. Did you say—" I have so many questions about Regina, the suffragists, what they're doing to stand up to the mayor, but the clock in the corner chimes three times, and a sour wave roils in my stomach. "Is it three already?"

Bea spins in her seat to check. "Sure is. Time flies, huh?"

"Regina is going to kill me." Before Bea even turns back to face me, I'm on my feet, gathering my packages and sputtering my thanks for the lunch. "I'm so sorry. I wish I could stay and help clean, but I'm afraid I could be in quite a lot of trouble if I don't get back to help start dinner, and I was supposed to be there at three."

My heart is pounding before I even reach the door.

"Of course. No, you should go." Bea follows me out the back door, pointing me down the alley. "Shortcut. I don't want you to get into trouble."

Sweaty and disheveled, I clutch my bags and race down Main Street. The door is open when I arrive, and Regina's eyes shoot daggers from the kitchen doorway.

"I'll just put these away and grab an apron." I apologize profusely, haul my shopping up the stairs, and knock on Emmett's door.

When he answers, I push a package of paper and two pencils into his hands. "Here. For school. I'm late to help with dinner."

"I'm sorry I took credit for the fish," he whispers after me.

"It's probably best you did."

Regina's kitchen smells nothing like Bea's, equal parts bland and sour. It's hot as the deepest depths of Hell, yet somehow manages to be colder than any other kitchen I've ever known. Whether kindness or neglect occupies her mind, Regina doesn't seem to mind my lateness. She merely makes room for me at the work table and motions to the knife and the pile of carrots.

She doesn't smile enough to be a true antithesis to Finn, but I feel a warmness toward her anyway, and I endeavor to make her smile. Mother had once said that even the dullest place could be improved with a bit of shine.

"I could sharpen this knife for you, if you'd like," I offer.

On second thought, maybe Regina prefers it this way.

CHAPTER SEVEN

As I force the knife through a carrot as thick as my finger, Regina kneads dough to within an inch of its life. It'll taste like a horseshoe if she doesn't stop soon. "Emmett can sharpen that knife if he ever comes out of that room. What's wrong with him, anyway? Coughs all night."

"He's sick. He'll get better, though."

I drop a handful of carrots into a soup pot of water that simmers on the stove. An entire chicken is crammed into that pot, little bubbles just beginning to rise to the surface. In another ninety minutes, I'll be straining the entire chicken and picking its bones clean, and nothing about it makes me look forward to dinner or any meal that follows.

Regina slaps the dough into a bowl and wipes her hands on a rag. She plunges her hand into a bucket of water and pulls out a herring, throwing it on a cutting board and fileting it with a small knife. I pick up another and do the same. "He has a spine, that brother of yours. Brought in fish just as he was told. If he gets caught, this whole house will suffer, though. Do you understand? Finn's family has been in this town forever. There's a certain amount of protection that comes with being from a founding family, but there are limits to what that reputation can do."

It seems like a warning that extends beyond fishing in the creek. And the way people consider me when I mention the Ryans, I'm certain Finn passed the limits of his reputation long ago, and that only makes me wonder how much protection he has. He seems to get away with an awful lot. Her voice is soft, almost scared, and the warning hangs in the air between us, trapped in the heat of a solemn kitchen. So much for brightening this place up a bit.

I've only been in this house, in this town, for two days, but all around me the world is peeling itself like an onion, showing its menacing layers, its shadows, the places where bitterness festers.

"Can I ask…" I put down the knife and run the back of my hand across my forehead. "I keep hearing about how much trouble we could be in, about people being taken to jail, curfews, and how dreadful the mayor is. Why? I don't want to cause trouble and neither does Emmett."

Regina doesn't make a sound. She doesn't look up or sigh. It's as if I haven't said a word.

"Please," I beg. "I'd like to keep my brother safe. Why are there so many rules about fishing? You're sending him out there to do it when they're washing up dead and the mayor says he could be arrested for it."

She swipes her hand across the table, pulling slate-gray fins into a pile. Then she coils another filet, tail end first, into a roll, and sets it aside on the slimy table. "We don't question the mayor. Emmett shouldn't be going down there at all, but I won't speak against Finn. Sometimes you got to choose between types of suffering. Going hungry is a lot worse in his mind than being in jail, and he's the man of this house."

"The punishment is extreme, don't you think? It's almost like they don't want you to have the fish. It's alright if the herring are sold to people outside town and the money lines the mayor's pocket, but they don't want *you* to look at them closely enough to see that something's wrong with them."

Regina drops the knife and places her hands on the table, hanging her head over the cutting board. I doubt I'm saying anything Regina hasn't already considered, but the darkness that takes over her eyes says the sin is in saying it out loud.

She grasps the knife and goes back to work. "It's the fish kills. They happen all the time now. There are less herring to be had and less to sell. Whitaker's just making sure the people at the top are the ones who make a profit. Money takes care of itself."

"But why go to all this effort when you can just find out what's killing the fish and stop it?"

Regina rounds on me. "It's not a conspiracy. They're just dead. Get back to work."

It's not that simple. Not to me. That many fish don't just all die at once for no reason. I've lived under a poisoned sky long enough to know that accepting fatal disasters is a terrible way to live with things. And the longer you let people with power tell you not to ask questions or think too hard about things, the more they profit from the truth.

That night when we sit down to dinner, I avoid the fish, cutting it into pieces and hiding it in my napkin. Emmett does the same. When Finn looks up and laces his fingers over his plate, clearing his throat loud enough to rattle the windows, I hold my breath and brace for backlash. There's no concealing what's in my napkin if I'm asked to shake it out. Still, I'd rather face the known menace of Finn's wrath than the darkness that lurks in the fish.

Finn sucks food from his rotten teeth and picks at them with his pinky nail. "I don't care what you children do, so long as it don't get me in trouble. You will be in this house when you're told. And there won't be any blatant disregard for the law in this town. I won't have you questioning the ways of this house."

Emmett flinches, rippling the air, but he isn't the delinquent one. He's been in his room all day.

Finn's head swivels, snake-like, to me. He's ready to strike. "I know you had a run-in with the law, and I'll not stand for your bullshit. Both your doors will be locked at night after the nets are set, and I'll unlock them in the morning when it's time to go out and collect 'em. And from now on, you both go. You better learn to pull your own weight in this house. No more showing up late to help with dinner and questioning how things are done around here. Do you understand?"

I say yes as I slice into a piece of boiled carrot, keeping my eyes down so he can't see my chin quiver.

A locked door at night isn't punishment to me. I can sit and sew for hours. But it's torture for Emmett and his night terrors. For as long as I can remember, he's panicked behind locked doors and from the blanket of night when it's all too dark.

Emmett's hand trembles. He can't handle this. He's not prepared for it. Neither am I.

His fork rattles against his plate.

Finn turns to him, pointing a finger in his face. "You'd better not screw up. Keep that girl in line, and quit that damn coughing, because you won't like what happens to you if you're found down there by that creek. Jail will be paradise compared to what I'll do. Don't act like fools. It's a man's job to keep a woman in line. You hear me?"

Emmett nods, his eyes fixed on his plate, and my heart breaks, seeing him sad and scared. At least his anger is in check this time.

Finn picks up his fork with his tanned, bony fingers and spears a hunk of fish.

"Finn?" Regina, red-faced, places her hands in her lap.

He wields his fork in her direction. "What?"

"I think… Perhaps…" she stammers. "I think these two ought to know what's been going on. They *do* have to stay out of trouble."

His eyes fly open wide. "Oh, you want to tell them that the police are scooping people off the streets, putting them in jail and holding them without charges? That when a man's in jail for two months without an income, his woman has to scrape to get by? And let me tell you, you will not rely on the kindness of strangers if something happens to me. We will not be indebted to this town." He turns to me, his eyes on fire. "The constables here aren't a joke. Fit in. If I end up in jail next to you, life will be a lot different when we get out."

Finn doesn't wait for the table to be cleared before he orders us upstairs. He climbs them behind us. I'm two steps into my room when the door slams shut and the key grinds in the lock. My heart pounds in my ears as I grab the handle and twist, pulling on the door, but it's no use. Short of tearing the door off the hinges or jumping from the window, I'm in for the night.

The key turns in Emmett's lock, and he erupts, pounding and kicking the door. I have to do something, but I don't know what. Em sobs and pleads, but his words are jumbled, and they catch in his throat until coughing takes over.

"Em, breathe," I plead through the wall, but he'll never hear me over his coughing and gasping for air.

I sit on the bed and pull my knees in, willing him to calm, praying to the God I don't believe in that he'll give us some peace for a while. And if we can't get peace, perhaps he can help me be the kind of person who can stand up to Finn.

In the room next to me, Emmett gulps, his breath ratcheting in swells of panic. It used to happen all the time when he was younger. Behind a closed door at night, he'd curl himself into a ball and wail until Mother came to calm him. Finn won't take kindly to weakness like this. I'll have to help him get through this. But how?

"Em. I know this is stupid, but do you want to play patty-cake through the wall?" I clap my hands together silently, then touch the wall. He's fifteen, not five, but it's all I can think of to distract him and bring him back to reality. "Patty-cake, patty-cake, baker's man. Bake me a cake as fast as you can."

It takes a few iterations, but he finally joins.

"We used to do this," I say. "Remember?"

"Yeah. Faster and faster until our hands couldn't keep up. I don't know why it worked." His voice is finally steady.

"Do you feel any better?"

"A little," he says. "It's too bad I can't summon up a fart when I want one. I'd like to fart on Finn."

I can't blame him. "Tomorrow morning will be better." I fold my arms and watch the tiniest of spiders weave her web between the window frame and the curtain. "It has to be. We'll get settled in school soon and get through this. We'll find a way to keep you from coughing so you don't get caught when you're fishing."

"I found mint growing outside, along the neighbor's house, and I took some leaves and saved them."

"That should help. I miss Mother's mint tea."

"Thought it was magic how she made it in the sun. Remember sitting on that scratchy old blanket under the maple tree, eating pie and drinking sun tea? I wish we could go back, Charlie."

"Me too."

I'd give anything to reach into my memory, grab that feeling in my hands and hold it to my heart. If I could just hold in my hand a hint of sunlight through my window on a spring morning, capture on my fingertips the way the first birds of summer sing as the sun comes up, I'd stash it in my pocket and hold it there forever.

This place is the opposite of home in every way. Cold, dark, and comfortless. Sharp, hard, and raw. We'll have to trust each other to make it through, and I've been failing Em since long before we got off the train. I wasn't asked to be plunged into this role, and I don't know how to go from being his sister to being whatever it is he needs.

I gather the sewing for Sidney and pull it onto my lap, spreading the fabric over my knees, studying the contours of delicate tulips I'd traced before dinner with my new pencil. It's all I can do. A small thing I can control. A tiny hope I can give myself. The tulips could use a hint of variation, some off-white thread to help define the petals, but Sidney only gave me one color. Nothing good comes without a bit of sacrifice, and knowing I could replace it later, I pulled some thread from my own skirt, unfurling the embroidery of a mock orange blossom and threading it into my sewing needle.

"Can you promise me something?" I ask. "Don't stand up to Finn. Promise me."

"I don't think it would end well if I did," Emmett says.

"Where did you go?" I ask. "When you found the mint?"

"Down to the brickyard, just to look around. I didn't go in. Oh, I saw that Pritchard man, that big boss from Stoke, down at the train station."

My breath catches in my throat, and chills run down my arms. I pause at the end of a satin stitch and leave the needle pierced in the fabric. "Are you sure it was him?"

"It was. By the train. He shook hands with that mayor guy from the meeting."

My chills swell into a cold sweat. The man who destroyed Stoke and killed our parents met with the man who makes this town hell on earth. They shook hands. It can't be a coincidence, can it?

"You're sure?" I ask.

"I'm positive."

"Do you think there's some kind of mayor network? Why would they even know each other?" I ask.

Emmett's bed creaks. "Maybe he's selling coal down here or something."

That seems like an obvious enough reason, but it doesn't sit well with me. Why would the coal boss be down here hocking coal when he has men for that? "I can't put my finger on it, but this doesn't seem good. Can you keep it a secret? Don't tell anyone you know who he is or what you saw?"

"Sure." Emmett yawns. Of course he doesn't care. He doesn't know I wrote Father's speeches, and I'm not sure telling him would be a great idea.

"Know what's worse than that?" he asks. "I saw what work at that brick foundry looks like. Man, that's a dirty job."

"Are you trying to find work?" I ask. "I can give you money. I have some."

"I don't want your money. I want to earn my own like a man."

"Emmett." I set my sewing aside. "You promised Father you'd get an education."

"Why can't I do both? Hey!" he exclaims. "Where would you get money if you didn't sew?"

"Here? I'd probably sell fish just to piss off Whitaker."

Emmett laughs. His mood is so improved that I don't see the need to argue with him about working while he should be focusing on school. That's a battle for a different day.

"Hey, I had an idea earlier," he says. "We could turn Finn into the cops for the fishing, so he gets in trouble instead of us. I found the police station on my walk. It's not far."

That would make life impossible for both of us.

"New rule, Emmett. No going to the police. Period."

"Why do you get to set all the rules?" he asks.

"Because Mother and Father told me to." I trace the contour of a tulip petal, creating its delicate curve. Then I start on the next.

If Em starts making poor choices, growing loud and angry, he will get us separated. Not once did it occur to me that my own brother might be our undoing. And there are even bigger things to worry about, such as figuring out how to handle Finn. Being compliant and amenable hadn't worked so far. And why was Pritchard here, talking to Whitaker? It could be as simple as two men exchanging greetings, but as Father often said, there is no such thing as an unhappy coincidence.

CHAPTER EIGHT

The riverbank is wet, spongy beneath my feet, and its petrichor perfume hangs thick. Women's voices float up from the grassy plateau where the river curves on its way through town, and by the time I reach them, my shoes and the hem of my skirt are soaked. Suffragists. Gathering against Whitaker's wishes. On a Sunday, even. Just the idea of it feels like danger. Good danger. Like mystery novels and whispered secrets and hope.

Two dozen women are spread out on blankets along the riverbank, some already working the twine in their hands, tying nets that fan out toward them, anchored by sticks shoved into the ground. Others are just getting started, chatting and laughing, spooling twine around their netting shuttles. The atmosphere is festive, almost the opposite of the edict in the park, but sizzling among the women and the petrichor is an unmistakable static of things not being quite what they seem. I'm determined to get to the bottom of it.

I feel in my pocket for the shuttle and find Bea among the flock. She scoots and shimmies, patting the space beside her, and I settle next to her on the gray wool blanket. I lean over to accept a warm hug from Leta.

"Thank you again for lunch yesterday." Shifting, I sort my skirt beneath me. "Sorry I left in such haste. I should have stayed to help you clean."

"Certainly not. You had somewhere to be. We don't let guests clean up after themselves in our house, and you are always welcome."

Leta's warmth draws me in, but only so close.

"I don't want to go stirring up hard things," she says. "But I know you've had some rough times, and if you want to do any talking, our door is open. I make good lemonade."

"Thank you, ma'am." I avert my eyes, pulling my shuttle from my pocket before a mist rises in me. I don't want to need this sympathy, but I let it soak into me all the same.

In the days that followed my parents' death, plenty of people told me how stoic I was, how proud they were of me for standing strong in the winds and gales. Sometimes I see Emmett, though, the way he carries his emotions around with him, on the verge of lashing out, and I envy how coiled up tight he is. No one asks him not to be. No one expects anything from him. He's eternally on a precipice, poised to leap, while I must shove my sadness down into my roots and be calm and still for both of us.

I flip the shuttle over, testing its fit in my hand. Leta's already gone back to looping twine around hers, around the peg and between the fins, and it looks easy. Meditative even. Like something I might enjoy.

"It's fun once you get the hang of it. Watch." Bea shoves two sticks into the ground, small poles on which she loops some twine.

"One for me, one for you. That's how you start a net."

"Bea says you do embroidery, and you're working on a wedding bodice for Sidney." Leta nods to my skirt. This one is light blue with white daisies and golden butterflies. "Did you do those flowers?"

"I did. My grandmother taught me. It fills the time and makes the world a little brighter."

Women on a blanket nearby crane their necks to see my hem, where daisies and poppies bloom. Some women are kind and smile. Others raise a critical brow, but I've lived in a dismal world of smoke and coal dirt for so long I don't have room to care about other people's gloom.

Their conversation turns to Whitaker, and as much as I strain to soak in every word, my mind keeps wandering to Pritchard and what he could want from this town. But I don't ponder it for long before one group of women gets loud, and another hushes them.

Not all the women seem to agree on what they ought to do, let alone what they can.

"Votes would be a wonderful thing," Leta says. "But we aim for more attainable things here. It was right here on this riverbank we hatched the plan to get that new school built."

"And it's right here on this bank we'll fail to do enough to get ourselves the vote." A woman with an infant sets down her shuttle and bounces the child on her lap. "I'm not here for a Sunday chat. I'm here for the movement. Some of you are just too scared."

A woman with dark red hair in a plait down her back and a freckle-spattered nose glances up at the bridge, then back at her work. "People talk big down here by the river, but they won't all have your back when it matters. My husband stuck up for what's right and paid the price. At least some people think it's shameful what I've been through."

An older woman tries to shush her, but the red-haired lady throws up her hand. Leta leans over and tells me her name is Minnie. She's small with thin fingers and deft little hands that work fast, but there's nothing miniature about her personality. It's as big as the sky, and you can see it in the flare of her nostrils as her temper flares.

"I don't mean you," Minnie says, nodding to the older woman. "I appreciate what you've done. David would have died if you and Annie hadn't come that night after they beat in our door, but I won't be silent." I wouldn't dream of asking what happened, but she turns to me anyway, answering my unasked question with her green eyes on fire. "The police accused my husband of stealing something from a store. It was a lie. Revenge for complaining that a cop was taking bribes. They dragged him out of our house at night, beat him in the street, and left him. I would like to vote so I can Whitaker and his men out of office."

"Don't scare the girl," a woman says.

"She ought to know what she stepped into," Minnie says.

"Something similar happened in the town where I lived," I say. "It was just a little village until they found coal. Then a coal town popped up. Eventually the boss became the mayor too." I tell them how, after my fifteenth birthday, I woke to voices downstairs. Father and his friends were swapping stories about Pritchard. They met at our house because we were just outside the coal town, just far enough away from prying eyes and loose lips.

I didn't tell the women the whole of it, how the next morning I found Father's first speech written out on scraps of paper. I rewrote it, reordering their demands so they sounded like a sermon, with all the points coiling into a crescendo, and I left it by his lunch pail. He didn't say a word about it. Days after a brawl broke out at the coal breaker, I heard Uncle tell my aunt how Father read a speech that started it, and I knew from the way he described it that he'd read my speech to the crowd. Days later, a dozen men were injured at a brawl, some of them gravely. Pritchard called in the police and gave them a list of lies. The policemen went door to door, dragging the men who started that brawl into the street. I felt responsible for a long time after that.

It wasn't until I got up the courage to ask Father about it that I realized how hard the coal work was, how people were getting sick and no one knew why. Father said it was all inevitable that Pritchard kept the people in chaos, and the more they tried to come together, the more comfort he took away. They had to force change. Later, when sickness and death circled our family and friends, I vowed to help the cause. He said no at first, but his friends demanded more speeches like the first. It wasn't until later I learned that the violence never stopped, it just took different forms. It happened in the dead of night, Pritchard lashing out at those who rose up for better treatment. I heard the stories at the dinner table and late at night, when men's voices traveled up to my room. I thanked God we lived outside of town and weren't in Pritchard's debt. Pritchard treated them terribly and called it consequences. Father called their uprising a just war.

The grief and pain in Minnie's eyes are so much like what I'd seen in Stoke that I realize how plausible it is that Pritchard and Whitaker would be acquaintances. They both feed off causing misery. Why wouldn't men like that be drawn to each other?

"All in the name of power," Minnie's friend says. "Her husband can't walk now. Can't work. He's a shell of who he used to be, just for doing what's right."

An older woman with sparkling white hair ties off a net and pulls it from its peg. "Constables followed two of his neighbors for weeks. Stopped and searched them, threatened them into silence. My brother was one of them. They forced their way into his house at night, kicked him out and locked the door. Seized his entire house. They make you afraid to talk."

"Or vote him out," says a woman further up the creek.

Another laughs. "Like voting would work. Whitaker stuffed the ballot box. Then he jailed his opponent. Coleman was in his eighties. Died of a heart attack and never got to say goodbye to his wife." Her plait falls into her netting, and she flings it back over her shoulder.

"At least he didn't live long enough to see these fish kills." A plump woman with rosy cheeks leans back against a rock, inspecting a knot of twine on her needle. "Taxes keep going up on what's left. They ain't using that much money to pay for that school. These men keep lining their pockets off our hunger."

All this time, Bea's been paying rapt attention, her shuttle laying idle. Leta nudges her back to work, and I follow Bea's motions as she works the shuttle and the net, looping the string around the flat rock I'm using as a gauge, wrapping and twisting, knotting the twine as the net grows out from the post in front of me. There's a rhythm to it, a cadence.

"Catching on fast." A woman in a brown dress pauses, her shadow casting over my work.

"Thanks." I squint up at her.

"Don't let the talk scare you."

"I've seen the same in a coal town," I say. "The workers got fed up from being injured in the mines, working all the time. The air was poisoned, and people got sick and died, but the coal boss wouldn't do anything about it. You can't vote out a coal boss, so our men fought back."

The woman turns back to me. "Did they win?"

I shrug. "I'm not sure. The poison killed my parents, and here I am."

She clicks her tongue. "Shame to lose them so young. Where are you from?"

"I grew up in Stoke," I say.

"Anthracite country. Been through there on the train. Heard a bit about it. You're staying with Regina and Finn?"

A million questions come to mind. Why they're so unkind. What Finn is so afraid of that he hides by drinking his last dime. Why Regina has no family or kin who can see her to a better place. But the trees have ears and the company could be mixed, so I give her a faint nod and the politest smile I can muster. "I hope we won't be with them for long, my brother and me. I'll graduate soon. Then I want to go back to Stoke. I want to make my own money somehow, maybe start a farm like my grandparents did. Rent some lodgings until I can buy a house of my own." And it occurs to me if she's heard of Stoke, she might know things I don't. "Can I ask a question? Have you heard the name Pritchard? Any idea why Whitaker would be at the train station meeting with the mayor of a coal…"

Church bells drown me out, pealing across the town. Around me, women gather up their things, pull their sticks from the ground and toss them in a pile beneath a towering tree. I'm disappointed I didn't get an answer to my question, but judging by their confused looks, they didn't seem to know anyway.

I yank my net from its stake and add my stick to the pile. My feet ache to run back to Finn and Regina's and find Emmett. I need to know every detail of what he saw.

Voices drift down from the bridge. Emmett's up there, walking with a group of boys about our age. They pass through a spot of shade and into the sun again, and I catch Pine's unmistakable silhouette. Of all people Emmett could pick to hang around with.

"Who is that other boy with them?" A woman shades her eyes and glances up at the bridge.

"That's Emmett. My brother."

Minnie folds her finished net over her arm, shaking her hair away from her neck. "Those boys are trouble. Watch what crowd your brother runs with."

"They're not all trouble," another woman snaps. "One of them is my nephew. Known them since they was small."

"Vernon is a good boy. He's always polite," Minnie says. "But that crowd is bad news, Martha. Those boys have grown apart. You'd be wise to keep Vernon from them."

I tuck my shuttle in my pocket and ball my net in my hands. I would have to warn Emmett.

Anne, the woman in the brown dress, pauses next to me, eyes narrowed at the group of boys. "I saw the lot of them roaming the streets last night after curfew. Last week they beat up old man Barlow. He was on his way to the pharmacy, and they took every penny he had. They're no good."

"Is that why we have a curfew now? Because of them?" I feel in my pocket for the netting needle. It's an odd sort of comfort.

"Hard to say. The only thing we know for sure is that whatever reason Whitaker says he has is usually not the real reason."

I have to get to Emmett. I thank Bea and Leta, gather my skirt and scramble up the hill, crossing the bridge and following the boys but keeping at safe distance. As they approach the pharmacy, I stick close to the buildings and, gaining on them, I tug Emmett's sleeve, pulling him into the alley next to the store.

"Pine will bring you nothing but trouble." I peek around the corner to be sure I'm not heard. "The women said that group boys is up to no good. And what's in your hand?" I pull on his arm and a pack of cigarettes tumbles from his fist to the ground. He bends to pick them up. "You can't smoke. Your hands will turn yellow. You'll go crazy and kill people."

"That's not real, Charlotte." He rolls his eyes and pulls his arm away. "That doesn't happen."

"It is true. I read it in the paper a long time ago. Where did you get the money for this?"

I know the set of his jaw, the glint in his eye. He won't answer. I grab his elbow, ready for an argument, and he wrenches away. I snag the cigarettes from his hand.

"You're not my mother." He spits his words. "You're two years older than me, and I'm not taking orders from you."

"These are bad for you. You'll turn into a cigarette fiend," I plead. "You just got out of a coal nightmare, and now you want to take up smoking? Are you batty?"

He shakes his head and his hair whips into his eyes, the tips of his ears flaring red. "You have no right to tell me what to do."

Pointing to the pharmacy, I shake my finger. "Everybody knows those boys are bad news. All the women said so, and you didn't see what Pine did to me."

"You walked right into him. It wasn't a big deal."

"No, Em. You weren't there when I broke his nose. You didn't see what happened after that."

"That was you?" He rolls his eyes and huffs. "What's wrong with you? Why are you breaking people's noses?"

"I was defending myself. And that's not the point. These boys will get you into trouble."

Through gritted teeth, he says, "Or they'll get me out of it."

"Are you talking about Finn? They won't help you there, I'm afraid. I'm only trying to help you. They aren't your friends. And I promised Father—"

"Stop." His eyes go wide and his lips pucker in as if he's trying really hard to keep the words in. "I don't want to hear about what you promised Father."

"Fine. Then I won't mention the promise, but you're still going to school. You will not work at a brickyard. And you will not smoke cigarettes. You just escaped choking on your rotting teeth as they fall out of your bleeding gums. I fought hard so you could have this opportunity."

"And you think I should do whatever you say for eternity out of gratitude?" His jaw flinches. "Father also said I'm the man in the family now. I don't see grown men taking orders from their sisters."

"Grown men don't do stupid things like smoke." I forced my voice back down an octave. "Don't look at me like that. I know they do. But they're stupid things to do, and you're not stupid."

"You're embarrassing yourself, Charlie." He yanks the pharmacy door open. "And you're embarrassing me. Leave me alone."

He storms into the store, and the door closes in my face. I spin on my heel, choking back tears, and storm up the street. Am I being too heavy handed? He's angry and grieving, and I understand all that, but he seems oblivious to the consequences.

I barely see the buildings I pass or the families walking to church. Rushing against their tide back toward the Ryans', I blink against the stinging tears, the net unraveling in my hand. I crash to a halt at an immovable wall, the hulk of a man in a black suit, and when I lift my head, I look directly into the eyes of Mayor Whitaker.

"What do you have there, young lady?"

At first I think he means the net, but I follow his gaze down to the crushed package of Emmett's cigarettes.

People stop and turn to stare.

I shift to my right, trying to dodge him, but he steps into my path again.

"It's not illegal," I say. "I'm seventeen."

"Yes, I know. And you came from Stoke. Your father was Frank Morris, your mother was Carla Denver. Your father made a lot of trouble for people, and your apple didn't fall far from his tree. You were lucky they died and left you penniless, because if he'd lived, things would have been far worse for all of you. If you're wise, you will use your time here to make some new habits. If you don't, you will further acquaint yourself with our constable, and your aunt will be very sad to hear of it."

Lucky? Lucky they died? Bile rises in my throat, and I swallow it back.

"I haven't done anything wrong," I say.

"You would be wise to keep it that way. Imagine how pained your aunt would be to find a constable on her doorstep too." He lifts his chin, smoothing the buttons of his velvet jacket. "You wouldn't want harm to come to Sophie, would you?"

More people dressed for church stop to witness the spectacle. From the corner of my eye, I see Anne in a fresh brown dress. Leta and Mitchell hang back in their doorway. Finn's warning to fit in, to lay low, is all but forgotten.

My hands are hot and slippery, and my mouth goes dry. Whitaker's smug look snaps something in me. I can't protect Emmett, but I sure can protect myself.

"Are you threatening my family?" I ask. "Why do you even care who I am?"

"I know everyone who lives in this town." He bends down to me with all the stern tenacity of a teacher who won't be defied. "You'd be wise to remember that you are nothing but a schoolgirl."

I can't stop myself. A thousand questions swarm within me, bouncing off my better judgment. "Why did you meet at the train station with Pritchard? How are you connected to Stoke?"

Whitaker lifts his chin, and his sneer makes my blood run cold.

"It's almost time for church." He checks the time on the pocket watch that drips from the chain at his waist. "Don't you think?"

"I wouldn't want to keep you," I whisper. He might miss out on all that forgiveness from his sinning club.

Ahead and behind me, across the street, people stop and stare. Whitaker brushes my shoulder as he passes, and a sinister heat ripples off him.

I take two steps, ignoring the eyes on me. As the church bells ring for the start of service, I hold the pack of cigarettes over a trash can, crush them in my fist, and let them fall.

CHAPTER NINE

I refuse to look back. Heart pounding in my ears, I rush back up the street toward the Ryans'. A few doors open and close behind me. Mothers warn children not to play in the street and sully their church clothes. Men scowl at me for rushing past them, but it all blurs around me.

With my hands balled into fists, gritty bits of tobacco grind into my sweaty palm, and I squeeze harder.

Whitaker knows about my father. That means Pritchard saw him as a serious threat, not just a noisy distraction. Should I write to warn Sophie? It seems absurd to send a terrified letter suggesting the mayor of some distant town might seek her out. Surely they would say I'm over-reacting. Aunt and Uncle already know about Father, and Uncle is still a part of the resistance there. Sending a letter could only complicate things, especially if it's intercepted.

I could find Emmett, pack our bags, hop on the train with my twenty-seven dollars and settle somewhere closer to Stoke. But no one will employ a teenage girl with no connections, and I owe Sidney the sewing. He's too kind for me to let him down, and if Emmett doesn't finish school, he'll be doomed to labor in the mines forever. He doesn't want to listen to me anyway, and running away won't solve anything. Finn's roof might be unstable, but at least it's over our heads.

I can't go back to the house like this, wild-eyed and frazzled. It'll raise too many questions. I'd have to tell Finn the truth if he asked, and no doubt he would. If I don't tell him, when he finds out later, there will be twice the hell to pay, and Emmett's already gone to bed hungry because of me.

I cross the bridge and slip down the hillside, the slick soles of my boots sliding on the grass. I reach for a tree trunk to steady myself just as I realize I'm not alone. Three women stand by the water where we tied nets not that long ago.

"I still don't understand how bringing back the water festival will help," one says. "We aren't supposed to gather."

"It's not about the festival," says another. "It's about the protest. Whitaker can intimidate us in small groups, but he can't stop the whole town."

"Hush," says Minnie. "You never know who could be listening. There are a few men who would consider a run against Whitaker, but they need a push. They don't feel safe. If those potential candidates see a big protest, they'll know they have support."

"And reinforcement," says the second. "Come, we need to be seen at church. We're already late."

I hide myself behind the trees as the women climb the gentle bank and make their way across the bridge. A sudden warmth grows in me for those women, especially Minnie, who lost so much, taking such a risk. I'd want to cling to every bit I had left.

* * *

Later that afternoon, I settle back in my room with the sewing, stitching tulip stems at the little table. When the house is empty, I sneak my jar of fish outside, cover my nose, and bury its contents, digging a hole in the soft earth with a spade I found against the side of the house.

I have more to worry about than poisoned fish. What if Pritchard found out I wrote Father's speeches? If he thinks I'm communicating with people from Stoke, he might just bring the fight to me. Pritchard could swoop in, destroy Emmett and me, and Bea is the only one who would notice. I need to confide in someone.

Leta. Surely, she must be in on the suffragists' plan to hold a protest and unseat Whitaker, and she's a safe person to talk to.

I wash the jar and return it to its hiding place in my mattress. Then, with plenty of time before dinner must be started, I take the shortcut behind the buildings, avoiding people, dodging down the alleys until I reach Bea's house. I knock and she flings open the door and pulls me in. Her eyes are wide, incredulous.

Her hand wraps around my wrist, and she yanks me through the sitting room. A sunny yellow wallpaper brightens the room. A corner bookcase teems with books, papers, and trinkets. Chairs with rose-colored embroidered seats flank the fireplace. Bea guides me through the dining room and into the kitchen where Leta tends to pots on the stove. I find myself plopped into a chair at the little table.

"Mother saw you talking to Mayor Whitaker this morning. She said he looked angry. What did he say?"

Leta takes two cups from a narrow cupboard by the stove and puts them before us. "I think it's time for lemonade."

"I don't want to impose." I blink down at the cup.

"Don't think of it." Leta fills the cups. "Whitaker seems to have a keen interest in you."

"Did it have something to do with Pine's nose?" Bea asks.

"No. Not that," I say.

Leta fills a cup for herself and places the pitcher back on the windowsill. "Then what was it, dear?"

It's hard to talk about, but I must if I want advice, so I tell them almost everything. "People were unhappy long before they started getting sick. Everyone knew it had something to do with the coal, but Pritchard and the doctor denied it. Some men threatened Pritchard, and he set the mine operators on them and seriously injured some of my father's friends. Father tried to reason with anyone who would listen. The doctor. The man who paid them. But it didn't work. Then some of the workers started meeting at night, in secret, talking in small groups and trying to organize. Father wasn't trying to be a leader, but it just happened. Then he died, and here I am."

I leave out the part about Father's speeches, because I have a feeling Leta wouldn't want Bea associating with me if she knew.

"That sounds familiar," Leta says.

Bea grabs my hand across the table. "That must have been terrifying."

"It was. The mine operators burned a man's house down. But Em and I were too worried about our parents to pay much attention at that point. They were getting sicker."

"And no one tried to stop those men?" Bea asks. "There's something to be said for turning the other cheek."

"Turning the other cheek hadn't worked. It was so much worse than I can express, Bea. They had no choice but to defend themselves." People couldn't just move away or find different work.

The coal company paid for their passage from Ireland and Germany, and Pritchard was of the mind that he owned those men until their debts were paid. But they couldn't ever pay him back. Pritchard harms those workers for profit. As Father was dying and the sky thickened, as people grew angrier and sicker, Pritchard intimidated them with beatings and arson.

"Thank you for listening to me," I say with a smile. "I'm glad to have a friend. *Friends.*"

"I'm glad to have you too," Bea says. "Everyone needs a smart, brave friend. I'm so very sorry, though. It must be so very stressful losing everything."

"What should I do? Nothing? Should I tell Finn?"

Leta gathers linens off a chair and carries them down the hall, her voice fading as she goes. "Heavens no. Tell no one."

"What if Finn finds out?" I ask.

"Then tell him Whitaker asked about your family and leave it at that. And for your own sake, don't reply to that man again. Smile and look pretty. You could make a reputation for yourself with the wrong people if you're not careful. You heard the women this morning. It doesn't matter if you deserve it or not. If Whitaker has it out for you, trouble comes your way." She returns with a pile of kitchen rags and dumps them on the table, folding them into squares.

I pinch the bridge of my nose. "I'll have to warn Emmett. He's having a hard time with all of this already. I know I have to be the strong one who knows what to do, but I'm lost."

Bea gives me a knowing grin. "He'll find his way."

Leta pauses, sets a folded rag on the stack. For a moment she glances between Bea and me with a look that borders on nostalgia. I realize she knows the side of grief that's like a battering ram, not just the sharp kind that carves away at your chest and sends you curling up under the covers. When she places a hand on my shoulder, I know she understands me in a way Bea can't.

"You always have a place here," she says. "No matter how hard you think it will be, you can always come here. I do wish we had room for you and your brother, because I'd bring you here in an instant. That house…" She shakes her head and nods to the door. "You two go into the market and get a treat. You need to eat. Skin and bones you are, and Regina doesn't feed you."

I thank Leta, take my last sip of lemonade, and follow Bea out the back door and into the market.

The store is closed for Sunday, but she slips behind the counter and takes a few pieces of fudge before we go back out into the blazing sun.

Behind the store is a span of trampled grasses where people tie their horses and walk along the creek. A stand of sweet gum trees has left a layer of prickly pods on the ground, but the little table and chairs are clear, so we sit across from each other, and I accept a piece of the most delicious caramel fudge I've ever tasted. Sweet and sticky, I let it melt on my tongue, resisting the urge to sink my teeth into it.

We spend the afternoon beneath the trees. She tells me about her friends Hazel and Ruthie, about classmates and teachers. We pluck little white chamomile flowers from the wilding patches by the tree line, and she teaches me how to string them together into a crown. When the sun dips, I shade my eyes in the patchy sun. Without the heavy cloud of Whitaker, and the heavy hand of Finn, I almost believe I could enjoy it here.

"It's probably nearing three," I say. "I should go soon, so I don't get in trouble. I'm trying to win Regina over, and I don't want to be late."

A flutter of motion in the shrubs along the creek gets our attention.

"What's back there?" I ask.

"Just the river. It comes past where the Ryans live, winds down here, and dumps at the park. A bunch of rivers meet just south of there, after the lighthouse, and become the Chesapeake Bay."

With a crash of branches, a figure emerges from the river's edge. It's Emmett, scrambling into the clearing from a shaded trail.

"Where have you been? I have to tell you about—" I start to warn him about Whitaker, one of his cheekbones is purple, his eye blood-filled.

"What happened?" I scramble to my feet and reach for his face to inspect it, but he swats at me. He smells of tobacco and beer.

"Did Pine do this?" I ask.

"Don't you dare touch me," he says.

"Is it Finn?"

Bea scrambles to her feet. "I'll get some ice from the root cellar for your eye."

"It's not Finn. It's you, Charlie." His voice is calm as falling snow. "You defied Finn, and he knocked me down for it. Leave me alone. Don't talk to me ever again."

Something changes in his demeanor, and he seems bigger, taller with his shoulders back and his chin up.

"I wish they'd split us up," he says.

"This isn't my fault." Except I suspect it might be. "I'm sorry. I'll talk to Finn."

He throws his hands in the air. "You're not listening to me. I want you to remove yourself from my life."

His words sting, and I wince. "Emmett! You don't mean that."

"Yes, I do. You and those stupid fish."

"I'm sorry. I know you're angry at me, but I don't know what you're talking about. Did Finn find the jar?"

"No." Emmett folds his arms like an indignant child. "He caught me trying to sell fish down at the train station."

I rub my eyes with the heels of my hands. "What is wrong with you? I told you I'd give you money."

"I want my own money, and that's not the point. I get in trouble for doing what you said you'd do—"

"We weren't being serious!"

"But it doesn't matter." He points at his eye. "Look at me. Don't act like I'm not supposed to be angry, Charlie. Why aren't you? You're fine with all of this."

Something foreign rises in me, hot and unsettling, rattling my bones and shaking my hands and my knees. It vibrates my senses. This is just another wedge that Pritchard has hammered into my life, cutting off more pieces and hacking me into bits.

"I am furious, Em. What makes you think that I'm not? I don't expect you to know what I think about at night, all the times I sat on the edge of your bed as you spit blood into a pail, hoping you won't die too. Both of us should be sick. Not just you. Do you know how guilty I feel that I didn't spend time in town like you and your friends, that I didn't get sick like you? Do you know how much I wish I could take it from you? But I don't have time to be sad or upset because I have to hold everything together."

Saying it out loud feels better. Not like relief or a lessening but like a conflagration. Like a bonfire raging in the darkness. It feels strange and foreign, but unlike all the other feelings lately, I don't want to tamp this one down.

"Stop trying," Emmett spits at me. "Leave me alone."

"Fine. I'm not saying what Finn did was right. Obviously, it's not, but just remember that if you keep pushing his buttons and trying to make friends with those boys you might get us separated after all."

My stomach's been tied into a hard ball for so long that I can't remember what it was like to live any other way. Every night I curl up and hope it will all be better by morning, but then day comes, and I have to stand up straight and choke it all back while trying to pretend it's all just fine. All those days, I had to get up every morning and act like I was perfectly capable of selling our things, cooking our meals, cleaning it all up, and doing all the tasks the state said I simply couldn't, while Emmett's teeth were falling out and death ran through the house.

Grief keeps knocking, but there's no room for it. All the things I ought to do, the ways I ought to be, echoed in my head all the time.

This new wave of hot anger feels different, though. An antidote to the powerlessness that's been hollowing me out since sickness first crossed our threshold.

Bea returns with chips of ice in a rag that grows damp. Water drips, leaving a dark spot on her skirt.

"Is he gone?" she asks.

I nod.

"Then I'll just use this for some tea."

I'll be gone too, eventually. I'll go home again. And I will find the sinew that connects Pritchard to all this pain, and I will cut him out and make him pay.

CHAPTER TEN

I don't know what I expected, but it wasn't this. The school is a box. A large, two-story brick box with windows. It's far larger than anything else in town, and it doesn't look very welcoming, but I don't need it to be. If it can give me an education and help me prepare for something after this, I'm sure I'll look back on it fondly as one of the most beautiful buildings I've ever known. But when I sit down to take my test, I realize Bea was right.

I should have known I wouldn't get the classes I want. Everything else has been going wrong. What's the point in sitting through half a day of placement tests if they're only going to insist my life's purpose is to sew buttons on shirts? I'll just have to read all of Em's books and beg him to teach me everything he learns, if I can convince him to talk to me again. Perhaps Mr. Benner will take pity on me and lend me some books. And if all else fails, I'll have more time on my hands to figure out how to use Whitaker to get to Pritchard.

A woman who looks as hard as the bricks themselves — sharp-angled, cold and unmoving — hands me a list of classes and a stack of books and pushes me into the hall. She tells me to wait outside the assembly room for classes to change, and as I lean there against the wall and ponder my fate, I have time to wonder why I haven't heard from Sophie yet and what I should say when I write to her again. I wish we'd established some secret code before I left so I could warn Aunt and Uncle about Pritchard if the mail were being searched. But there isn't much time to ponder, because doors fly open and students flood the hall from every angle. Bea rushes at me and grabs my arm.

She glances at my tower of books. "You got your schedule?"

I nod at the paper tucked between my books. Bea snags it.

"We're in most of the same courses. They're not so bad. Look, we both have civics after lunch. Come on. I'm starving." Bea steers me into the assembly room, a vast empty space with chairs and tables scattered about. We settle at a table by a sunny window.

Sharing a schedule with Bea makes things feel less bleak, but I still struggle to muster a smile for her friends. The twisted grin feels unnatural. I'm glad I wore an old, plain work skirt so I don't stand out.

"This is Ruthie and Hazel." Bea unwraps her lunch of bread and cheese. "I told you about them."

Ruthie is a pretty girl with wide green eyes and thick, dark lashes. Her curly blond hair is held back with a blue ribbon, and her dark blue dress is perfectly pressed. She has an angular chin, and her gap-toothed smile makes her seem younger than her years.

"It's marvelous to meet you. Brilliant, even. We heard someone new was coming. I hope you've found the town delightful." She blinks, enthusiastic, and I try to twist my face into a grin while I say how wonderful everyone is, and how quaint and perfect the town seems.

Hazel cocks an eyebrow and I can tell she's the suspicious one. She wears her dark brown hair parted in the middle and tied back in a low bun. She has a tired expression that borders on a pout, unaffected and natural. It's refreshing, in a way.

"Nice to meet you." Hazel plops down onto a chair without fanfare.

Bea squeezes her sandwich. "Charlotte is from Stoke."

"Where's that?" Hazel asks. "North, right?"

I nod. "Coal country."

Hazel inspects her rather smelly deviled ham and curls her lip. "How'd you end up here?"

"Against my will." I tell them the story as I pick at my sliced chicken. It's better than it looks, which is more than I can say for the other aspects of the day and things that come from Regina's kitchen. "My choices were either to stay and become the young bride to a man in need of a maid or accept being an orphan. And here I am."

"Well, welcome to hell's outhouse, then." Ham falls from Hazel's sandwich. "It really is as ghastly as it seems."

Ruthie flicks her hand, shooing Hazel's notion away. "It's not so bad."

"Look at it this way," Bea turns to face me. "If you get through this, you can go to college. You could be a teacher!"

"Certainly," I say with a laugh. "If I embroider eight billion wedding dresses, I can afford to pay for that. I'd much rather learn how to run a business."

Ruthie perks up. "You want to run your own business? Gosh, that sounds fun."

Her eyes are twinkling, and it sparks a bit of excitement in me. I start to tell her about my grandfather's farm and how he fed the whole town before the coal company came in with their promise of wages and their company store.

"Want to join our literary society?" Hazel's suggestion is met with silence and wide-eyed blinks from the other girls. Ruthie clucks her tongue and shakes her head as if Hazel gave away a big secret.

Yes. I want to join whatever this is.

"Don't talk about that." Ruthie hisses. "You know we aren't supposed to have clubs. She could run and tell everyone or let it slip by mistake."

Suddenly, school is a lot more interesting. "What's this? A covert group of women forming a subversive literary society? I want in. I won't tell. Why can't you have clubs?"

Ruthie rolls her eyes. "It's not a conspiracy. We read books and talk about them. It's a book club."

"We write stories too." Bea keeps her voice down. "And we publish them in a journal that we run on the mimeograph machine in the teacher's lounge. But we never say who writes them because girls aren't allowed to be in clubs. We pretend the whole thing is written by the boys, but it's all anonymous and no one knows who we are."

I duck my head and whisper. "I still don't understand why girls can't be in clubs."

The three of them exchange wearied glances.

"Why not?" I beg.

Hazel takes in a big gulp of air and sits up straight. "We aren't supposed to be like *that*."

"Like *what*?" I ask. "Readers?"

Ruthie smoothes her skirt over her knees. "We're supposed to be at home. Not endeavoring for things." She laces her fingers and throws her elbows on the table. "Our mothers banded together. They wanted us to have a real education, like they have in cities, with better books, so they raised taxes to make it happen. It made a lot of people angry, and because it showed what women can do when they make a plan… Well, they don't like it when we do that anymore."

It explains a lot: Leta warning the women not to get too chatty, saying that the woods have ears. The town doesn't trust women.

Bea swallows her bite. "We have to be quiet when we get together. They fired Miss Walters for having a sewing club. She was just teaching girls how to make quilts. That was months ago. She had to answer questions down at the police station and everything. Please don't tell."

I agree. I don't need to join a literary society. I need to find Pritchard's Achilles heel and clean up Stoke. Figure out what connects Whitaker to Pritchard before both of them come for me, and I have every reason to believe they're both watching. With Whitaker on my tail, the fastest way for Bea to lose her literary society will be for me to show up. They don't deserve that. "Don't worry. It's not for me. Thanks for the invitation, though. I won't say anything. I promise."

I push to my feet and toss the last of my sandwich into a trash can on my way out the door. Let them incinerate it.

Everything in this town is as cold and dull as the brick walls of this dim hallway. Everyone accepts these arcane rules. It's no way to live. It makes me even more determined to get home, so I don't end up the same way.

I pause outside room 105, where I'm supposed to learn about civics for the next hour, but I'm early and I'm not alone. Emmett paces in the recessed doorway like a caged lion, but when he sees me, his eye purple and black, he freezes in place, then storms down the hall and around the corner, into a growing crowd.

"Emmett?" I call after him. He doesn't come back, and I don't expect him to, but the permanent knot in my stomach twists and coils tighter knowing a whole day has gone by, he won't talk to me, and I still haven't told him about Whitaker's threat.

The hallway floods with laughter and footsteps. The door flings open to our classroom, and younger students tumble out. Bea joins me by the door, and Emmett slinks past us for a seat across the room. I can feel everyone's eyes on me as they enter the room. They chatter in clusters, and I know they're talking about me. I shouldn't care what they think, but I do. Bea and I make small talk about the weather until the teacher calls for quiet and asks Emmett and me to stand and be welcomed. I glance at Emmett. I don't know why. Some instinct to present a united front so we don't look so weak and vulnerable. I'm surprised when he glances back at me, and there's a coldness in his eyes. A chill runs down my spine and keeps me ramrod straight when I take my seat again.

"That was icy." Bea leans toward me and whispers. "Still not speaking?"

"Seems we're not."

"Today, we're discussing Thomas Paine," the teacher begins. "The famous pamphleteer. He's famous for being the first to make a public call for independence. Does anyone know why *Common Sense* was so persuasive?"

A boy in the front row raises his hand. "Because he wrote it like a sermon."

"That's right."

My eyes glaze over by the time we reach Paine's comments on Monarchy and Hereditary Succession. And my mind is stuck on Pritchard. He knows far more about me than I know about him. Why chase me all the way down here? Why would a man of that stature with so much to do with his days take the time to tell Whitaker that my father led an uprising? Pritchard won that battle when my father died. Pritchard must know I wrote Father's speeches then. But how? And why does he care?

Around me, everyone shuffles their papers and closes their books. It snaps me to attention.

"If you can help our new classmates acclimate, please do," the teacher says. "They may have questions before the next test, so don't hesitate to show some kindness. Does anyone have questions about the homework?"

"I do." A vaguely familiar voice calls from the back of the room.

I glance over my shoulder to find Pine with his hand in the air. Of course, we'd be in the same class. I snap forward, eyes fixed on my book.

Pine clears his throat, and silence falls on the room. It's a small comfort that he has a reputation for terrorizing everyone. At least it's not just me. But it doesn't bode well that no one's knocked any sense into him yet.

"Are orphans entitled to help from the town? To use the school?" he asks. "They don't contribute anything. They only take. Doesn't that make them servants who must repay their debt to society?"

Bea bristles and hunches her shoulders, glancing at me as if she has something to say, but I am physically incapable of looking up from my desk. I don't need sympathy or pity from Bea or anyone else, and I definitely don't need to see Emmett's reaction. Scratching little daisies in the corner of my paper, I will my burning cheeks to cool.

The teacher places her hands on her desk. "I didn't expect that kind of question from the mayor's son."

I drop my pencil and it falls to the floor. Bea scoops it up. The mayor's son?

"To answer your question, no, orphans are not asked to repay their debt. The foster system is one of many social programs that benefit everyone. We take care of each other because that's what God intends. We love our neighbor, and it's in everyone's best interest to ensure that we all become healthy, productive members of society."

Outside the classroom, doors open and the hall fills. The teacher glances at the clock. "Don't forget your homework. See you all tomorrow."

Pine is the mayor's son?

I take my pencil from Bea and fumble with my books, pretending to scan the chapters. My knees are weak, and if I stand I'll only wobble and give away how helpless I feel. How alone.

"You go on ahead." I motion to the door. "I have a question for the teacher. Lots of catching up to do." Bea doesn't argue, but she lingers a moment, and I can tell she wants to offer to wait. "It's all right. I'm not offended. Like you said, I only have to deal with Pine for a little while. He has to live with himself forever."

When Bea makes it far enough away, I give the teacher a polite smile and pretend to be enamored with a page in my textbook. When the classroom is empty and the hall nearly quiet, I stack my books and tie them together with the leather strap, hug the bundle and stand.

Pine might make me teeter, but I refuse to let him distract me. He can taunt me all he likes, but he won't get an ounce of my dignity. It's all I have left, and I refuse to waste it on him.

The hall is nearly empty. Except for a few quickened footsteps echoing off the walls, most of the students are already in their classrooms. Doors close all around me. With a good, cleansing breath, I make it five paces toward my next class when someone grabs my shoulder from behind and spins me, pushing me against the wall. A warm hand presses against my shoulder, and I lift my chin defiantly because I know it's Pine's eyes I'll meet. My heart thunders in my ears and my palms sweat.

We're not alone. Some boys shuffle in behind him like the cards of a sinister deck, along with some stragglers running late for class who pause to ogle. Seven or eight boys at most. I recognize some of them from the police station. I set my jaw and narrow my gaze, commanding my racing heart to run cold.

"Are you following me?" I ask.

"You owe me." His breath smells like rotted meat. His nose is still bruised and crooked.

My stomach churns. "I don't owe you anything."

"Ungrateful bitch. We put the food on your table," he says.

"You certainly do not. If you did, I'd rather starve."

He moves closer, his leg pressing into my thigh, and I feel the netting shuttle in my pocket. Clutching my books in one hand, I let the other drop to my side. My fingers inch for it. I wrap my hand around it. That netting needle could do a lot of damage, shoved in the right place.

"Eat this." Pine reels back and hurls hot spit on my cheek.

I recoil, but I let it drip down my cheek as I grip the netting needle tighter, biting my tongue. Fighting back will only make it worse.

Pine and his father are dangerous, and he has his claws in my brother.

A menacing smile spreads across his face, and I lose my weak grasp on my temper. The hot spit on my cheek becomes fuel for my fire.

"Nobody feeds me." He'll pay for this. Not right now. Eventually. "I feed myself."

Pine pulls his arm back, spooling up for a blow, and I brace myself to lift my knee, to take my pound of flesh in return, but a boy rushes down the hall, reaches through the crowd, and grasps Pine's shoulder.

"Stop," he says. "Enough. Leave her alone. She's not bothering you."

Pine's sneer doesn't budge, but he glances away, and I peek over his shoulder into the kind dark eyes of the Greek Poet. Whether he's Pine's only reasonable friend, the lone voice of dissent in a mob of hyenas, or prolonging the torment for his own amusement, I don't care. The whole lot of them can burn in hell's outhouse, as Hazel so aptly called this place.

"Let's go," the Greek Poet with kind eyes says, pulling back on Pine's shoulder.

Pine slings his last arrow. "See you around, Blondie."

CHAPTER ELEVEN

I nudge the bathroom door open and find it empty. At least I have the place to myself while I clean Pine's spit off my face. My hands are shaking, and I'm not sure if I'm more angry or scared, but the water is cold and my breath hitches when I wipe at my cheek.

I feel like a cannon went off and struck me in the chest, like I could implode and fall to pieces so small no one would even notice me. I refuse to cry, though it swells inside me, closing my throat. Gripping the edge of the cool sink, I stare, wide-eyed, at the ceiling, hoping the tears will dry before the fall.

The door creeps open. Ruthie tumbles in with Hazel and Bea behind her.

"One of the younger girls saw you in the hall with Pine," Bea says. "Are you alright?"

I insist my feelings aren't hurt, but I suppose it's obvious I've been wounded. Bea spins me around and tucks in her lower lip, inspecting me as if I'm a muddy kitten she found on the porch as Hazel fusses about my hair. Meanwhile, Ruthie warns me about tangling with Pine, as if I didn't already know.

"He likes you," Ruthie says. "That's all."

She means well, but the notion doesn't shift my mood. "Even if it's true, it's no excuse," I say.

I accept a handkerchief from Hazel and dab at my eyes in the mirror, but it's no use. Between the anger and the sorrow, my eyes are red and puffy.

"I just want to go home," I say. "I want everything back the way it used to be."

"Join our literary society," Ruthie pleads. "Even if you don't write, you'll feel loads better if you have something to do."

"I do write. And it would be nice to have something to take my mind off everything," I say.

"I can't imagine how hard all of this must be," Bea says. "I always feel better when I have something to think of other than my problems."

"It would take my mind off Pine," I agree.

Maybe I was being rash before, thinking I couldn't have friends. They were already running afoul of the rules. I couldn't truly make it worse by joining.

I return Hazel's handkerchief and walk with them down the hall to our next class. As they chatter around me about boys, I can't help but think about how cathartic the literary society might be. I could even use it to get back at Pine. If their writings are anonymous, perhaps I can satirize those awful boys without anyone realizing it's me.

Emmett approaches the classroom just as we do. I tell Bea to save me a seat, and I grab him by the arm.

"What do you want?" Emmett barks. His eyes are pure fire, but they don't rest on me long. He spins to peer out the window.

"Two seconds." Inside the classroom, the teacher calls on a student to read a passage from Tom Sawyer. It buys me some time. "I need to talk to you about Whitaker."

He makes a noise from the back of his throat. He has every right to be angry, but so do I. He could make friends with anyone, but he chooses Pine?

"Please forgive me," I plead. "I'm sorry I got you into trouble with Finn."

"At least Finn's predictable." He drops his books and paces, hands in his pockets. "You're worried about my behavior, and you're the one getting into trouble. He's also right. You should be seen and not heard."

Ouch. "Emmett, I'm trying to help. We have to look out for each other."

"I don't want you to look out for me," he says. "I want to go home. I didn't ask for any of this."

"You think I did?" I hiss. "You think I woke up one day and said, 'Gee, it'd be super if our parents get sick and slowly die while the state says I'm incapable of putting food on the table, but they can't find any place we can stay together, so I write a hundred letters and annoy a dozen people until they find a place out of state that'll take us both?' While you wouldn't come out of your room? We have to make the best of this. You're busy hating me, and I'm counting how many times you cough every night because I don't want you to die too. And I don't sleep because I'm listening at the wall in case you have a night terror. You're having more of them, you know."

Eighteen days. It's only been eighteen days since they died and Emmett isolated himself in his room. Seventeen since our aunt said she was sorry they don't have room for two more mouths to feed, and I told Emmett I'd find a way. Fifteen days since the state came and told me I'm unfit, and I swore I'd keep us together. Twelve days since the bank showed up and people started carrying off Father's chair and Mother's drum table, and Em yelled at the buyers. I have counted every day, logging them all like inventory I could take back to the company store and return. All the while, Emmett has been losing control piece by piece, and maybe I haven't given him enough room for his own grief.

"I'm sorry." I roll my neck and look at the ceiling, rubbing my eyes. "I'm trying. Things will get better. They have to."

"Whatever." He pushes away from the wall. "What's Whitaker's problem, anyway?"

"He knows about Father. About the uprisings in Stoke. Look, I'm sorry I've been so wrapped up in losing the house and keeping us together. I should have been... Every time I focus on one thing, ten more things fall apart. But Whitaker knows."

And he probably knows something Emmett doesn't. That I wrote those speeches. With the way Emmett's temper has been, letting him in on the secret now could only put it at risk. If he told Pine, and it became common knowledge, I could be in trouble.

Em swallows hard. "So what if Whitaker knows what Father did?"

"Pritchard must have told him. That means Pritchard doesn't think we're so innocent. His suspicion of Father followed us here."

"Then you could at least try not to make it worse by going to some women's meeting. It's like you're trying to get me pummeled. Just leave me alone. Do not speak to me anymore."

For so long, I've been cycling through numbness and sharp pain, hollow voids that ache for comfort and so many tormenting, stinging heartbreaks I swore no more feelings could fit. Now this?

"Fine," I say. "Go out on your own. You'll see how hard it is with no family, and you'll come crying back to me for help."

"I don't want help. Why don't you understand that? Worry about your own future instead of mine."

"What future?" I hug my books. "I can't imagine my future, thank you. I'm worried about you and getting out of this place, and I don't have a plan."

Emmett's eyes fill with fury. "Then get out of my life, and you'll have plenty of time to figure it out."

How can he say that? He refused to help. I gave him every opportunity, but he wouldn't come out of his room to feed the pigs and the chickens, tend the garden, talk to the bank, or sell the furniture. He sat in his room, angry and wallowing, and I had to fix everything. He can fight his own battles from now on. He'll regret it once he gets what he asks for, hanging around with those boys. And instead of worrying about Emmett, I can write for the Literary Society. Maybe I can even help the suffragists and get to the bottom of the mayor's hold over this town and his ties to Pritchard. Without Emmett, I'll have nothing left to lose.

"Fine." It hurts to say it. The words burn my throat. "Take care of yourself, then."

Emmett flings open the classroom door. "I will."

* * *

The rest of the day passes in a daze of books and notes, and by the time the last bell rings and we all tumble out into the afternoon sun, I have plans to go to Bea's after dinner to talk about the Literary Society. We all part ways at the top of the hill, and I walk back to the Ryans' house alone, to sit in my room and sew until it's time to cook fish and salted ham. I finish dismantling the lilies of the valley on my skirt to use the white thread on the tulips.

If only I could rewind the clock and go back to Stoke, to one of those moments when life was good: Father in his chair, shaking his newspaper upright, Mother pulling bread from the oven, autumn light painting our house a warm orange. If only I could go back there, knowing what I know now. I would shake sense into them, beg them to pack our things and board a train to some faraway place.

Now, I only have this room at the top of Finn's stairs, a knot in my stomach, and an endless pit of burning rage because none of this would be happening if it weren't for Pritchard.

Why haven't I heard from Sophie? Did someone harm them? I could write to one of Mother's old friends. They might know. And what did Pritchard tell Whitaker about us?

No one in this town cares a lick about Pritchard, but plenty of people are outraged about Whitaker, and some of them want to do something about it. But what? We have no Thomas Paine here, no one to write pamphlets calling for common sense.

Then it hits me. If the Water Festival is as big a gathering as it sounds, it's the perfect chance to print a message and put it in everyone's hands. Printing the truth would be easy, if only I knew what the truth was. And if the Literary Society publishes everything under men's names to get around the ban on women gathering, then maybe I can take a card from Father's deck and drive a wedge in Pine's feral boy colony.

If I pretended to write as one of his friends, Pine might grow suspicious and distrustful of them. Whitaker might even tell him to stop associating with them. Without his friends to prop him up, he won't feel so powerful. He'll leave Em and me alone. Meanwhile, if I can find the link between Whitaker and Pritchard, I might come up with a way to break it. Maybe they're doing something illegal that I could prove. The faster Stoke is cleaned up, the faster I can get home.

After dinner, Em retreats to his room. Regina allows me to go to Bea's and I promise not to be late getting back, so I sprint down Main Street toward Bea's to meet with the girls. I keep my chin up and smile at a man outside a small law office, and I nod at a woman who emerges from the pharmacy. The whole town looks different in this new light, knowing there's resistance in so many corners.

Bea welcomes me in. Ruthie and Hazel beat me there, and I join them at the dining room table, talking about what to wear to the dance. Ruthie is honor bound to wear something blue of her mother's, but Hazel is salvaging lace from her grandmother to sew it in cuffs of an old green dress. Bea hasn't decided, and neither have I.

"But we have to talk about our stories for the next issue before curfew is up." Bea places a stack of pages in front of me. It's all short stories and poems.

"What do you think about a little non-fiction?" I ask.

"What do you mean?" asks Hazel.

I chew my bottom lip. Bea trusts Ruthie and Hazel, so I do too. I tell them about Stoke and Pritchard. I tell them things I've never told Emmett, about my father and his speeches. My chest twinges, and it feels like a betrayal to tell them things my own brother doesn't know, but they need to know the truth.

"There's a connection between Whitaker and the coal plant that killed my parents. There has to be," I say. "I need to find it."

"Golly." Ruthie chews the inside of her cheek, her lips pursed in a mix of confusion and consideration. "I wouldn't know where to start."

Hazel's eyes gleam. "I don't either, but I sure want to find out."

"My cousin and her family are still in Stoke, so I have to be careful about it. Whitaker threatened them to me, and I haven't received a letter back from my cousin yet."

"The mail runs so slow," Hazel says. "My father was complaining about the trains just this morning."

"Speaking of trains," I say. "Whitaker and Pritchard met at the train station and shook hands. Whitaker knows much more about me than any ordinary mayor would. Something is wrong, and I can't put my finger on it. I don't expect anyone here to care about Pritchard, but Whitaker will get worse if he's taking tips from the man who killed my parents."

"In that case, we need a measured approach," Hazel says. "We have to think through every angle before we act.

"It seems like fate, doesn't it?" Ruthie asks.

Hazel nods. "Like the universe wants you to do this. Something seems to connect our towns. It almost seems as if you have no choice but to find out what it is."

I bounce my foot, and daffodils in the jelly jar on the table nod their heads. "It feels that way to me too. I just don't know what to do."

The resolute coil tightens within me, and I fall back in my chair. I want to tell them about the Water Festival and what I overheard at the creekside, but I can't. Not without betraying what I heard. And if Leta is involved, it would break my heart if their secret plans got out, and it was all my fault.

Bea's lips thin, pressed into a line. Her eyes are focused on some distant spot. She knows something.

"What is it?" I ask.

She glances between the grandfather clock and the back door, rising to her feet quietly and putting an ear to the stairs. She motions for us to follow her outside. The sun hasn't set yet, but the town is quiet, nothing but cicadas and the burbling creek. A window is lit upstairs where Bea's parents must be.

With her eyes fixed on that window, Bea speaks softly. "There's something you should know. Whitaker is up for election next year. Father has been talking to some of his friends about running."

"Your father might run for mayor?" Ruthie asks.

"Other way around. He's trying to convince his friends. I heard them talking last week."

I'm relieved on all counts. Bea already knows so I don't have to be the one to tell them. And Leta is definitely involved. "I heard something about a water festival. What is that?"

Ruthie gives a little jump. "It was such fun. Down at the park. It was grand. Streamers and boats, games and music. We had duck decoys, quilts, we'd tie nets and sell them. There were clothes and crafts. The women used to run it."

"They're talking about doing it again," Hazel says. "My gran mentioned it. In June."

"That's not far," says Ruthie.

My pulse quickens. "We have work to do." We just have to figure out what it is first.

CHAPTER TWELVE

I spend the week with my head down, focused on my classes like a horse wearing blinders, surrounded by Bea, Hazel, and Ruthie as we move through the halls. We take to walking home together, lingering at the bridge before parting ways, me doing all I can to avoid seeing Em. Up and gone before the sun each morning, he returns in time for dinner each night. Whatever he does with his time after that, I do not know.

I spend my evenings at Bea's talking about the literary society. I've never written poems before, and my first attempts reduce us to tears of laughter.

Every other waking moment I scavenge threads from my skirt to use on Sidney's wedding dress as Finn's pipe smoke ekes between the floorboards. One by one, I strip the skirt of peonies and chamomile, lily of the valley and daffodils. The little clusters of hydrangea flowers lose their tips as I take every shade of white I can find and layer it into the wedding bodice. As one tulip takes shape, another becomes a ghost of its former self. A younger version of me would care, but I need the money to get back home. It's an investment, I tell myself. For my future. And I can always buy more thread to replace them once Sidney pays me for the work. I'm even better at embroidery now than I used to be, and I can easily cover over the holes left by the old thread.

No reply from Sophie ever comes. Regina assures me that she collects the mail each day, and I have no reason to distrust her on that count, so I shove my worries and disappointment down into my shoes and carry two more letters to the post office on my way to deliver the finished skirt to Sidney. He's so enamored with my work that he asks me to do something more colorful on the finished bodice. With my profit in my pocket, I go back to Russell Street and dismantle lavender stems until it's time to dress for the dance.

My cream skirt with hundreds of flowers embroidered at the hem is no longer an option. There are too many voids, too many pinholes where threads once were. So I choose a different skirt instead, with less skilled stitching, more leaves and fewer flowers. But it's night and the gas lighting will make for plenty of shadows, and no one will notice the flaws but me.

Emmett leaves ahead of me, presumably to catch up with Pine and his pack of feral gamins. Regina catches me on my way out the door and lectures me about not being late, but promises the door will be unlocked and demands we be quiet when we return. I'm not sure if it's the excitement of the dance, the hope I feel about the literary society, or the fact that I'm more worried about Whitaker and Pritchard than I am about Finn, or even the trusting look Regina gives me, but it feels like progress.

The time it takes to offer my assurance makes me too late to catch up with the girls at the bridge, so I make the walk to the school alone.

The building is lit up, its first-floor windows glowing golden yellow. Little clusters of students stand in the darkness outside. Even after a week of school, I still can't tell who is who. I'm only here to see my new friends, anyway. Without thin walls, Leta, and Whitaker to worry about, I hope we can talk about the festival and a possible new mayor. Maybe even come up with some story ideas that would nudge it along.

Steeling myself with a big gulp of crisp night air, I follow a giggling group of girls in pastel dresses up the sidewalk to the school, but Emmett's voice stops me in my tracks. He leans against the wall by the door, a lit cigarette hanging from his lower lip. He roars at some joke Pine tells. I recognize the entourage. One of them lights a match behind his hand, his face glowing as he sucks in the smoke.

Something in the way they carry themselves, as if they own the town, makes my skin crawl. They ogle a girl from my civics class, whistling and hissing. Seeing Emmett — my little brother, my playmate, my friend who always had my back — among them, leaning back against a wall with his cigarette and joining in mockery, sends ice through my veins.

My feet are heavy as I enter the school, and my heart aches to see him this way, but his battles aren't mine to fight anymore. If he wants to ruin his life, so be it.

"Save a dance for me, Charlotte." The twinkle in Pine's voice makes my stomach boil, but I refuse to let him know, so I keep my chin up and step inside.

Puddles of gaslight illuminate the hall to the lunchroom. It's full of students and teachers, but no one's dancing. They cluster about the room, holding glasses of punch and picking at pastries from a sparse buffet. Girls in soft dresses with cinched waists and full skirts, puffy sleeves and lace collars, bat their eyelashes at boys in suits with their hair slicked back. With no sight of the girls, I aim for the punchbowl, scooping a small glass cup of it, but it smells bitter and tastes worse. Any fool can tell it's spiked, but it'll keep my hands busy while I scan the crowd. Besides, it might give me something to throw at Pine later.

As if summoned by my thoughts, he slithers through the crowd with Emmett and his roving band of blockheads. Beyond them, across the room, I spot Bea, Hazel, and Ruthie with a group of girls, and I wind my way to them.

Just as Bea comments about the pastries, a sharp whistle by the punch bowl catches everyone's attention, and the girls all swarm in a haze of skirts and giggles toward a growing pack of boys in dapper suits. Some of them I don't recognize. They seem to be older, like they don't belong, and it turns my stomach sour.

I catch Bea's arm. "You know it's spiked?"

"Of course," Bea says.

"I hope you're not drinking this." I swirl the red punch in my cup. "But now that we're away from ears, can we talk about the literary society? Have you ever read Jonathan Swift?"

"Satire, right?" she says.

Ruthie returns, Hazel at her side, pushing a glass of punch at Bea. "I have news. I don't know if you heard yet, but Laura's grandfather died last week, and both of her parents are sick."

Hazel frowns into her drink. "Laura's grandfather used to take his flat-bottom boat upstream to shoot ducks with his long gun. He hauled in fish all day. Everything her family eats comes out of that water. Those fish are making people sick."

"Why does Whitaker tax them if they're making people sick?" I clutch my unsipped drink with both hands, a little proud of myself for realizing something wasn't right about the fish, though I don't know how anyone could convince themselves otherwise when they kept washing up dead like that. "It doesn't make sense. People will just stop eating them, eventually. We should write about it. I'm thinking of a story where the fish are symbolic of something, maybe."

Hazel holds up her empty cup. "I'll be back."

"It has to be related to those fish kills." Ruthie flattens a hand against her stomach and whispers. "It only happens in this river. The other two aren't like that."

I can feel someone behind me. I spin around and bump right into Pine, standing way too close for comfort. I'm not even a tiny bit sad about the spots of red punch that splash from my cup and stain his shirt. A wave of heat washes over me, and I bite back the urge to flee.

Unwilling to step back, to lose ground to him, I stiffen my shoulders and set my jaw. I owe him for spitting on me in the hallway, and I start to say so, but behind him, Emmett sneers, and the barb sinks in.

I roll my eyes and fake apathy. "You're looking better, Emmett." It isn't a lie. The black of his eye has faded to purple and green already. He looks better than Pine, whose nose is bent and still bruised.

Pine's nostrils flare. "Why don't you come hang out with your brother? We're a fun group. We'll take *really* good care of you."

The sea parts as Hazel pushes her way through, cups of punch in both hands. "This looks like a party." Her voice is rich with sarcasm. "She doesn't want you, Pine. None of us do." She leans toward me as if she's about to unleash some big secret, but her voice is loud enough to wake the dead. "That over there is Max. His father's the police chief. There's Vernon. He works at the train station. His father handles the mail. A bunch of these morons think they run the world because their fathers are constables. Just your typical group of toddlers who think they're entitled to whatever they can wrap their fingers around."

"Or whoever." I barely get the words out because as I'm scanning the sprawl of Pine's hangers-on, I make accidental eye contact with the tall man who defended me in the hall. The Greek poet who pulled Pine away at the train station. He has the air of being not with the crowd, and I can't tell if he's passing by or lingering among them, but something sets him apart. The hair rises on my arms, and for the tiniest of moments I wished Hazel had included him in the introductions. Heat rises in my cheeks, and I look down at my cup, praying no one notices.

Lucky for me, Pine spins into my orbit.

"Are you enjoying the slow torture as much as I am?" he asks. "Can't wait until next time. Hazel's right. Everything in this town belongs to us. You'll get used to it."

I sit my cup down next to Ruthie's. A tiny red drop of punch sloshes over the side and bleeds into the white tablecloth like an omen.

I curl my lip with disdain. "I would rather row myself out to sea than ever get used to your presence, Pine."

"Don't be rude, Charlie." Emmett scoffs.

"I'd rather be honest," I say. "It's not nice to meet these people. I haven't enjoyed a moment of their company, and I already know how you feel about mine lately."

Emmett steps back. There's a flash of something in his eyes, a reluctance threading through his warning. "They can make your life miserable."

"You should take your own advice." I fold my arms. How did he turn into this? "Pine can only make me miserable if I let him. At least you found a crowd you can fit in with for once."

Hazel's laugh cuts the tension. She wobbles on her feet.

Pine bows to the drunken Hazel and turns his back on us, striding away, his horde in tow. "Enjoy the punch, *Charlie*. Have another glass. Or three. We'll be back."

I snatch the cup from Hazel's hand. "Stop drinking this."

"I'm sorry Emmett fell in with them." Bea pulls out a chair and pushes Hazel into it. "He'll come to his senses."

Hazel reaches for her cup and downs what's left in it. "And good for you for finding a better group to run with." She holds the empty cup aloft. "Cheers."

"Did you hear me?" I ask a little louder. "They put alcohol in the punch."

Hazel cocks an eyebrow. "You're clearly missing the point, Charlie. Of course they did. It's delicious."

It hurts to watch Emmett stroll out with that crowd, to make his bed with such poor fellows, but I can't fault him for building up his own defenses. Grief does strange things to people. He's only trying to get by in this new world on his own terms.

"They're insufferable." I turn to Bea. "Anyway, about the fish and the literary society… it's time we came up with a plan."

CHAPTER THIRTEEN

I huddle with Bea in a shadowed corner, sipping the sweeter, and therefore safer, version of the punch. The buffet spread around the punchbowl holds little of interest — mostly vegetables, muffins and a few pastries with jams and jellies — so we nibble on fruit and the last of the eclairs while I keep one eye on Emmett and the other on Pine.

The roving clan of boys splinters, some outdoors probably smoking cigarettes and terrorizing the neighborhood, others huddling in their own corner, flirting with blushing girls.

"Sure you don't want the spiked punch?" Bea nudges my shoulder and grins. "Hazel seems to enjoy it. You deserve to relax a little with all you're going through."

"No way." Across the room, Emmett and the boy named Vernon approach a group of girls. A brunette fawns over Em, blushing at his attention. "I watch Finn stumble around, and that's all the drunk I need in my life. I'm staying sharp. Besides, I really want to talk about the literary society, about that story."

I'd been starting lines on scraps of paper, getting nowhere and burning them because I couldn't figure out an angle.

"I know what it needs to accomplish." Rubbing at my forehead, I lament my growing headache. "All Whitaker's crimes and sins need to be put in print, for once and for all. All the better if it comes from within Pine's camp. I'm just not sure what to say. Or how to do it."

A brunette in a mauve dress with a frilled high collar reaches out and touches Emmett's bruised eye. They're too far away for me to hear what she says, but it's clear from Em's body language that he's reenacting a fight that never occurred. How did my sweet little brother—who used to nudge ants off the porch rather than step on them—turn into this?

I pick at a pastry and toss back my punch. Bea rambles about the first three chapters of *Wuthering Heights.* All of it is lost behind the ringing in my ears. I turn to the bowl to fill my glass again, and the room spins. Gripping the table's edge, I try to sit where I swore there'd been a chair, but I stumble, my foot catching the hem of my skirt. I teeter like a baby deer. Just before I land on my rear, a pair of hands grabs me from behind, scooping me up and pulling me back into the shadows.

"Get off me." Shuffling my feet to disentangle myself from my skirt, I steady against the wall and run my hand over my hair, but the arms still hold me up, and the sour stench of cigarette smoke kicks off a wave of nausea. Emmett?

I wiggle free of his grasp.

Bea giggles. "Charlie, I think you're drunk."

"You need help," he hisses.

"I most certainly do not." The words tumble out slowly, drawn out, like the large, italicized writing in a child's picture book. "Even if I did, I wouldn't ask you."

"Yeah, well. I'm not exactly thrilled to be over here, but I'm trying to help, despite my better judgment." He grabs my arm and tugs at me, but my feet are planted. My eyes spit fire, even though I can't focus them.

"Get off me," I say.

I don't hear Pine approach until he's next to me, his hot breath on my neck and his clammy hand around my waist. "Thanks for taking care of her for me, Emmett."

People and voices swirl around me, glistening in the flare of the lights. Bea is here, her voice like shards of broken punch glasses, whistling about teachers and not being seen. It's all Pine's fault, she says, for spiking the punch.

"She's my sister, and she's off limits." Emmett sounds far away and furious. "Bea, go back to your friends and leave us alone."

It's getting harder to stay balanced as the room spins. I gulp air and try to stay still, but every time I open my eyes, the room wobbles like a ride at the World's Fair. I try to hide it, but I must be doing a terrible job, because Bea pushes a chair against the backs of my legs and shoves me into it, not missing a beat while she argues with Pine. The room tilts on its axis.

The dizzying motion sets off a fit of giggles. "You're in over your head, Emmett," I say.

"No." His finger is very close to my face, and I go cross-eyed looking at it. "You're in over *your* head."

The only thing in focus is the floor. A new set of shoes appears, shiny and brown with punched toes, a diamond pattern scattered like buckshot across the leather. I trace the shoes up to a pair of knees, a vest buttoned over a crisp white shirt, a dark jacket draped over the broad shoulders of the Greek poet who helped me at the train station and pulled Pine away in the hall. He may have done me a favor that day, but I owe him nothing, no matter how handsome he is or how good he smells.

I try to stand, to prove myself perfectly competent, but only half my body complies. I fall into the chair again and squeeze my eyes tight.

"Leave her be, Pine," the Greek poet commands. His voice is soothing and it slows the spinning a bit. "Don't be a goop. It's not her fault she's on a bash. Teachers are around. You'll get us all in trouble."

"Alright, Weisenheimer." The biting sarcasm belongs to Pine. "What's up your ass lately?"

"My ass? You're the one spiking the punch and being rude. Leave her alone. What's your problem with her, anyway?" The fireworks behind my eyelids subside, and I open one eye, focusing on the leather shoes.

"She's a bitch," says Pine. "Ungrateful. That's my problem with her. Don't know her place."

Leather shoe guy tugs on Pine's sleeve. "You're a gas. Come on. Let's go."

Pine touches my hair and runs his finger down my ear. "I'm not done with you, Sunshine."

My mouth waters as my stomach lurches at his touch, and I'm about to be sick. A cold sweat runs down my spine. Suddenly my insides seem made of slurry, and I catapult back a decade to being small, my feet dangling off a chair in our kitchen, Mother telling me that boys can be bullies when they think you're cute. I let spit collect in my mouth, ready to repay him and hurl it at his cheek, but he peels away, tugged aside by the Greek poet with the kind eyes and the leather shoes.

Emmett lingers, crouching beside me, and as hard as it is to fix my eyes on any one thing, I find his.

"What is wrong with you?" he asks.

"I appear to be drunk. I didn't mean to be." My voice is a few seconds behind my speaking, like it's coming from across the room.

"You drank the sweet punch?" He shakes his head. "It's all spiked."

"Clearly. Do you think Sophie will ever write back to me? I keep writing, but she hasn't sent one letter yet."

"She will. It's only been a week."

"A bit more. And a letter only takes two days."

"It's still not long. It's probably stuck somewhere." He looks like he resents having this conversation.

"You're doing much better. You don't cough as much." I grab his chin. If this is my last chance to pull him back, to convince him to be my brother again, I have to try, but all I see in his eyes is ice. Cold, hard, unmovable ice. "You used to be so squishy and soft. Now you hate me, and they're going to use you to get to me. The mayor and the police here are bad. Em, you have to stay away from them. Find some other crowd."

He puts his hands on my shoulders, glancing up at Bea. "You're smashed, and you're being dramatic."

"I'm telling you the truth. I'm going to take them down, and you don't want to be in the way."

"You're always looking for a revolution. Just like Father."

With a sigh, he rises to his feet and studies me for a second, like he can diagnose my pain. I wish he were a doctor who could find my problems and cut them out. I can't pinpoint the moment he gives up on me, but it's there, in the slump of his shoulders and the roll of his eyes. There may be a hint of sorrow in him, but he walks away all the same, aiming for Pine and his cast of clowns. He chooses anyone but his own sister.

Tears well in my eyes, and I brush them away, scolding myself for being so sappy. It's embarrassing. Bea materializes next to me, skirt puddling on the floor, and she rubs my arm. She whispers soothing words, but nothing Bea can say will make this any better. My heart is shattered. I've lost my brother. Months of nursing our parents through sickness and that town doctor in Stoke saying there's nothing he can do. It seems like there's been nothing but grief for months, and I've formed this hard shell to protect myself so I can keep moving forward. But Emmett? He was all I had left, and my shell is cracked.

Everything fractures into tiny continents, leaving me adrift, clinging to a bleak little life vest with no shore in sight. A few friends and a literary society will not fill this void. I'm alone.

"Bea. How do I help him?" My breath catches, hitching in my throat.

"Emmett's strong. He'll be alright," Bea says. "You need to help yourself."

"But..." Fiddling with my skirt, I smooth out a pulled green thread from an embroidered fern leaf. "I have to stop Pritchard. And I have to figure out how he's connected to Whitaker. He knows about me. He knows I wrote speeches for my Father. Did I tell you that? My father started a riot. More than one, actually."

"I know. You said. But let's not talk about that here."

I fish my handkerchief from my pocket and wipe my nose. "It's all money to these people. If stopping Whitaker makes Emmett hate me, then I guess I have to live with that. He's better off without me, anyway."

"That's not true." Bea chews on her bottom lip. "He's not better without you. Can you do me a favor, though?"

I spin, looking Bea square in the eyes. "What's that?"

"Talk quieter? Little whispers, alright? And don't be too hard on Emmett. This thing with Whitaker… Emmett could be the weak link you're looking for."

I don't know what she means, but I nod, ratchet back a breath, fill my lungs and steady my heart. "Are my eyes puffy and red?"

Bea's eyes shift as she studies my face. "You look great. Are you alright to go home now? I think you need to sleep this off. Hazel is worse for wear, too. We'll go together."

My chair makes an impolite scrape against the tile when I stand. I swear I don't need Bea's arm but take it anyway, letting go when my feet figure out how the floor works. Part of me knows that if I don't leave now, I might be embarrassed in the morning by things I say when I'm not myself, and if this is what drinking is like, I'm happy to never do it again.

We walk side-by-side down the hall, arms entwined as we push through the big oak doors and into the night. We reach the bottom of the stairs, and I loosen my grip.

"Thank you for helping me," I say.

"Never trust the sweet ones." Bea gives me a knowing smile as we pass from the glow of the school into the shadows. "I didn't know both punches were spiked. You'll be fine in the morning."

We collect a reluctant Hazel, who loops her arm through Ruthie's, and the four of us make the short walk to the bridge. But there, we part. Bea and Hazel live to the south, Ruthie to the east.

"I'm fine," I say. "It's just a few steps and four houses down."

"We didn't think this through," Bea says. "I should have asked Emmett to walk with us."

I wave a hand. "He wouldn't have done it, anyway."

Bea clicks her tongue and we all push on. At the bridge, Hazel and Bea head in one direction, Ruthie and I in another, and just before Ruthie peels off for home, I mention my regret that we never had time to make a plan.

"Tomorrow," she says.

"See you in the morning."

I turn to go down Russell Street but sounds behind me get my attention, a strange, echoing mixture of footsteps and voices. I pause to see if Emmett's among them, and I think he is, but I can't be certain, so when they turn to go down Main Street, I change course and follow them.

The distance between us is great enough that they don't realize I'm tailing them. I don't know why I'm doing it, except that the one form taking solid shape is Pine, and the crisper his edges become, the more bones he has for me to pick with him.

"Hey, Pine," I yell.

They all turn to stare. All seven of them.

"Blondie," he says. He strolls in my direction, hands in his pockets. His head is down and his hair flops over his eyes.

I stop in the middle of the street. "I have a few things I want to say to you." What has come over me? What could I possibly have to say to Pine in the middle of the street? At night? "I want you to leave my brother alone. Don't talk to him. Don't talk to me. Just leave us alone."

"Or what?"

"Or I'll make you. I'll make you wish you'd never met me," I say.

He tilts his head and the moonlight traces his features. Everything about him is limned in blue. His slow-spreading smile seems innocent enough at first, almost like he's realized something for the first time, but when it reaches his eyes, the glint is ominous. He takes a step closer. The memory of his spit on my cheek makes me shiver, but I refuse to move.

"I can make you wish you'd never resisted."

His arm snakes behind me, his hand finding the small of my back. He pulls me toward him, and I stumble. I shove the heel of my hand under his nose and push up, shoving his head back, hurting his raw nose again. His free hand wraps around my wrist and twists. I wheel away and stomp on his foot, digging my heel into his toes, and he lets out a grunted moan.

I hadn't heard the footsteps, but now that I'm not in Pine's embrace, I realize we're not alone. The ground rises up and connects with my knees, and a strong hand yanks me up. My eyes won't adjust to the dark. My mouth is drier than the cracked earth four months into a drought.

Voices swirl, leaves in the eddy, and the night is a wash of color and movement. Someone says I'm drunk. Someone tells me to get lost, and I pinwheel my arm free of their grasp. Light glimmers off something metal and a sharp, cold blade plunges into my right arm, piercing, slicing deep, taking the breath from my lungs. How? Why? I clutch the wound, blood seeping through my sleeve, running between my fingers.

"Why the hell do you have a knife?" Pine cries out.

"I always have a knife," someone says.

"He's been carving up those strawberries he stole from Miss

Glisson's garden all night. Putting them in the punch."

My arm sears and pain wells in my eyes, tears falling down my cheeks. I curse them beneath my breath.

My feet start moving before I'm ready, and I tumble forward, scrambling for balance. I take off in a run, blood streaming between my fingers, dotting the dry earth.

"Wrong way, Blondie," Pine yells after me.

"You're going to the hoosegow," one of them says to the boy with the knife.

"My father won't let that happen," says Pine, his voice fading behind me. "Go after her. Stop her."

I duck into the shadows.

CHAPTER FOURTEEN

My pulse throbs in my neck as I run. I yearn to be back at the Ryans', in my room behind a locked door, soaking in Finn's cigar smoke, with Pine nowhere in sight. Everything in my stomach is about to make a grand reentrance. I let it push me faster.

"If you scream, you'll regret it," Pine hisses from somewhere behind me.

His voice mixes with all the others in my head as I run. Mother saying that boys confuse wanting or sadness for anger sometimes. Bea saying that Pine's mother had left him. Part of me wants to reason with him, but my mind is fuzzy from the drink, and I have every reason to question my own judgment.

I stumble through a stand of trees by the road where my knees buckle and my legs give out, and I fall against a wooden fence.

Tears sting my eyes. Forcing my legs to bear my weight, I hurl myself forward. I have to hide. I rush along, between the fence and the trees, evergreen branches snagging my skirt. I emerge in a dark field beneath a blanket of clouds.

Crossing it takes all I have left. By the time I reach the edge of a narrow street beyond, my legs won't hold me, and my feet feel foreign, like a newborn horse's hooves. I wobble at the edge of the road, blinking through the warbled panes of my splintered vision at a red barn I've never seen before.

I am irretrievably lost.

Panic rises in my chest, tingling my hands. It's after curfew. If I'm caught, I'll be in big trouble. Finn will find out. The night is callous in its dusk, blanketing the town. There are no lights, no landmarks. I collapse on the soft grass. The earth smells like summer, and I gasp, gulping down gallons of wet earthen air. At least it's soft. I can sleep here, safe beneath the boughs of the trees that canopy the road, and in the morning I can rise and find my way back home. I tell myself this, though it's not that simple.

Voices stir me, laughing and taunting me.

"Charlotte. Where are you?" Their jeers lure me from sleep. "We know you ran this way. You left a trail."

I scramble to my feet, squinting against the head rush. I cross the road, and my steps echo off the barn. Leaning against the wall, my weight on my good arm, I peel my fingers back from the wound. The bleeding is slowing, but it burns like the sun, and every time I wiggle my fingers, pain shoots straight to my head. I grip the netting shuttle with my left hand. It's comfortable, like an old friend. Even if it's in the wrong hand and no match for a sharp knife.

Their steps grow closer.

"If she squeals, we're in it deep," says Pine. "Find her. We have to make her keep quiet."

I have no way of knowing what's in this barn, but the uncertainty of what lies ahead pales in comparison to the danger of what's on my tail. Their heavy breaths pulse in the night air, louder and louder.

Tracing the walls, I find the door and use my weight to test it. If it squeals in its tracks, it'll give me away. It swings open enough to let me in, and I roll against the wall, pushing the door until the gap closes.

I hold my breath. All I can hear are footsteps outside, rustling and rummaging, voices calling my name.

Please don't let them find me. I swear, I'll never tell a soul.

My skin prickles. I'm shivering. No, trembling. Taking shallow breaths, I will every inch of my body not to move.

Something rustles in dry leaves or hay, and it's close. Very close. Inside the barn.

I squint to see in the soupy dark, expecting a horse or a cow, but a sliver of moonlight creeps through the chewed boards of the far wall and glints off a dewy pair of very human eyes. They blink to life. A man steps forward, hands in the air.

"My name is Otto," he whispers. "I can help you."

CHAPTER FIFTEEN

"You're hurt." Otto points a crooked finger at the blood streaming from my ripped sleeve. He says it as if there's a chance I hadn't noticed. "I can stitch it."

I scramble, sliding farther along the wall. He's a few years older than me at best, with scruffy brown hair clouding his compact frame. He lifts a wooden beam across the door with an effortlessness that seems unnatural, latching us inside.

"Are you real?" He can't be. I'm dead in a field, and this is some ludicrous purgatory.

"I'm real. I'm Otto." He moves without sound, peering out through knotholes and breaks in the walls. "This is my father's barn. We have a feisty cow with a history of breech births. Should be along any day now. Afraid to leave her alone at night or we could lose both of 'em, so I sleep in the loft."

"I didn't mean to break in. I'm sorry. They're chasing me." There isn't enough saliva to dampen my throat. "I hate to impose, but do you have any water?"

"The well is outside, but you need more than a drink. You're hurt, but not too bad." He peels back the tatters of my sleeve and squints at my wound. His deadpan expression gives me a bit of comfort. If a man who deals with breech birth calves thinks this isn't bad, I'll survive it.

The barn smells hot and sour, like cattle and piss. My lungs won't fill with enough air, and my body can't hold me up any longer. Everything's running on half steam, and the barn is tilting on an axis. Sliding down the wall, I thump to the ground, landing hard. Otto squats beside me, hands on his bony knees. Outside, voices call my name.

He raises his head. "That's Pine. He's bad news. Steals chickens. Stay quiet for a bit."

"I can't stay here. It's past curfew. I need to go…" I stop myself from saying *home*. It isn't a home I'd be going back to, just a different type of hell.

"We can make a diversion." He pushes to his feet and snags a slingshot off a nail on a post. "Is there anything on the ground we can throw?"

I roll onto my side and search the dirt, pressing my face to the cool earth. Moonlight sparkles off pale pebbles scattered along the outside wall. It will be risky to stick my hand out and grab them, but with nothing else to lob at Pine and his lackeys, I take a chance. Plunging my hand through a hole in the wall, I collect half a dozen rocks, most of them too small to go far.

Otto rolls up his sleeve and lies on the ground beside me. He reaches his arm through the hole and claws in more gravel.

I squint one eye so the earth'll stop spinning and study the shadows, waiting for one of them to come into view. My head is full of red-hot pain and my tummy churns.

Pine and his friends round the barn. I can't tease words from their knotted whispers, but I see their shoes and the cuffs of their pants wet with dew and grain chaff. Another sound cuts the night air. Gruffling low murmurs. Muddling large feet.

Cows.

I shift to see and grind my teeth against the shot of lightning that runs from my bicep down my spine. Beside me, Otto raises the slingshot, squeezes one eye shut, and takes aim with the other.

"What are you aiming for?" I ask. "Pine's on the left."

"I'm going to hit the ground near the cow," he whispers.

"Don't hurt her."

"I won't. I'm aiming behind her. It'll startle her, that's all. There's a bull out there for mating. Once they hear him snorting, they'll run off."

I hold my breath as he lets a pebble fly, but it lands quite wide of the furry white leg. He tries again. And a third time.

"They're going to find us," I gasp.

"Just one more." Otto promises.

He rests the pebble in the leather cup, aims high, and lets it go. A cow's huff breaks the night, and warm relief washes over me.

"She heard it." Otto pats my shoulder, peering out into the darkness.

Face pressed to the dirt, I blink through the dust. The cow shuffles and stomps, skipping to the side. Otto lets another stone fly, and a puff of dust goes up a few feet to the cow's left. She bucks and bellows. A protective bull comes out of nowhere, rattling the ground as he heads for Pine and his cronies.

At least four sets of feet rush past, the bull gaining on them. They zigzag across the field, going back the way they came, followed closely by a growing stampede.

Exhausted and relieved, I lower my head to the ground as the scene unfolds.

Behind me, Otto scuffles upright, walking around and rummaging through hay and wood boxes and tins.

"That'll teach 'em to break into my pasture. Sit up. Let me fix your cut." Otto crouches next to me. "Do you have thread? Something from your hem?"

The loose green thread. With my good arm, I heave myself upright. The fern leaf will be hard to replace. It came from leftover sewing supplies after my mother made curtains for a neighbor. I pluck at it and chew it free with my teeth.

"I'll clean your cut with moonshine. It'll hurt." Otto's voice is soft, too soothing to be real. "I'd offer you a swig, but I think you had some already."

I smile as best I can and hold in a breath of air that tastes like hay. Otto tugs on my sleeve and pours the spirits into the wound. It stings like nothing I've ever felt before, and a screaming pain flares from my arm through my whole body. I bite back a whimper.

He doesn't waste time plunging a needle into my skin, and it hurts a lot less than I thought it might. It's like being hit with musket fire after surviving a few dozen cannon blasts to the gut, I imagine.

"I need to get out of here before I get caught." There's already hell to pay.

He jabs the needle through a flap of my flesh, and my vision goes dark, but I can't tear my eyes away as my spotty vision returns.

"I think you should eat something," he says with a crooked smile. "I have beef jerky." He pauses and drops the needle. It swings from the green thread dangling from my arm. I can't stop watching it, a gruesome little pendulum. He scrounges around in a wooden box and returns with a paper-wrapped slab of dried beef. "Here. This will help."

"Thanks." I tear off a strip of the dried meat with my teeth. It's spongy in places, stringy in others, yet dry and salty at the same time. "This is delicious."

"Can be a whole meal. You never ate beef jerky?" His brow pinches, and he squints at his stitching. It's a little hard to watch, but mesmerizing. Down through one side, up through the other. Tie it in a knot. Bite it off. Start another stitch.

"We don't have this where I came from." The more I chew, the more gratifying it gets, and my stomach growls for more. "I'm feeling better already. I think you might be an angel or a fairy or something."

"Not even a little bit, but you're welcome." Otto glances between my wince and my wound. "Where'd you come from, anyway? I've never seen you around here."

"I grew up in Stoke. North. We were coal people."

The past tense clings to me along with the sweat and grit. I'll never get used to the fact that my life is in the past, that every day takes me further from my family.

"Were?" Otto tugs the thread through my skin. "Moved for the change of scenery?"

"Orphaned."

Otto gives me that look of pity with the puckered lips and the drawn-in eyebrows. It never looks good on anyone.

"Don't," I say. "I can't stand sympathy."

He goes back to stitching. "I'm convinced life ain't easy, no matter which slice of it you get. Especially with the rules in this town. Guess I don't have to tell you to watch your back."

"Whitaker making you suffer?" I ask.

"Yep."

"How so?"

He pulls the thread taut. "It's always money with him. We used to have more breeding cows, and we'd sell calves and send them out on the trains. Delivered milk. Had a store to sell butcherings and sold hides to a leather guy. All we can do now is take it to the butcher 'cause there's a fee on every cow you sell. We got to pay Whitaker to breathe the air. We tried sheep, but they're damn awful, full of diseases and picky as sin. If you've never picked June Bugs out of a sheep, you're living right. Now we do mostly chicken, and they tax the life out of that, too."

"That doesn't seem fair." At least they only tax the chickens. They could be poisoned, too.

"It don't matter what we do, Mayor Whitaker is going to make the biggest profit."

"He really is a horrible person. Why is he like this?"

Otto ties a knot in the last stitch, bites the thread free, and wraps the excess around his finger. He drops the coil in my palm where it lies, wet and bloodstained.

"I don't know what broke that man," he says. "Greed, I guess. I don't want to know, either. The more you know, the more opinions you got to carry around. Feelings slow me down, and they don't change nothing."

"That's a really good policy. I'm the opposite."

"It takes all kinds to run the world. You all should run the world. Women. You'd fix all this."

I swallow the last piece of beef jerky. It's salty, and a lot like eating shoe leather, but it's filling, and it steadies my stomach. "It's nice of you to say, but we're probably just as prone to greed as any man."

He pours moonshine over the needle and places it back in his tin of supplies. "You all seem more willing to think about other people. Empathy or whatever they call it."

"Maybe." I stand, wobble, and brush dirt and hay from my skirt. It's in my hair, too. With any luck, I won't have to explain all this when I get back to Finn and Regina's. It won't be easy to hide this wound while it heals, and I'll have to clean and mend the sleeve without being seen. But first I have to avoid being caught outside curfew or running into Pine. No amount of optimism or determination to make the best of things is a match for life in this town.

Otto must sense my hesitation. He waves a hand at a mound of hay. "You can stay if you want. There's plenty of room in here for two. I sleep in the loft. Won't bother you, I swear."

"If someone found out I slept in a barn with a man, my life would be over." Peeking through the gap in the wall, I can't see any sign of Pine and his friends. I'll have to make a run for it.

"Well, I swear not to write it up for the town newspaper if you stay," he says.

Newspaper? "What did you say?"

"I won't write it up for the Record. The newspaper. Well, I wouldn't if we still had one."

Newspaper.

I squint through the gap in the wall. The cattle have settled back in the field. "There's no newspaper here?"

"Closed down years ago." He scrubs at his nails with a

moonshine-soaked rag. "Only way to learn things here is by rumor."

Home was rough, but this place gives me a new perspective. At least Stoke had a newspaper. Full of lies, but it showed up every week. And I was never stabbed in Stoke.

"Thank you for this. I owe you," I say.

"No, you don't. It's what neighbors do." He hangs the slingshot on its hook, scrambles up the ladder, and tucks his tin of tools in the loft. "Don't worry much about Pine. He'll be out of school soon. He's just trying to make his mark on the world."

I inspect my skirt, where blood's soaked into the embroidery, stiffening the stitches. I slip the coil of thread in my pocket. "Well, his friend made his mark on my arm. And I'm not happy about it."

"You look hard enough, you'll find something in common with him. You should see Bradford to get real stitches in the morning. The chemist. He can clean you up good."

I peel back my sleeve, peering at his handiwork. These look good enough to me. I can skip the chemist. "Do you know the Ryans? Finn and Regina? They live down by the river, near the train station? I need to get back to their place, and I'm lost."

"I don't, but the station is that way." He points back the way I came. I'd run in the wrong direction. Of course. "Go through that field, you'll come out to the school. Keep going and cross the creek."

"Thanks again." I lift the bar from the door and nudge it with my hip, inching it open. Cool air refuses to cross the threshold, hanging low over damp earth. I hadn't noticed the smell of cattle before, but it lingers, fresh and pungent compared to the sulfur air I'm used to. I'm glad the bull is on the other side of that fence.

I slip out the door and into the night and retrace my steps. At the school, the lights are dark, the people long gone. From here, it's a short but tiresome hike on failing knees through air that's damp and thick with moss back to the Ryans' house. It makes my hair stick to the back of my neck, my skirt heavy and hot.

Every step is an uphill trudge, wearing away the last of my energy until I reach the door, but the fatigue doesn't blanket one bit of my anger. I clench it down in my jaw, between my teeth, where I hope it will stay if I encounter Finn. The front door is unlocked, as it always is, the empty fishing pail under the bench. All I have to do is get inside, past that drunken slough of a man, and into my room. The whole downstairs smells like his booze, and Finn is asleep at the kitchen table, his pipe still clutched in his right hand.

And there, by his left, resting on the table, is the key he uses to lock our doors at night.

It's warm and heavy in my hand. And it's mine now.

CHAPTER SIXTEEN

I climb the stairs on the outside edges to keep from creaking in the dark, and every step sends a bolt of pain down to my fingers and up to my scalp. I grip my arm as I reach the top step, cursing those boys the whole way.

A thin band of blue moonlight stretches across the floor from my open door. Emmett's door is open, too. His room is empty. And he says I'm the one making trouble?

I close the door behind me without making a sound, and all the tension and stiffness seem to drain out of me and into the floor. I made it back. Now I can rest.

Winding my clothes into a ball, I hide them in the back of the wardrobe, then slip into night clothes without ripping my stitches by some small miracle. I tuck the key in the mattress, shoving it as far in as I can, and I curl up in the bed where I shiver in my clammy skin, kicking my sweaty feet from beneath the blanket as the room spins. How can I sleep, let alone wake in a few hours to haul in a net full of diseased herring and then go to school? Where is Emmett?

Rolling over takes effort. I can't get comfortable. I press my hot wound against the cool wall, anchoring myself to the mattress as the ceiling spins. Sleep puts up a good fight, but eventually I drift into the soft arms of a dreamland, where my mother cooks breakfast on a warm spring morning, eggs sputter and crackle when they hit a hot pan, and the tangy spice of apple butter glosses over as I spread it on a warm roll. The scene tilts, and I move down the aisle of a railroad car, crinkling in taffeta with Sophie on my heels. We're chasing the sunrise eastward on our way to become silent film stars. My nails would stay clean forever, and I'd never have to pretend to eat another fish again. But I'm catapulted awake by a yearning for what I once had and can never regain, and everything seems strange and unfamiliar in that first moment of wakefulness.

Waking in a fugue state in this dismal house is like opening my mouth to let out a guttural scream and finding my voice has been stolen. Everything is wrong. All my things belong to other people now. My brother's gone. Someone else is in my home. All I have to my name is the burning urgency to rip the authority away from Pritchard and make that man pay for what he's done. I've been telling myself I want to go back because Stoke is all I know, because I love the land, but it's a bloody lie. I want revenge, but I can't admit it, because I'm afraid it will make me a bad person. That it'll eat me alive.

All this time I thought alcohol made people lie, and here it is, telling me the truth. Suddenly I wonder what truth Finn knows.

No, I don't care. Not about Finn, not about pretending I don't want revenge. I want them all to burn. Finn. Whitaker. Pritchard. I want everyone to pay.

The sun comes up and limns the room a dusty lavender, and as the earliest birds rouse the world, the seething fury resolves to a simmer. I know three things for sure: I'll never shake the urge to collect morning eggs, I'll never grow fond of herring, and no one will ever stop me from learning the truth, no matter where it leads.

Through the wall, Emmett snores. Part of me wishes he were awake so I can thank him for helping me at the dance. He can't hate me as much as he said he did. Still, he can't find out about my arm. If he learns one of Pine's cronies stabbed me, he'll be forced to pick sides, and his life is hard enough already.

I have to get out of bed before Finn wakes up, though, and life becomes even more miserable for everyone. I have to wash my dress and get to school. At least Whitaker can't get to me there. As long as they don't have a reason to expel me, I'll have a safe place.

With my hand clamped over the throbbing, swollen wound, I put my feet on the cold floor and peel my fingers away to admire Otto's work in the light of day. I find my old skirt in the closet, pinholed where embroidery used to be. It isn't much use to me like this, and I can always fix it later, so I cut out the waistband and cut off a strip. I wince as I wrap it around and around my arm, and it compresses the stitches. In a fresh skirt and blouse, I collect my soiled clothes and rags. With a lump of lye soap from the kitchen, I cross the deserted street and slip down to the creek.

Cold water babbles over weathered rocks, eating away at the storm in my head and calming the raging tide. With the sleeve of my blood-stained dress draped over a boulder, I run my thumbnail over crimson dried blood and the creek carries it away, mine and Pine's and whoever else's blood I wore, all gone in a backwater swirl of claret and silt. I hold the blouse up to the dappled sunlight, filtered by darkening clouds. It can be fixed. Sidney has plenty of embroidery thread in his shop. The sleeve isn't even destroyed. I can patch it with a bit of embellishment. Those are the best scars, Mother had said, the ones that become something beautiful.

I drape the clean clothes over the low branch of a maple, and wind lashes through them. A storm is coming, the horizon growing dark. The leaves are turning up their silvery sides, shimmering under the dark gray sky. Unlacing my shoes, I peel off my stockings and slip into the stream, aiming for the herring net, curling my toes in the silt and letting them freeze and go pale in the frigid waters.

If I had my way, I would dump my memories right here. Just unhinge my heart and dump it all out and let the memories float away on this river. And when they were gone, I'd be a blank slate. Clean and new. I could build myself up again in some other shape better suited to war, because this hole in my arm hurts like hell.

What little horizon I can see through the trees is drenched in darkness. I've wasted too much time already sharpening my purpose on the whetting stones of this bank.

I haul in the night's net of herring and release them into the bucket as voices descend the hill. Other women visit the river in the mornings, but they come much later. Their voices confirm the late hour. Scampering for my things, I gather my clothes from the maple's branch.

"I heard that dance was a scene last night. Charlotte confronted Pine in the street."

The voice is familiar. I twist around the tree to see who it was, but their backs are to me. It's women from the net tying. I stand, frozen, out of view, with my shoes and wet clothes balled in my arms. Someone must have seen us from a window. I'm not surprised, as much noise as we made. Hope it doesn't get back to Finn.

"Word is, she got the better of him. I don't know what he's trying to prove." I recognize Minnie's voice.

"He's no match for her, by any definition."

Minnie laughs. "Did you hear what happened between her and the mayor? Caught her with cigarettes. Someone said she took them from her brother, but Whitaker got red in the face and threatened her family. The way he talked, it sounded like he did a lot of digging on her and that brother of hers."

"I heard her father was a big organizer up in Stoke. He led those miners in an uprising. Did Leta talk to you?"

"About pulling together shopkeepers to sell wares at the Water Festival again?" Minnie asks. "She did. I'd go, and I'd wear my sunflower pin. I got plenty to say. I'll stand up in that gazebo and talk."

"You could talk for a year. We just got to make it plain that we want someone other than Whitaker. That the whole town is united against him."

"I'm afraid it won't be that easy. People here are too timid. It'll take somebody with no sense of self-preservation to put it out there in black and white."

Black and white.

"A lot of people around here have been terrorized by that man. When word gets out—"

The literary society.

A bolt of lightning creases the sky, and the treetops whirl in a bitter wind. The women scoop up their nets and run. When they're out of sight, I take off in the opposite direction, back to Finn and Regina's, water soaking into my blouse from the laundry I'm clutching to my chest.

Black and white. Just like Thomas Paine.

It makes perfect sense.

I need to get to Bea, to convince the literary society to be the voice of the people, and time is running out.

I race to the house in pelting rain with water sloshing from my minnow bucket. After I drop it under the bench where Finn will find it when he wakes, I rush up the stairs, leaving wet footprints as I go. There isn't time to clean up my tracks. Being late for school will only draw unwanted attention, and I must find Bea.

CHAPTER SEVENTEEN

I drop my books on the floor and fall into my seat next to Bea, out of breath with my pulse throbbing in my temples.

"You got home alright last night?" she asks, looking at me as if she knows I didn't.

"Ran into Pine. One of them stabbed me."

Bea hunches over her books, head down, her face contorting with a you-can't-be-serious glare. "They *stabbed* you?" she whispers.

"Right here." I touch the swollen wound, hidden by my long sleeve, and I instantly regret it when sharp pain radiates down my arm.

Bea gapes at me, opening and closing her mouth as she fumbles for words. "What did Finn and Regina say?"

"Haven't even seen them. I ran in the wrong direction and ended up at a barn where a man named Otto stitched me up." I glance around. A few of our classmates glance our way, but no one seems to pay attention. "Listen, I had an idea…"

The teacher lowers her glasses to the desk and calls out a chapter. The class pulls out books. I glance over the shoulder of the girl in front of me to figure out what page we're on.

"I almost forgot." Bea whispers, glancing around us. "That… the festival is on."

"I heard. And—"

"Charlotte?" The teacher blinks at me, and the class falls silent. The gentle rustling of papers stills, and a few giggles spatter the room. Oh God, here it is. She knows about Pine. I'll be made a fool, forced to eat poisoned fish, thrown from school, evicted, banished to a deserted island. I'll have to sew together leaves to make a shelter.

I sit up straight in my seat, folding my hands on the desk. "Yes, ma'am."

"Have you seen Emmett? Is he joining us today?"

He was gone when I returned from fishing. Yet his seat is empty. "I don't know. Haven't seen him."

I let out a sigh and give Bea a smile, trying to look unconcerned, and I sink back into my chair, wishing I could melt into the floor. Though my math book is open to page sixty-three, my mind is split between Emmett and the literary journal. Where *is* he? Did Finn snag him on his way out the door? Did he give up on school and get a job, or join the circus, or take off for the East Indies?

Bea nudges my elbow and hands me the assignment. Letters swim on the page.

The town has no newspaper. That means there's no competition. No one to refute the truth with a barrage of lies.

With class in the way, I pretend to pay attention, scrawling notes in the margins of my paper, jotting the names of women whose stories we might collect and tell, but I don't know the town half as well as Bea does, and I can only come up with a list of names like *the nice lady with the red hair* and *the woman who wore a brown skirt.*

All the while, the seat where Emmett is supposed to be is empty.

When the class is over and everyone slams their books shut and scrambles to their feet, I do the same, pulling my classwork into a pile and following Bea into the hall, but I lose her in the stream. On my tiptoes, I scan for her or Emmett. I don't even see Pine. And when I turn to head to my next class, I find the Greek poet leaning against the wall beside me, hugging his books. His shoulders curve when he adjusts his grip. Strong shoulders that were built for work, but the neatness of his nails says the rest of him is made for something different. He notices me noticing him, and his grin looks sincere enough. The corners of his eyes lift in a way that makes him seem less menacing than his friends.

"I suppose I should thank you for your intervention last night," I say.

"Think nothing of it." He shifts his weight against the wall. "I'm Weylan."

"Aren't you friendly with Pine?" I ask.

"I wouldn't say *friendly*. We grew up together. I'm sorry about all of this. That's all I wanted to say."

The smell of him is heady, like leather and the best kind of wood smoke, like burning branches on a crisp fall night with warm cider and cawing crows. It's the same exciting type of comfort-laced energy that ripples in the air as the world is about to change, to slow down, take over my senses. I can't tear my eyes away from him. Dear God. Pritchard and Pine I could classify, but this is an entirely different kind of dangerous man.

"It isn't your fault." I hug my books tighter. "Unless you spiked the punch."

"No, I mean what happened outside. After. I'm sorry I wasn't there." The lilt of his smile and the narrowing of his eyes sends a flutter through my stomach and makes my knees a little weak, and I need my knees to find Emmett and run as far away from this man as possible, so I look down at them. It brings me to my senses.

Who does this guy think he is? Does he think I'm stupid? No one who spends his time with Pine is worth trusting.

"Anyway," he says. "I heard him boasting about it after the fact, worrying that you would say something, and I felt bad. You're just trying to get by in this new place, and you've been through a lot, so—"

"First off, I have no intention of telling anyone anything. And so what? You know nothing about me." I push away from the wall. The last thing I need is some guy thinking I owe him a debt of gratitude. "Stop defending me."

Weylan shakes his head, and soft, sun-kissed auburn hair falls into his eyes. "People need to start standing up to Pine. He's a jerk. Everyone knows that. The older he gets, the meaner he gets. I don't want to think of him as a lost cause, but he's definitely not the same kid I grew up with, so if you think I—"

"No offense, but…" I raise my hand. "Class will start soon, and I need to find Emmett."

"He was looking for Max."

"Why?" I ask.

He shrugs. "I don't know. Something about Finn."

Heat rises up my chest, creeps up my neck. Forget Pine. Finn's the one who needs to be stopped. "Who's Max?"

"What do you mean, *who's Max?* What do you want to know? He's Max." He holds up his hand at about my height. "About this tall. Dark hair."

I roll my eyes. "Why is Emmett looking for him?"

Weylan shrugs. "His father is the chief of police. Maybe he wants to turn Finn in."

"Blazes." That's the worst thing he can do. I have to stop him. "That could get us both in a lot of trouble. Where do I find this Max guy?"

"He could be anywhere," Weylan says, pointing up the hall. "But he went that way."

"Thanks." I mean it, though it doesn't sound like it. I squeeze my books and leave him sputtering as I slip into the crowd, volleying through lingering students and impatient teachers.

The last of the footsteps quicken on the tile floor, and doors close up and down the halls. I turn the corner and catch sight of Emmett ahead. My boots slip on the hall floor, and I pray I won't be chastised for running by a nosy teacher, but I finally reach him and I grab the back of his shirt and spin him around.

"You're going the wrong direction," I hiss. "Class is back there."

"I'm looking for Max. Leave me alone."

"What happened?" I ask. There are no marks on him. No bloody nose or raw chin. "What did Finn do?"

"He came in my room this morning when he found you gone. He doesn't trust you to go fishing on your own. Says you're sneaky. And he wants his damn key back or he'll kill me for taking it."

I sink back against the wall. "He won't kill you. He needs the money. And I have his damn key."

He inflates and deflates with a sigh. "How'd you get his key?"

"He was asleep at the table with it when I got in last night, and I guess I was too drunk to think straight. I took it. I'll give it back to him and tell him I did it."

Emmett grabs my good arm, thankfully. "Don't you dare."

"I know you don't want to be locked in that room again, so if we don't give him the key back, we need a plan. He could blame Regina, and that would be unfair. I should put it in a cabinet so it looks like he misplaced it."

"No." He grips the back of his head like it will make his thoughts settle. "There has to be a way we can use this to make him stop."

For the first time in a long time, he locks eyes with mine. The rift between us has grown so wide I barely recognize the pain and resolve I see there.

What if I can kill two birds with one stone? "We have to find his weak spot. What if people found out about how abusive he is in an anonymous way? Like in a newspaper. Then you can get your peace without him blaming you for the key."

Emmett sighs and looks away. "What's that gonna do? The last thing I need is to be written about in some stupid newspaper. We could tell that lady from the state, though."

"They don't care about us. How would we even find her?"

"She'll be here on Friday, but it could backfire if she doesn't believe me."

"What?" I step back and stumble over my books. "She's coming here?"

"Regina got a letter. She told me while you were off with Bea talking about dresses and school and whatever."

I count the days. They're all running together. "That's in four days. Does she want to talk to us? Is it only Regina and Finn? Maybe we're lucky, and they want to send us closer to Stoke. There's still poison in the air, but your night terrors would get better if you're away from Finn. And maybe we could find a place a little further from town. What else did Regina say?"

"We're not going home, Charlie. It's just some kind of inspection. Finn would never leave us alone with her long enough for us to tell her the truth, anyway. They might not even believe me, and that would make things worse. I need a sure thing, and Max is my best chance. I can turn Finn in and let the constables handle it."

"Emmett, Max isn't going to help you. He'll only make things worse. He's Pine's friend, and he can't be trusted. Even if you did turn Finn into the constables, they're not on our side. Look at the laws they enforce. Are you certain that turning Finn in will make things better instead of worse?"

"Yeah. Maybe you're right," he says.

Thank God. At least something got through to him. "Let's talk it through later. We'll come up with something."

He chews his bottom lip. Raises a shoulder. If it weren't for the raised eyebrow, I'd mistake it for resignation.

As Emmett turns and heads for class, all my fears and doubts and worries coil into a tight ball in my chest. We can't go to the state and ask for another place to stay. This was our only option to be together. And Emmett's no match for Finn. Not because he's young or strong but because rage makes a man powerful, and Finn has more than enough of it. Until we have a surefire way to make him stop, anything we do could backfire. But the longer this goes on, the more Emmett fills with his own rage, and that scares me as much as seeing him hurt does.

Something has to happen before all of us break.

* * *

I plop down in the chair next to Bea. The cafeteria's buzzing voices, scraping chairs, and the crinkling of sandwich wrappings echo off the tiled floor and concrete walls.

Bea slides her lunch over to make room. "I was just telling Hazel and Ruthie about your arm."

I made a sound in the back of my throat that didn't begin to express my disdain for how much it hurt. "I'll spare you the details, but it's gross."

Hazel wrinkles her nose. "This whole place is becoming a Dickens novel."

Bea looks around before whispering, "What were you trying to tell me this morning about the Water Festival?"

"I had an idea." I lean, reeling in Hazel and Ruthie, too. "All this time, we thought we should publish stories. What if we publish news instead?"

"News?" Ruthie leans back. "How? What would we even say? A feral gang of heathens is running around stabbing people?"

"That's a start." Hazel's doubtful look takes on a hue of consideration.

"More than that," I say. My skin tingles. I need them to agree to this. "We need to collect real stories, like Minnie's. Like Ruthie's uncle's and stories from the suffragists. All the violence and injustice, the poverty, the illnesses, the high taxes on the fish. We'll print those stories, like a newspaper, and distribute them to every house in town before the Water Festival. It'll draw everyone there. And we'll add a slogan, something clear. Precise. And when the festival happens and everyone protests, they'll have their rallying cry. From there, the suffragists can find their candidate to run against Whitaker. With all the public support, someone will be willing. It doesn't have to be Jonathan Swift and snappy satire. It just has to be the truth."

"This is crazy." Bea's voice was small but hopeful.

Ruthie blinks at me. "This could actually work."

"I know." I smile and dance in my seat. "But it's risky."

Hazel leans back and tucks in her chin. Ruthie's eyes grow even wider.

I can't give them a moment to think too hard. "We have to tell the stories. That man who was beaten and the one whose house was raided. The woman who's trying to raise her children on her own because her husband's still in jail without charges. We're writers, aren't we? Either we interview everyone in town or get them to write it down themselves. We can publish anonymously, but we'll have to plead with them to keep our identities safe. At least until there's a new mayor."

"They can still do terrible things to us and our families if we publish something like that." Hazel raises an eyebrow.

"But the whole town would be watching at that point. They'd already be talking," I say.

Bea dabs at her mouth with her handkerchief, and I swear I see the hint of a smile.

"I always wanted to write for a newspaper." Ruthie chews her bottom lip.

"It sure sounds better than being hopeless." Hazel opens and closes her mouth, taking in little gasps of air. "Most of our class wants to move away after graduation. No one wants to live here anymore. My family's here. I can't just leave. What happens if we stay, and it becomes a ghost town? At least I'll know I tried to make things better."

Bea shifts in her seat. "I hear a lot of talk at the market. I can come up with a list of people we can speak to. And it is exciting to think we could change things. We *should* all speak up."

Hazel snorts. "I never thought I'd hear you talk like this."

"Why?" Bea reels back, surprise furrowing her brow.

"You're such a wallflower," Hazel teases. "And you never complain about this place."

"I am not a wallflower. I hate that people think that about me." Bea slumps in her seat. "And what's the use in complaining? It's easier to accept it."

Ruthie gives her a playful nudge. "She's teasing you. Come on. What do you say?"

"Does that mean you're in?" I look from Ruthie's wide eyes to Hazel's flushed face to Bea's faint but growing smile.

Bea clears her throat. "We're already breaking the rules. What's one more?"

"If it's a one-time deal, I'm in," Hazel says. "As long as we're anonymous. We only print the facts as people tell them to us."

"Of course." I nod. "We'll print so many facts that Whitaker won't be able to manipulate the truth anymore. And we'll give them a rallying cry."

"I'm in." Ruthie puts her hand on the table.

Hazel places hers on top. "I may not be the best writer, but I had a Christmas poem published when I was seven. If it helps us understand why people get sick and some never recover, I'm in."

Bea places her hand on Hazel's. "Me, too. I know men who will talk."

I put my hand in and look between them. "We should get started right away and meet with everyone we can. And we'll publish it a week before the Water Festival. The timing has to be perfect. Early enough for outrage to grow but not so much that people forget. And we must swear everyone to secrecy so we aren't found out. If they're brave enough to talk, they'll be brave enough to keep our secret."

Hazel pulls her hand back and plucks at her sandwich. "We could be punished for this."

"Brutally," I admit.

CHAPTER EIGHTEEN

I wake to angry footsteps stomping up the stairs and fight my way through a groggy haze. There's far more sun than there ought to be. I've overslept and not gone fishing. Emmett's bed creaks, and I realize he didn't go fishing either, and those footsteps can't be a good thing. My door is shut but not locked, thanks to the key being shoved in my mattress, but that only means Emmett has less warning than usual. Before I have time to kick myself for my poor choices, I hear the scrape of his door on the floor as it deepens its groove.

My hands fumble for the windowsill in search of the netting shuttle.

"Where's the damn key, boy?" Finn's voice claws through the wall.

"I don't have your damn key." There's no hesitation in Emmett's speech.

I throw my feet to the floor and find the shuttle. It's all I have to defend him.

"I told you what would happen if I don't get that key. And you didn't go fishing."

There's a scuffle. Feet on the floor. Emmett rising from the bed. I slip into the hall and into Emmett's room, and I find him on his feet. Finn has yanked him up by his nightshirt, and the two of them are nose-to-nose. It's unfair that Finn can be that strong, as gaunt as he is.

"Emmett, no," I warn.

"Stay out of this, Charlie."

Emmett's gaze lands on the shuttle in my hand, and he gives me an almost imperceptible shake of the head. It's a bad idea, I know, but I'm not letting go of my only means of defense, and I'm not letting Finn pummel my brother one more time. Especially not for something I've done.

I wedge myself between them, using my good shoulder, trying to make space.

"Finn. Don't touch him. Please."

He smells like cigars and last night's moonshine, and he loosens his grip on Emmett enough to shove me aside. My foot catches on his, and I start to fall, twisting myself to the side to avoid landing on my hurt arm, but I land on my left hand instead. My pinkie finger bends back. I feel it break.

The shuttle skitters under the bed.

I reach for it, but my hand lands on a shoe.

"Let him go," Regina says.

She stands by the foot of Emmett's bed, just inside the door, squeezing her elbows. I scramble to my feet, holding my finger straight. She snatches the shuttle off the floor, and my heart plummets. My only defense is in Regina's grasp, but it's more than that. Leta gave that to me. It ties me to this place, to the women I met at the creek, and it makes me feel less alone.

"You'll *ruin* this, Finn." Her voice is soft but stern. "That woman will be here in three days."

There's a hint of trepidation in the fear that etches her brow, and I realize this is probably the first time she's ever stood up to him.

She looks me up and down and asks, "Are you hurt?"

"I need a splint," I say. "*And* my netting needle."

Regina unclenches her jaw. "Get ready for school. Take your books and stop at the pharmacist on the way. He'll splint you up. Tell them to put it on Finn's account."

Behind her, Finn mutters obscenities at both of us.

"Don't, Finn." Regina folds her arms, her head down. "You can't get in trouble over this. They can't be late for school."

Regina points at the door, glaring at me, and as I push past her, she slips the netting needle into my hand.

"Be here in time to start dinner." Regina says. "And you best be perfect angels when that woman shows up."

Finn clomps down the stairs behind Regina, leaving us alone to get ready. I'm already running late. I fling open the doors to the wardrobe, pull out a wool skirt and a simple shirt, and throw them on the bed, ignoring the questions Emmett lobs at me from the doorway. I couldn't care less if Regina was merely being selfish, stepping between Finn and us. She doesn't deserve the retaliation she'll get for it. I fall to my knees, fling back the blanket, and dig in the mattress for the key.

"What are you going to do with that?" Emmett asks.

"I don't know yet."

The pain in my arm seems to lessen a bit now that my finger hurts so bad. Funny how an old pain hurts less when a new one shows up.

"You want help?" Emmett asks. "I can carry it for you."

"It's almost curfew. I don't want you to get in trouble." Between my right arm and left hand, I'm not sure which to use to brush the rat's nest that's become of my hair.

"I'm sorry you got hurt." He leans in the doorway.

"I'm not sorry." I hold up the hand with the drooping finger. "Small price to pay."

"But you did it for me."

"Partly my fault. If I hadn't taken the key, he might have left you alone today."

He looks at me as if I'm being ridiculous, and maybe I am.

Something has changed his tune. He used to chew his bottom lip when he wanted something. He would stand in the kitchen, too short to reach treats cooling from the stove, blinking up at the pie safe, chewing a hole in his bottom lip. There's a flash of that little boy leaning in my doorway. He wants something.

"What is it, Em?"

"You're up to something that's a lot bigger than the key, and I want in."

"I'm not up to anything. Get out. I have to get changed."

He spins into the hall, and I slip into my skirt, trying to figure out which hand to use to button the damn thing because neither of them works very well.

"I need to do something," he says. "I can't just sit around and wait for things to get better."

Emmett deserves the same sense of relief I felt when the girls agreed to work on those stories together, but I can't trust him with something that big. Not while he's still friends with Pine.

"There's nothing going on, Em."

"There is. You and Father. You both get this faraway look like you're plotting something."

The present tense in his words sloughs off some of my anger. Even though action feels so much better than wallowing, I can't help wondering if he'd be proud of me or wish I'd give up the fight.

"Once I'm dressed, I have to go to the pharmacist. We can talk more at school?"

"Sure."

He goes back to his room and, at least for a moment, things are closer to normal between us, and that makes everything else seem a little easier to live with.

I slip the key into my pocket and pull my books into a pile, tie them with the strap. Then I close the window in case of rain, and find strips of fabric from my skirt on the windowsill. It's a small battle, tying the netting shuttle to my finger to keep it straight.

While I'm wrapping up my arm and cursing my splinted finger, Regina's voice leaks around the joists and seeps up through the floor. The argument beneath my feet is punctuated by stomping and slamming drawers. Regina tries to reason with Finn. They need the money. Two orphans bring in more cash than one child, and we're easier than having someone younger running around. She's worried a neighbor might hear or the school might notice Emmett's eye or my finger, and what will become of her if Finn is locked away? She won't survive on lies and excuses.

But Finn can't stand to hear Regina calling it abuse. In his mind, he's adjusting attitudes. By his estimation, he was a man when he was Emmett's age, and I have no right to act with such boldness. He blames Regina for running a lax household. She claims he started it by hitting Emmett at dinner, and Finn says he has no excuse for how he acted that night, but does have plenty of reasons. The boy is lazy, and I talk back. To cap it all off, Finn hates the way Emmett whimpers at night, and he wants his damn key. He demands Regina find it and set the house right before the woman from the state arrives.

"If you don't come up with a decent story about those injuries, you'll regret being our undoing," he tells her.

I can't let him hurt her. I'll have to tuck the key in a place where he'll find it. Somewhere only he goes, so he can't rightfully blame Regina. But where? And I only have seconds to spare because they could come out of their room at any second.

Finn has a wood toolbox that he leaves in the kitchen, on the floor by the back door. I've nearly stubbed my toe on it half a dozen times. He carries it every day he's sober enough to leave the house, but it has a thick padlock on it, so I lift it just enough to slide the key under it — beneath the back corner. With luck, he'll find it, assume he dropped it, and be too unwilling to admit his own failings that he'll never mention it again.

Emmett taps on the doorframe with his knuckle. "You ready?" He mouths the words and reaches out for my books. I nod my thanks and we creep out the back door. Any sound we make is drowned out by the feud.

We trudge around the house, and toward the street, then pause at the bridge for Emmett to shake a pebble from his shoe. Just ahead, Main Street stretches to the horizon, and to the left lies the school.

"You sure you don't want me to go with you?" he asks.

"No. You shouldn't be out here anyway, or you'll be caught out after curfew." My finger throbs. It's turning a purplish red. "I never should have taken that key. It was stupid."

"You were just trying to save me."

"But it wasn't enough. It made things worse. Everything I do seems to make things worse."

"That's not true. You got us this far." A gale nearly rips Emmett's hat from his head. He tucks it under his arm as his dark hair swirls. "April showers bring May Flowers."

"But it's May," I say.

"Then God help us."

We part ways. The dense air of another coming storm hangs over the town. Everything seems slower, thicker, as if the very air is molasses. Shopkeepers sweep the night from their porches, tipping their hats, offering waves. Their attempts to rid their shops of debris send leaf chaff and litter out into the street. A woman drops her mail in the postbox, and my heart clenches. Every time I think about Sophie, about the letters I sent and how I haven't heard back, this hollow place in my chest opens up. Sure, it's possible that someone is taking my mail. I believe Finn when he says I haven't received any. But Pritchard or Whitaker might intercept it. It hurts like hell that I haven't heard from her.

A light is on in the pharmacy, and a bell rings out when I nudge open the door. Otto rests on a chair by the counter, hands on his knees. He smiles when he sees me.

"What are you in for?" I ask.

"Something for the animals." His eyes drift to my hand. "What happened?"

I tap the netting needle against my books. My finger throbs, but it has nothing on the itching wound healing beneath Otto's stitches. "Broke my finger. It's been a fun week."

The pharmacist emerges from a back room and places a bottle of salve in Otto's hand. He lowers his glasses and considers my haphazard splint from beneath pinched brows.

"Who do we have here?" he asks.

"My name is Charlotte, sir. I broke my finger. I was wondering if you had a splint, and if I could put it on Finn Ryan's account?"

"That man…" He clicks his tongue and shakes his head. "Call me Bradford." Pharmacist Bradford smells of menthol and tea. He mutters instructions at Otto and waves me behind the counter. Laying my finger flat on the countertop, he unties the fabric strip and slips the shuttle from beneath my finger. If he notices it's been filed down to a blade, he doesn't show it.

I've only ever known one doctor, and he'd been a reprehensible man, to put it mildly, picking and choosing who he healed and who he hurt. He ranked his patients based on their value to the company. But Bradford seems more interested in the wound and hasn't yet looked me in the eye.

He spins on his stool, collecting gauze and a splint from glass jars on a shelf. "I hope Finn isn't leaving an impression."

"Oh, he is," I say.

He frowns and slips a slat of wood beneath my finger, wrapping it with a strip of muslin. "That family's buried one kid already. They said it was an accident. That was the official conclusion, but I have my doubts. And you cannot tell a soul I told you that. You must swear to it."

"What accident?" I ask. Why aren't men of science more forthcoming with the facts? "I won't say a word. What happened?"

"Years ago. I don't know the entire story, but it was a boy, about eight years old. His body was found one morning. The circumstances were suspicious, but nothing could be proven."

Around and around my finger, he wraps the muslin gauze.

It might not be true, I tell myself. Just a small-town rumor. The state wouldn't put us in a house where a child died. And if it were true, small-town justice would have been severe. Finn never would have gotten away with it. But a pharmacist would know, wouldn't he?

"It seems like a lot of people protect Finn," I say. "Or he's just lucky."

The pharmacist lifts one shoulder. "A bit of both, I suspect. His family's been here for as long as there's been a town, and its branches cast a lot of shadows to hide in."

"So we shouldn't fight back. Is that what you're saying?"

He ties the muslin tight and pats my good shoulder as he stands. "I'm saying you're a very brave girl, and you should be careful."

"Everyone keeps telling me that." With any luck, Finn got the message, and this will be the last time. I debate telling Bradford about the way Finn treats Emmett, but if Bradford warns someone, things could only get worse. So many possibilities swarm my thinking, and I choose silence instead. Collecting my books, I thank the pharmacist, and he tells me to keep it splinted for eight weeks and keep the secret to myself. The moment he finishes, I'm out the door, rushing past businesses and cutting through yards. I cross the street and catch up with Emmett in front of the school, tugging him away from whoever he's talking to.

Emmett isn't any more surprised by the news than I was, and it changes nothing for him either, but at least he knows. All day, I wonder which of us sleeps in the same bed as that little boy. Had he gone fishing in the mornings, too?

On my way home from school, I stop at the train station to talk to the man who handles the mail. He pulls in his bottom lip and says he's seen nothing yet, but he promises to set aside anything that does come for me.

Every day, for the next three days, I drop off a letter and leave the station empty handed. Then I cook dinner every night in silence with Regina. Finn warned her to make this place look like we're a happy family before the woman arrives, so I do my best to help her tidy and clean as the week wears on, but she won't speak to me enough for us to come up with a unified story about my finger.

On Friday, I walk back to the Ryans' with Emmett at my side, and I try to make a joke to lighten the air, but Emmett won't budge.

The matron from the orphanage is settled at the kitchen table when we arrive, an assortment of papers before her and a carpet bag at her feet. She sits up straight with an air of civility that seems unnatural in the Ryans' kitchen, like a sudden burst of summer flowers blooming in a blizzard's squall. The windows are open and a breeze washes in. Crisp curtains I've never seen before flutter against the windowsill.

Finn sits to the woman's left, dressed in a suit at least thirty years old with shoulders broader than his form can fill, still chewing on his split lip. Regina wears her best day dress and sips on pale tea, with a smile that doesn't mask the jittery tension in her eyes. But her hand is steady when she sets her cup down and waves us to the table.

I sit across from the woman and fold my hands in my lap. Emmett asks about her trip, but Finn clears his throat and the room quiets the way flocks of birds do when they sense a hungry cat is near.

"I'm quite glad for this arrangement," the woman says. "We don't place our young people into indentured servitude any more, thank heavens, so we are packed to the rafters with younger souls. We strive to keep families together where we can—"

Finn laces his fingers on the table like a dutiful student. "But like I said, we can't handle two children like we thought. We'll keep the boy. The girl needs to go."

"What? No. You can't." I reach across the table with my good hand, and pain sears in my bad shoulder. I mask the wince with my shock. Pleading with the woman, I say, "They promised we could stay together."

After everything that's happened in this house in such a short time, part of me wants to pack my clothes, carry my bag to the train station, and thank the good Lord for my fortune, but I'll never leave without Emmett. And I won't leave this town until I've lassoed Whitaker and used him to beat Pritchard. Unless, of course, they'll send me straight home under better conditions than I left. I might be able to live with that.

I've already tried the argument once, but I have to try again. "Please, ma'am. We have to stay together. I'm old enough to work, and so is Emmett. We could find a place to live, and—"

She heaves with a sympathetic sigh. "That is true, but at Emmett's age, a parent has to give permission for a child to be emancipated. If you were an older brother or a married older sister, we could sign him over to your care, but like they told you in Stoke, you don't have the ability to make it on your own. You're simply too young, and his health…"

"Is much improved," I say. "Listen to him. He isn't coughing like he was. He's better now."

"And this is way too rural a location for proper oversight. You have no family here." The woman shakes her head in tight, rapid increments as she scribbles in a ledger. Her objection is stained with judgment.

"Ma'am, please." I glance at Emmett, hoping for some inkling of support, but he merely blinks down at his hands.

She slams the ledger closed. "We went over this weeks ago. Your aunt and uncle have too many children to provide proper supervision. There are no houses in that part of Pennsylvania that will take two teenagers. The system is here to protect you, and this house is perfectly sufficient. If the Ryans think they can't handle two of you, Emmett can stay. We can find another place for you."

Emmett stands. "No. I won't stay here without Charlotte."

Finn lifts a hand to the heavens. "Do you see what we have to deal with?"

The woman clicks her tongue. "I was afraid two teenagers would burden a household. I was hesitant after that last boy died here..." The woman trails off and opens her ledger again, running her finger down a list.

"What boy?" I ask. I want to hear someone in this house say it out loud. "What happened?"

"Just a former boarder," Finn grinds out. His right eye twitches. If I keep pushing, things could get worse, so I sit back in my chair.

The woman shuffles pages. "I have nothing near here. It's rare to keep two teenagers together. The best I can do is make some calls and visits. I'll see what I can do."

"She has to go. Tonight." Finn's voice is hard as a rock.

I place my hands on the table loud enough for the splint to clap against the worn wood. Regina blanches with fear. I feel bad about making her face the wrath of Finn, but not half as bad as I'll feel if I don't take care of myself.

"What happened? Are you two fighting in school?" The woman

points her pen between my broken finger and Emmett's black eye. She lands on Emmett. "You first."

"School." Emmett wastes no time. "Wasn't my fault. Bully hates new students."

I meet the woman's expectant raised eyebrow with a vacant, barren glower.

"Well?" she asks.

I lock eyes with Emmett. If I'm honest, it will be our word against theirs. A small part of me wants to stand up and tell the truth, but if I do, I may be torn from this town and I'd have to start over. I could be separated from Emmett and end up further from Stoke and further from the truth. There's more to do. I can't give up now.

"Accident." I stand, refusing to look away from Em. An idea comes to me, such a bold imposition, but it's the only chance I have to stay near Emmett so I seize it. "Leta and Mitchell live down the street. They run a market, and I'm friends with their daughter. Leta said if I ever needed anything, I could ask. If they agree, can I stay there?"

Emmett flinches ever so slightly. One eye quivers. He doesn't want to live here alone with Finn, and I can't blame him, but Bea's house is small, and it would be too imposing to ask if they would take both of us in. This is better than being shipped to opposite sides of the world.

"Tonight," Finn grumbles.

I feel awful imposing myself upon Leta and Mitchell like this, assuming my friendship with Bea can extend this far, but it's my only chance. The worst they can say is no. Leta did say she wished she had room for both of us.

"It's not far," I say. "Just a short walk down Main Street."

The woman puts on her glasses and gathers her things. "I don't understand the urgency, but I can appreciate your desire to have Charlotte and Emmett settled. As long as Emmett continues not to work, there's no reason to think this won't be a suitable arrangement. If Charlotte will introduce me to Leta and Mitchell, perhaps we can make some adjustments."

I didn't hear Leta and Mitchell agree to let me stay, because Bea and I were exiled outside while they spoke at the dining room table. We sat instead on the front porch of the Mitchell's adjoining market with the men who seemed a permanent fixture there, having the same conversation about taxes and fish that they'd been having for generations. They were of the mind that Mitchell would agree to it for no other reason than Finn had a running account at the store that he would never pay. By their thinking, having Charlotte under their roof would increase Finn's debt and make him all the less likely to show his face there again.

Whatever their reason for agreeing to it, I could barely contain my gratitude. I offered to work at the market to pay for my keep, but Mitchell wouldn't hear of it, so I walked back to the Ryans' alongside the woman from the state, equally eager and hesitant to pack my things and leave Emmett behind.

"It's not goodbye, you know." Emmett leans in the doorway. "I'll see you at school every day."

"Of course." I glance around the room, peeking into the dark corners, making sure I've left nothing behind. I'm not coming back here if I do. My skirt with the fern leaves is cleaned and packed away. My favorite with all the flowers is now reduced to tatters but carefully folded and packed away with the blooming wedding bodice for Sidney. Money is in my pocket with my netting shuttle, the coal lion, and the mermaid's purse. I bequeath the fish jar to Emmett, which I won't miss a bit. "That's everything, I guess."

Leaving feels like a failure in some ways, a broken promise to our parents and an apology I can never make. I can't protect Em if I'm not here, but he doesn't want me to anyway.

"Don't fight back," I say.

The room is orange, like a watercolor version of itself. I'm running out of sunlight, short on time. I'll be racing against curfew if I wait too long.

"Oh, I will," Emmett says. "Finn's not stronger than me. If I'm lucky, I can get the same deal you got and stay with Max or one of the other boys instead of being here."

"Oh, at the chief of police's house? That'll be great." Has he lost his mind? "Finn won't ever let you leave. Your meal ticket lasts longer than mine."

"I hate that you're right." He gestured to the window. "It's getting late."

"And I don't want to get caught up in curfew."

He pulls me into a hug, and my chin fits onto his shoulder. When did he get to be so tall? He'll eclipse me soon.

I put some money in his hand. "Keep this safe. If I don't see you at school every day, I'll come looking for you. Remember what mother said about not losing track of each other?"

"I'd tell you to stay out of trouble, but I know you too well for that." I should be looking into the face of a little boy, but I'm not. Em gives me the cocky grin that looks increasingly like Father's, and I know that he'll be some version of fine.

His smile fades. "I know you have something up your sleeve. If it's about Finn or Pritchard, I want to know about it."

"I'll tell you tomorrow. I'll meet you at the river to fish if I can."

"You'd better."

I can't handle a teary farewell. I carry my bag down the stairs alone. The house feels eerie. Regina rustles in the kitchen. Finn kicks off his boots in his room while Emmett's steps creak overhead. I don't want to think about how quiet it will be up there for him with me gone.

The suitcase weighs a ton by the time I reach the bridge, and the stitches in my arm burn and gnaw. Switching hands doesn't help, not with the swollen, splinted finger. I'm too proud to admit, even to myself, that I should have taken Emmett up on his offer to carry my things. With curfew bearing down on me, I need to race the setting sun, though the bridge does look like an enticing place to rest. Just for a second.

"Charlotte?"

Regina is behind me, clutching a shawl around her shoulders.

"Just a word? I won't keep you long."

Unable to resist whatever she could possibly have to say, I lean my bag against a tree.

"What is it?" I ask.

She clutches the violet shawl around her shoulders. "I'm sorry. He's not the man I married."

I try to peel apart the helix of my feelings, to disentangle my blame and anger from my sympathy for her situation, but I can't, and I'm so tired and frustrated that I don't have the energy to hold it in anymore. Regina is the only thing standing between Emmett and Finn now, and to hear her say she's sorry makes me want to scream. She could have stood up to him a million times, long before we ever showed up on their doorstep. But I understand why she doesn't.

"That shouldn't have anything to do with me," I say.

"But it does. And I'm sorry." Her tongue probes her tooth. She glances up at the gloaming sky.

"I don't even care, Regina," I start to turn from her, but there's more I need. "Watch out for Emmett. Promise me."

"I'll do my best," she says.

"If anything happens to him, I will dig up every fact about that boy who died in your care, and I will not rest until you're both behind bars for the rest of your lives."

Regina stands as still as the trees, her eyes as vacant as a cloudy night sky. A distant fox lets out a torturous wail, crying out for its mate.

"You have my word," she says.

"And he will not work at that brickyard."

"No." She shakes her head. "If Emmett works, the money stops coming. Finn won't risk that."

"And you won't want to risk life without Finn. If he goes to jail, you'll be even worse off, so we both agree that not a hair on Emmett's head should fall out of place?"

She doesn't respond, but there's a change in the fine lines around her eyes, a smoothness in her puffed cheeks that looks a lot like resignation.

"I have to go," I say. "There's a curfew."

Wind picks up the fringe of Regina's shawl. "Why did you lie to that woman about your hand? Why didn't you tell her the truth?"

"So Emmett and I could stay together. If I told her Finn did it, we could end up in different towns, many miles apart." I don't need to mention the unfinished business that ties me to North East. If I left this place, I'd lose my only source of information on Pritchard. "Emmett's all I have left, and I'll do anything to protect him."

Regina doesn't have to say she understands. It's there in her nod, in the solemn shrug of her shoulders. We're both survivors in our own ways. Regina keeps her head by staying quiet, taking what comes, bending like a willow. I feed off of the lightning bolts, standing in the storm with a rod in my hand. We'll never be friends like I hoped, and I won't ever understand how Regina can spend her life on her knees, but she understands me, and that's all I need.

The first hints of stars should take the stage, preparing for the evening's show, but lingering clouds from the day's storm race overhead, casting a curtain. The clock is ticking.

I gather my skirt and collect my things, then I cross the bridge and head down Main Street, past the shops where shopkeepers sweep the day from their doorsteps and children dart from house to house.

Leta's house is only a few blocks away, but it feels like another country, and my arm is near the end of its use for the day by the time I arrive. How can I possibly apologize to Leta for imposing myself on her kindness? How will I face Mitchell and thank him for allowing me to stay?

It's just a door, a few inches thick, not a locked cell a million miles away, but it feels like a giant wall between me and Emmett, and suddenly I'm afraid to face my first night so far from him. I've never slept a single night away from my family before. What if he has a night terror? Regina might not let him starve, but she certainly won't comfort him.

He isn't a child anymore, I tell myself. He's made that abundantly clear.

He's nearly the same age as some of the men who organized alongside our father. The same age as men who vowed to raise an axe against the managers. He's gentle and wise, and his chin fits on my shoulder, and maybe it's time to stop protecting him from everything and let him face his demons.

I knock on the door with all the strength I have left. Leta greets me, pulls me into a warm hug. It's no trouble my being there, she says, no trouble at all, and she carries my bag upstairs to where Bea is already making up the spare bed in her room for me.

I feel awful invading her privacy. I apologize a hundred times for imposing, but Leta pays me no mind. She says she'd have done the same thing, considering the circumstances. Leta shuffles off for lemonade and something to eat, and Bea gives me the sad sort of smile I expect in these moments of tribulation. It makes my stomach churn, but I refuse to be reduced to a needy orphan on the cusp of despair, so I help make the bed and apologize again. But once Leta is out of earshot, Bea plops on her bed, mischief dancing in her eyes, as she says having me there will make our efforts so much easier. In fact, she's already gotten started interviewing the men who gather on the market's porch, and more of Whitaker's victims are crawling out of the woodwork.

Bea doesn't get into much detail before Leta returns with lemonade and demands to know what happened to my finger, dragging from me the truth that it was Finn's doing when I stood up to him. I tell her I don't regret it for a minute, especially since I hope it will keep him from ever doing it to someone else again. But Leta disagrees. It's about power and control, she says, and Finn will never give up either. But the state has Finn on their radar now, and being under Leta's roof means I have more freedom. The suffragists are working hard on the festival, and as long as I keep my nose clean, I can join in all the preparations I want.

A moment later, Mitchell reaches the top of the stairs and gives me a hearty welcome. I thank him for the kindness, but the true purpose of his trip up the steps is to relay some puzzling news. An officer stopped by the store during his rounds to say the curfew has been lifted.

"You'll be able to see Em," says Bea.

"Yes, it's a blessing," Leta declares. "But I don't trust him."

"It's curious." Mitchell strokes his wiry beard. "Because those boys are as mischievous as ever. However, Whitaker's own son causes most of the trouble, and the curfew was never designed for him. That can only mean Whitaker wants to see where people go when they're free to roam. We must all be on guard."

When Leta and Mitchell head downstairs, chattering away about curfew and the dinner boiling on the stove, Bea gives me a look as serious as any I've seen from her, and says the news doesn't sit right with her.

"Whitaker only taketh," she says. "He never returns."

"It feels like a trap. I wonder if he knows we've been talking to people. Perhaps he's giving us the rope to hang ourselves."

CHAPTER TWENTY

I wake not knowing where I am, but knowing it isn't where I'm supposed to be or even where I'd been the morning before. The pieces fall into place with Bea's soft snores and Leta's gentle shuffling of pots and pans in the kitchen below. The heavy curtains obscure the hour, and with a twinge of panic that I've slept until noon, I peek out and am surprised to find the day is still new.

Terrible scenes play out in my mind. Emmett locked in his room, gripped in the throes of panic while Finn taunts him. Em would be fishing soon. I wonder if he knows curfew is lifted, and I'm eager to know how the night was after I left, so I throw on my clothes, negotiate a fast breakfast with Leta, and take my books and lunch down the path along the woods' edge. Behind the market, the woods are thirty paces deep, leading back to the river where the land dips down to a small clearing, and a wide flat rock rests on the bank. Steam comes off the water, inviting me to sit. I will, but not today.

I find Emmett at the fishing spot, his pants rolled up to his knees and an empty pail at his side. He fights with the net.

"Stupid thing's all tangled up." Emmett crouches in the water, his pants growing dark and wet. "It was too loose, I guess."

To spare my skirt from the waters, I make pants of it, reaching down between my legs and drawing the back up to the front, tucking the hem into the waist. I grab one end of the net, Em takes the other, and we untangle it from itself. It did manage to collect some fish, though. Feisty herring splash into the pail.

"What did Finn say last night?" I ask. "Was your door locked?"

"No. For once." Emmett sits on the fallen log and unrolls his pant legs, dark brown striping them where the water soaked in. "He sat in the kitchen, smoking in the dark. Went to bed drunk."

"That's as good as it gets, I suppose."

"My turn." He flicks water from his fingertips. "You're being secretive again like you were in Stoke when you were writing for Father. What are you up to?"

"How do you know about that?" I ask.

"I'm quiet, not stupid. I watch," he says. "So, what's this plan you have?"

I want to tell him the truth, all of it, about the literary society and the interviews, the protest, the suffragists' plan to take down Whitaker, and how I'm certain there's a link between Whitaker and Pritchard. I want to tell him how good it will feel when we find that link and press on it like a bruise until Pritchard hurts enough to squirm. I want Emmett to feel what I feel, the warmth of hope as it glimmers like a starting fire and the anticipation of knowing it will grow into an inferno. If he can take control of his own fate, he may let go of the anger that drives him to befriend people like Pine. But then, there is Pine. Whitaker's son. And his horde of friends connected to the root rot in this town. If Emmett lets anything slip, even by mistake, it will ruin everything.

"Can I ask you something?" I kick at a muddy rock, and it splashes into the creek. "Do you think there's a chance Pine is trying to get close to you because Whitaker knows who I am and what Father did?"

He thinks about it for a while, chewing it over the way you do notions you'd rather not consider at all. The wound to his ego shows on the tips of ears, which grow redder by the second.

"You think I hadn't considered that?" His frown says he hasn't. "Tell me what you're doing."

"I can't, Em. What if you let something slip?"

"Well, I already know you're doing something which is half the way to knowing what it is, and I hate Pritchard as much as you do, so why would I tell Pine what you're up to? Besides, if you make people angry, they'll assume I'm in on it anyway, so you might as well tell me what I could be blamed for."

He has a point. "Just as long as you keep your mouth shut."

"I'm quiet, remember?" His pleading eyes look like he means it, and I know when he's telling the truth. I push aside my objections, because it's nice to have his support, and it gives me a little confidence knowing I'm not the only one who wants revenge. These waters must be tread lightly, though.

"They lifted the curfew." I rest on the downed tree, letting the water dry from my feet in the morning breeze. "They're trying to trap us. They'll follow us to see what we're doing."

"Not surprised." He leans back, crossing his ankles and squinting into the rising sun. "What's the plan? Set the town on fire? And what do you want me to do?"

"We're going to fire Whitaker, to start. And somehow, along the way, I'm going to figure out what ties him to Pritchard." Someone who tells us their story must have clues for me to follow. Deep down in my gut, I'm sure of it.

Emmett flops his head back, chest heaving with a sigh. "I thought you wanted to know what happened to Mother and Father? Now you're trying to take down Whitaker? Can't you just get a hobby and paint pictures of ponies or something?"

"No. I can't paint pictures of ponies. Listen to me. Whitaker and Pritchard are linked. You saw them shake hands at the station. Pritchard warned Whitaker about me, so he must think I'm dangerous. What if Father was close to something, and they think I know? If I can find out what it was, if I can prove that Pritchard knows he's killing people with poison, then I can figure out how to stop him." I grab Emmett's arm. "We can go home, Em. But it starts with Whitaker. Pritchard could have just been happy we were gone, but he came all the way here, and he needed to tell Whitaker about me. Why?"

Emmett chews his bottom lip, staring at his shoes like they have an answer. "Let's say you're right and taking down the mayor will lead you to Pritchard. You just got here. How are we going to destroy Whitaker?"

"The suffragists are already working on that. We'll just help it along. I'm working with Bea and some girls from school, talking to everyone in town who's been punished by these people. We'll write up their stories, and print them a week before the festival. Everyone will wake up and read it. They'll whip themselves into a fury, rightfully, and show up at the festival madder than hornets. It'll become a protest. It'll be too late, and too big, for the mayor to stop it."

Dappled sun freckles the bank. I search his face for signs he thinks

I'm crazy, or it's impossible or, better yet, that he thinks it'll work, but he only gives me the kind of exasperated look he gives me when we played gin rummy, and I threw down a card he wished I hadn't.

"I can't believe you're doing this," he says. "Have you thought this through? These are people with power, not childhood games in the woods. You know what Pritchard did to people. Helping Father was one thing, but this is—"

"Helping the suffragists," I say. "It's not all that different." Of course, I know how dangerous it is. I've been stabbed by a member of Whitaker's apprenticeship program, and these are scrapes compared to what Pritchard can do.

"He bricked a guy up in an empty mine shaft, Charlie. He's not going to let you go because he thinks you're a harmless teenager."

I tug at my sleeve. "That's why you can't tell a soul. Not a single person."

"You're going to trust Bea, who's so meek she can barely be heard, and a bunch of suffragists who could throw you under the bus to save their own hides, but you yell at me for trusting Vernon and Max and Weylan."

"Don't talk like that about Bea. Max's father runs the police." I roll my eyes. "And I've met Weylan. Alright, one of them seems normal." And dangerous in the way an innocent-looking pair of eyes can be. I've never been one for church, but I remember that Easter sermon when the minister said the devil wouldn't be as ugly as you'd think. For all I know, the Devil has wavy auburn hair that tumbles into his piercing eyes, he wears nice shoes, and he smells like leather and wood. "Bea is more trustworthy than they are. You can't deny that."

He sighs as if he figures I'll change my mind. "What can I do?"

"Nothing. Just listen to people when they talk. Pine, especially. And let me know if anyone in that circle has access to Whitaker's office, or if their father might be willing to speak out or something."

"I think it's a mistake to discount Max so soon." Emmett plucks at his shoelace. "He's not like his father. Doesn't want to be one of those constables. He wants to be an engineer, he says. He has access to people, and I bet he hears a lot of talk. If I take my time, I can get him on your side. I'm sure of it. Vernon would probably help, too. He's a good one, and he hears everything, being down at the train station all the time. He and his father handle the whole town's mail. I heard him say things that make me think they're not happy with Whitaker."

It's a leap to trust Emmett on this, but I'm far too curious to know if Vernon thinks the mail is searched, and maybe his father has seen Pritchard here more than we know.

"Only Vernon," I say. "Find out if he's seen Pritchard here before, and ask if he's seen any mail for me. I still haven't heard from Sophie. And promise me you won't say anything until we're absolutely sure they're on our side."

Emmett holds up his pinky finger. "I promise. Pinky swear."

I link my unbroken pinky finger with his.

"Sophie never wrote you back?" He wiggles his feet into his shoes.

"No. There's a chance she never got the letters or didn't know what to say." I shrug. "I'm trying to think positive."

"Yeah." He throws twigs into the stream one by one, where they swirl among the rocks. The last one misses and lands among dead fish that cling to the bank. "I still don't think this is a good idea," he says. "The world is full of things you're better off not knowing. You can't put the cork back in this thing, Charlie. You won't be able to change your mind and make it stop."

"Well, I'm on the right path then, because I don't want to stop. I don't want to put the cork back in."

"I know." Emmett stands and brushes dirt from his pants. "It's the regrets I'm afraid of."

CHAPTER TWENTY-ONE

I spend the next few days coiled tighter than Bea's rag curls at night. It sets my fingers alight, and I finish the wedding bodice for Sidney, unraveling poppies and bachelor buttons, lavender spires and foxglove trumpets. When Sidney pays me for my work and I have one less skirt and fifty whole dollars to my name, I feel rich, though it's hardly enough to start a life on. He's delighted and says he'll send a note for me at Leta's when he has more work, but I'm in no hurry with the literary society taking up so much of my thinking.

Bea and I sit at the table with Leta each night, and she tells us tales of what the Water Festival was once like. Women would stroll around the park, the little thumb of land that dips into the river just as it really opens up wide enough for flat bottom boats. They carried umbrellas and walked with their beaus and played with their children there. She speaks of it with such reverence, that even I long for the thing I never lost.

Whatever Minnie sees in me — a younger version of herself, perhaps — she agrees to talk to me, and her story is the biggest of all. I meet her in her sister's kitchen, prepared to ask a hundred questions, but she talks for three hours without pausing to breathe, so it's more like taking notes in school than it is doing an interview.

"Do you know that house?" Minnie asks.

I hadn't realized I was staring out the window. "No. I don't."

"Seen a lot of tragedy, that house. Half the family died from these waters."

"Do you think they'd speak to us?" I ask.

She shakes her head, pushing out her lip. "No. They shut themselves up. Some people do that because the grief is too much to bear, but others have no choice. Nobody wants to hear about sadness all the time. They think it's contagious. That's how Whitaker gets away with it. Nobody wants to talk about difficult things, and that's all the more reason we have to be brave. I'm surprised you don't know them. You go to school with the son, Weylan."

So that's where Weylan lives. There's where he hides from the world.

Minnie reaches across the table and puts her hand on mine. The look in her eye says she's proud of me, urging me on, but it feels like sympathy to my heart. The kind that makes you feel less alone. That makes the mountain easier to climb because you're not the only one to try.

It takes me a few days to put her words into prose, not just because her husband went through so much, but because it hurts to write it all out. Then I swap writing with Hazel. She's far better at commas than me.

After helping clean up after dinner and putting away the dishes each night, Bea and I stay up late writing stories from interviews, exchanging our work with Ruthie and Hazel. During the days, I give Emmett his space and keep my head down, listening for hints that people are onto the plan, but so far, everything is silent. By the time I leave school on a blazing hot Thursday, I'm convinced no one is paying attention to a group of high school girls. I'm exhausted from getting up early to write another letter to Sophie and deliver it to the post window at the train station, and I go through the motions of walking home, with Bea on one side and Ruthie on the other. Hazel gives me her notes on my article and I skim.

"We can't meet at my place tonight," Hazel says. "There'll be too many people around. Uncle is coming over to help Father hang some new doors, and it'll be chaos."

"Tomorrow will do just as well," says Ruthie. "I drew a poster for the festival. An alternate poster. I heard Mother talking about their ideas, and they seemed too cheery. I thought, once people read the news, we could hand out something different."

I prop my books on my hip when Hazel puts it in my hand. It's beautiful and water-colored with silvery herring swirling in the corners. The date, June, catches me off guard. So soon. As I pass it to Bea, Emmett catches my eye from across the street, twenty yards ahead, walking with Pine and his band of laughing madmen. Pine nearly doubles over, probably over some horrible joke at someone else's expense. My arm itches and strains against the stitches as if even my skin wants revenge, but I have to keep my eye on battles worth waging.

"Hello? Charlotte?" Weylan waves and steps from the sidewalk into the street. He gestures for me to meet him in the middle. Alarm bells go off in my head. He's a distraction. A ruse. More than that, he reminds me of witchcraft, the way he makes the world around me go fuzzy. I wish he weren't so damned handsome.

"What happened to your finger?" He casts a long shadow on the street.

I hold up the splint, tied to my finger with a piece of my old skirt. "Accident. Broken."

"Does it hurt?"

"Not really. It swells a lot. Not the worst thing I've ever experienced."

He nods. "I heard you moved in with Bea. My father runs the brickyard. He's friendly with Mitchell."

"The brickyard?" Where the Ryans' former boarder died.

My curiosity must look a lot like confusion because he puts up a hand as if he feels the need to explain. "Don't worry, my family isn't part of the ruling class, if you know what I mean." He keeps his head down, his shoulders hunched. The slouch seems natural on him, as if he grew faster than his peers and wearied of standing out. "I might as well just say it. Emmett told me everything."

His voice is nearly a whisper.

"Told you what?" I ask.

Emmett is dead on his feet. I'll kill him.

Weylan switches his stack of books from one arm to the other, and I notice his hands again. How clean his nails are. He doesn't work in his father's world, that's for sure.

"It's dangerous, what you're doing. I want to help," he says.

I specifically told Emmett not to trust anyone, only to talk to Vernon in the narrowest of senses. No one can be trusted. Not even unassuming young men who smell like new leather, with broad shoulders and strong hands and soft, kind eyes. It's a short leap in this town from a fisherman to a policeman, and an even shorter leap from Weylan to Pine.

"I have no idea what you're talking about." The words spill out of me so fast they sound like one word.

"I think you do. Emmett trusts me." He raises an eyebrow, an expectant sort of quizzical look that edges on flirtation, and I refuse to acknowledge it. Whatever he's hoping for, the only thing he's about to receive is an earful of threats aimed at Emmett.

"I can tell you're angry," he says. "You need allies, and he's just doing his best. My mother and my brother were killed by whatever's in that water, and it's time to set this right."

I'm going to kill Emmett as soon as my heart stops racing. "Look, I'm sorry to hear that, but I haven't a clue what you're talking about."

"I think you do. My mother spent all her time in the river, and my brother loved to fish. He ate herring like candy. She smoked them, pickled them. Their skin got redder, and their eyes burned more until my mother said it felt like she swallowed fire. Their gums bled, and they lost their teeth."

I couldn't take another step if I wanted to. It's like my blood has turned to lead and fixed me to the street like a statue.

"I'm sorry about your parents." He stops, stands before me, gripping his books to his chest. "It was the worst, watching them get poisoned by their own food. I understand."

His smile is the sad sort that can't break through the persistent melancholy. I wonder how often I make that same expression.

Suddenly it occurs to me, and my blood drains to my toes. "It's not the fish," I say.

Why didn't I see it before? My tongue is thick, and my hands go clammy. The rest of the world dissolves away.

"Are you all right?" he asks. "You're pale."

"It's not the fish. It's the water."

"Do you want to lean on a tree or something? You don't look all right." He holds my arm just above my elbow, and the now-familiar stab of pain threads from my bicep down to my fingertips, but it's distant. It doesn't even matter.

"The water's poisoned," I say. "Did you know that?"

"I thought it was the fish." He lets go of my arm and narrows his eyes, shakes his head a little. "Anyway, about a year ago, I was down at the station waiting on Vernon. I was sitting in the office by myself, and I heard the mayor and some other guy in the mailroom. The guy rattled off a bunch of science and said he found something in the fish. Said he was with some company in Baltimore, and he'd been studying the waters that go into the bay. But maybe it is the water, and the fish are sickened by it."

I step back. Pritchard knows. That water flows through Stoke, continues downstream into North East, and that's why Pritchard was here.

I thought having the answer would make me feel better, give me some sense of direction, but it makes me heavy. There's no way it was this easy, that some charismatic, attractive boy with kind, sad eyes and matching story shows up with the clue I need. Life doesn't work this way.

It can't be true. Can it? Why didn't Weylan look into it himself?

Students file around us like water around rocks. A group of younger girls giggle as they pass and turn their heads to stare. It jolts me back to reality.

I close the space between us by half. "I didn't realize... I'm sorry about your family."

"You, too."

"What else did that scientist say?" I ask.

"That's all I heard." His voice is low and hard to hear in the rolling tide of students. He steps closer. "If you think it's the water, not the fish, there has to be a way we can prove it. If Whitaker knows, and he's intentionally keeping it a secret, he has to pay for what he's done. Let me help."

No. It's too convenient. Way too easy. It has to be a trap.

"Bullshit." I hug my books and turn on my heel, heading for Bea and Ruthie.

"Wait." He scrambles to catch up with me, shuffling papers among his books, laying on top a piece of homework. The purple lettering of a mimeographed vocabulary list facing me. "You're going to need some help."

"With vocabulary homework? I don't think so." My tongue is stuck to the roof of my mouth, and my books slip in my hands.

His head lowers to mine, his voice low, rippling across my skin. "The school is the only place that makes these mimeograph copies. It's the only place for miles with purple print. Unless you have access to a press with more normal looking ink, you're going to narrow the focus on the school. They'll find you in no time. And you'll take down teachers with you."

I hate that he has a point, and I'm even more infuriated for the girls that their secret is no longer safe. Anger warms my cheeks.

"Emmett told me the plan," Weylan says. "Mitchell told my father about the festival and the search for a mayor. Before you ask, no. He doesn't want to be the mayor, but I figure you're aligning your stories with the festival. If you use the machine from the school, they'll figure out who you are, and you can't wait around for a window of opportunity to print it when teachers are away. You need to put it in people's hands as soon as you can. Before the festival, so they're angry and ready for change. You may not care if Whitaker finds out, but you should."

"Emmett was wrong. He lied." The words rattle out of me, though Weylan is right.

The way he looks at me, eyes narrowed, makes my insides turn to aspic. My entire plan is cut up into pieces, suspended in his syrupy gaze.

"You know exactly what I'm talking about." He heaves his books into his arms, shrugging his shoulders. "It could work. I want it to, for my mother's sake. What can I do to prove you can trust me?"

He raises his eyebrows and cocks his chin like he's just won an Olympic-sized battle of the wits. I match it. "You can't possibly expect me to—"

"There's a printing press in the old North East Record office, where the newspaper used to be. They have almost everything you need. There's even miles of old paper in there. I can take you."

"I'm not interested." I dislodge my feet from the tarmac, shuffling my weight. He's right, though, and it's the perfect solution, but it's far too convenient, and he's annoying, with his gaze that sends butterflies through my stomach and makes my hands slippery.

"Suit yourself." He squints at the horizon where Pine and his friends push each other. One of them stumbles from the curb. Why can't teenage boys just walk places? "I'll meet you behind the pharmacy at sundown if you change your mind. Wear something dark. We'll be in the shadows."

The whole thing sounds like a set-up. First, curfew is called off, then Weylan shows up with some plan to drag me out of the house at night. Whitaker's already threatened my family. And if I'm caught alone with Weylan, breaking into a building, I'll be branded a harlot. The entire plan would crumble. After my last encounter with Pine,

I can't just go running around town with one of his friends at the first hint of a quick fix.

"No." I shake my head. "I'm not listening to this anymore."

"You think it's too convenient? It's a trick? I can't force you to trust me, and I wouldn't want to. We have to go at night because the place is abandoned. We can't break in there in the middle of the day. I'm not trying to feed you to wolves. Bring friends. Bring Emmett. Just don't bring the whole town, because this is just as much a risk for me as it is for you."

"I doubt that." I turn away.

"If you're not there by nine, I'll know you're not coming. And the Ryans are dangerous people, by the way. Did they hurt your shoulder? I can tell it's hurt by the way you hold your books. Dislocated?"

"No. It wasn't Finn." Shame makes my voice small. It isn't any of his business, and I don't want to talk about it. I've been doing a good job of hiding the searing pain that shoots down my arm all day, and I'm not giving into it now.

I take a few quick paces, trying to catch up to the girls, but his stride is longer than mine, and I can't outwalk him.

"What do you know about a young boy who lived with the Ryans who died at the brickyard?" I ask.

"It was sad," he says. "The Ryans had that boy doing small errands at the brickyard. He was scrappy. My father found him dead one morning. Officially, they said it was a work accident, but it was a lie. My father thinks Finn dumped him there. I warned Emmett to be careful, not to go after Finn. You'd be wasting your energy on low hanging fruit."

He looks at me like he knows me, or like he thinks he does, either of which is equally exasperating. I clench my jaw even harder and feel my cheeks warm which makes me even angrier because it gives me away.

"I have no intention of tangling with Finn," I say. "You're right, though. This is all too convenient. Why should I trust someone who's friends with Pine?"

"They're not all my friends. And you know I'm right about the printing."

I want to tell him it doesn't matter to me one way or the other, that I have no intention of trusting him, but I don't have to consider it further because we reach the end of the road. We pause at the intersection, and he fidgets, tugging his sleeve down over his wrist.

"I go right here," he says.

"I don't." The sun is at an angle now, aiming into my eyes as I turn my face from him.

"Maybe I'll see you tonight."

I risk a glance at him as he walks away, and when he's just out of earshot, I mumble. "Maybe."

CHAPTER TWENTY-TWO

By the time I catch up to Bea, Ruthie and Hazel have already peeled off for home.

"What did Weylan want? Do you think he likes you?" Bea asks, hugging her books. "He's such a dream."

"He doesn't even know me. We've barely spoken to each other."

She halts and faces me. "But you said he saved you from Pine at the train station. Then the dance." She counts on her fingers. "He's saved you at least twice. And he never talks to anyone."

"He hangs around with that crowd." I glance over my shoulder.

"Not really. Just Max and Vernon. But he keeps to himself. I've never seen him speak to a girl. What's he like?"

I laugh and nudge her on. "Stop swooning."

"You're not getting off that easily." She skips to catch up with me. "Tell me everything. He always seems so mysterious. Silent and broody, but when he smiles his eyes light up. You just want to run your fingers through that hair."

"Bea!" I glance around. Nobody is close enough to hear, luckily.

"What?" She gapes at me. "He looks like an angel."

"I wouldn't go that far," I say.

"I would." Bea blushes and lets her books dangle from their leather strap. "You two set tongues wagging. You should have seen Hazel's face. Thank God curfew is over because every girl in town will run for the rumor mill."

"But that doesn't mean I can trust him." I tell her about the ink and his invitation to see it. The thought of me alone with him sends her into a fit of giggles. "Bea, I'm serious. All our work could be for naught if he lets it slip and we're caught before the job is done."

"Oh, I know," she says. "And he's absolutely right about the ink and the trouble we could all be in. What else did he say?"

"That he thinks the fish are poisoned. He heard a scientist tell Whitaker at the train station some time ago. Then I realized—"

"Wait." Bea chews her lip, her eyes on the street a few paces ahead. "I remember that. Last summer. Weylan told Father at the market and said we should all stop eating the fish and selling them was bad. We never had any trouble with the fish. Ours come from Stony Run. It's a different waterway."

So he didn't lie. Everything about Weylan seems to measure up. His reasoning makes sense. The school's mimeograph machine *would* give us away, and we could be expelled. Bea can confirm he's been worried about the fish since before I arrived. And there was that look, that unmistakable loss that you can see in someone who carries it around inside them like Pandora's box, this thing that takes all their energy to protect, lest it open and all the demons fly out.

"Maybe the tax was Whitaker's way of steering people away from the fish," I wonder aloud.

"I don't think so. The tax started well before that. But it might save a few people."

And it might tie Whitaker to Pritchard. Maybe Pritchard knew all along and warned Whitaker to steer people away from the waters so no one finds out. But how did the scientist know to come looking?

"Even so, something about Weylan feels off," I say. "It's all too convenient."

"You think he's trying to set you up?" Bea asks.

"Perhaps. But I'll have to trust him for now. And you have to tell your mother to warn the others. It's not just the fish. The water is poisoned. I'm sure of it. Stay out of that creek."

"The water? Golly," she says. "I will. I promise."

"Weylan wants me to meet him tonight at sundown. Hey, you don't think it's strange he's friends with Pine and Max?"

"He's not friends with Pine," Bea explains. "Max and Vernon, yes, but I don't see him with Pine much. Not since we were all young."

"Can we trust them?" I doubt it. "Isn't Max's father the head of the police?"

"He is, but he's not like his father. I mean, he's a little rough around the edges, so he's not someone I would hang around with, but he's an honorable young man." Bea quiets and smiles at a woman we pass on the street. "Why?"

"Emmett trusts him, and I'm not so sure."

Bea raises a shoulder. "Well, I can't believe I'm saying this, but I think you should go tonight. Weylan doesn't have a single enemy. You said he pointed out a flaw in the plan, right? And he wants to know the truth as badly as we do."

"I don't want to take advantage of your parents, though. They're so kind, and for me to sneak out—"

Bea grabs my wrist. "I'll cover for you. If you don't go, we still have the flaw, and we'll need a solution."

"I can't argue with that." I could ask Em to go with me, but that would only get him in trouble with Finn. So I would go alone.

The market and house are just ahead. We slow our pace to finish our talk. "How did your interviews go?"

"It's been a whirlwind. I think Mr. Vickers was the last one. We've talked to all the women downtown who don't leak like a sieve and all the men who've been jailed and are brave enough to speak out. We're very close to being finished. Maybe tomorrow."

"Then we need to move fast," I say as we walk up the alley. "Can I borrow a dark shirt?"

"Of course." Bea opens the back door with her hip. There must be a dozen women in the dining room, their voices carrying through the house and into the kitchen. The air is saturated in the smell of fresh bread and tension so thick you could cut it with a knife.

"Girls!" Leta exclaims as we step around the corner. "I thought you had plans."

"Canceled." Bea shrugs.

"We're working on the festival. I don't need to tell you how imperative it is that you keep anything you hear to yourselves."

I start to warn them about the water, but she waves her hands, shooing us upstairs.

"Yes, Mother," says Bea. "We're going."

"Of course, ma'am," I agree.

Bea waves me to follow, and we climb the tight spiral stairs. We drop our books and Ruthie's poster on the table inside the door. She slides hangers along the pole in her wardrobe as quietly as she can so we don't miss a thing they say downstairs, tugging a dark blouse free.

"Back on topic, ladies," Anne says. She runs through the vendors, because it is, after all, a festival. Jacob will sell decoys. There will be a table with nets and lures. Sidney will set up a table with sewing wares, and Anne will sell her quilts. There will be games for the children, and Otto will set up a petting zoo near the gazebo.

"That's where the candidates should speak," says Anne.

"Finally. Back to the good part." Something akin to ire drips from Minnie's voice.

Bea drapes the blouse over the foot of my bed, sits on hers, and hugs her knees.

It makes sense, I think, that the water is poisoned and there isn't something wrong with the fish. They only die like that in one area. And sometimes the water has a hint of the stink damp, that funny rotten egg smell we had all the time in Stoke.

"I want to go down and warn them," I say.

"I wouldn't interrupt that."

"Where does that water flow from?" I ask.

Bea shrugs. "Somewhere north?"

"Has the water ever turned teal?"

Bea wrinkles her nose and shakes her head. I have a feeling it will before long. Then nothing will live in it. "If you're right, and the water is poisoned, we have to tell everyone we know to stop eating from that creek as soon as it calms downstairs."

I agree. "Did your mother already spread the word about the fish?"

Bea nods. "Father is letting people know at the market, too. Some people already suspected but others…You know how people don't like to talk about sickness."

I do know. There's a certain shame that comes with illness, like the isolation is contagious.

"The candidate must speak out," Minnie demands. "Otherwise, there's no point to any of this."

"This must be a peaceful event, Min," says another. "So people feel positively about change, and things don't get worse before an election."

"They should be screaming demands," Minnie argues. "Call it a festival if you want, but it should be a protest. More people will come if they know it means change."

Bea tucks in her bottom lip, chewing on the hard truth.

"Surely it will be a show of unity against Whitaker." Leta settles the women. "But it should be just enough and not too much."

"Waste of talking, those girls and their interviews," Minnie says. "Your own daughter and her friends going to all that effort, and you reduce it to a social party."

"Hush," says Anne. "You weren't supposed to say a word. We all swore to secrecy."

"How dare she?" Bea clamps a hand over her mouth.

I press the heels of my hands to my eyes.

"What do you mean?" Leta asks. "What interview?"

She's going to kill us. Leta mumbles something more, and chairs scrape the floor as the air fills with the bustling of skirts.

Bea has gone so white I'm afraid all her blood has drained into her feet. The back door opens and closes as women leave, and Leta's footsteps climb the stairs. All the while, Bea shrinks smaller and smaller, and I am frozen still.

I hold my breath as Leta knocks, hugging my knees. The door opens and her eyes land on Ruthie's poster.

"Girls — What is this?"

We never hid it away. We came in from school and dropped our books and never gave it another thought.

"Minnie seems to think you've been interviewing people. And what is this poster about the Water Festival?"

"It's mine," I say. "Bea has nothing to do with it."

"It's not yours." Leta clicks her tongue. "Admirable of you to stick up for Ruthie, but I know her watercolors. She's been painting at my table since she was knee high to a bumblebee."

Bea and I speak at the same time. She says we just want to promote the festival, and I say it was all my idea.

"It isn't Charlie's idea," says Bea. "Don't listen to her."

She tells her mother about the literary society, how for two years they've been writing anonymous short stories about youth and growing up that everyone just assumed were written by boys and how we all stumbled on the idea of the interviews.

"We have a right to care too," Bea says.

"Minnie can't keep her mouth shut in a friendly room," Leta argues.

"But she trusts you," I say, just barely louder than a whisper. "And she knows where the unfriendly people are."

"That she does," Leta agrees. "I forbid you to do this. I'm at a complete loss for words. Why did you not tell me?"

Bea swallows hard. "Because I thought you'd tell us to stop."

Leta's nostrils flare. Her lips press into a thin line as she glances about the room. Without another word, she leaves and closes the door behind her. Bea and I blink at each other, uncertainty rippling like summer thunder. I can see the tenterhooks of decisiveness sink into Bea, and I brace for her to say it's over, but she purses her lips and wrinkles her nose — looking a lot like her mother — and she huffs like a raging bull.

"There's no way you're going to quit, is there?" Bea asks.

"No."

"Me either," she says.

"I heard that," calls Leta's voice from her room. "I'm going to pretend I didn't."

CHAPTER TWENTY-THREE

I'm growing used to feeling like I ought to be somewhere other than where I am, but as I trace the mortar along the bricks of the pharmacy's wall, I feel like I'm in another world. The world of night bandits and villains. It's exhilarating in a way, like being in a Sherlock Holmes novel, but the danger is real. The last purple hues of day pick up shiny bits of rock in the cement, and they shine like stars. I pause at the corner, face to face with Weylan. He's dressed in black, and he doesn't waste time on chatter, waving for me to follow.

We weave between stores as the sky darkens, across streets, through yards, and into the woods, moving deeper into a town I don't know with a man I'm not sure I should. My pulse races as we pass a cluster of dogwoods, and I recognize the path I took fleeing from Pine. I make note of the landscape as we go in case he's leading me on a path to disaster and I need to retreat, reaching out to break a twig from time to time to mark my path, but the night sets in, and darkness blankets the town. If I do need to find my way back alone, it'll be difficult until the morning.

Nothing about Weylan's behavior seems sinister, though. Quite the opposite. He stops often and turns back to guide me, helping me find my footing over wet patches of grass. My fears lift as we walk. I don't need his help, but as friends of Pine go, I much prefer attentiveness over being stabbed.

When we're far from the ears of a listening town, he says, "The building is just up here in this clearing. I tested the printing press already. It still works."

"You know how to run a printing press?" I ask.

"I looked it up in the library."

I stumble over a stick and wobble like a baby deer before catching my balance. "How long have you been planning this?"

"A while. I didn't test the machine until yesterday. I didn't want to propose anything and drag you out there if it wasn't possible. We need ink, though, and I know where to get it."

"Why are you helping? Why do all this when you can just not eat the fish?"

He pauses at a break in the trees and holds up a hand to stop me, squinting across the field. A distant dog barks, but the coast looks clear to me.

"You don't have to do anything, either. You can just graduate and leave." His voice is barely a whisper. "My home is falling apart. It's not just Whitaker. People are leaving, going bankrupt. They aren't building new houses, that's for sure. Maybe I want to run a newspaper one day. Plus, I care about the water. My mother grew up a herring snatcher."

"What's a herring snatcher?" I ask.

"Us. We are. It's not a bad thing. People say it like it is when they come through town on the train, but my people spent their whole lives up to their knees in these waters. My mother did. A lot of her family got sick. Been like this for a while now, and it's getting worse."

The hurt in his voice is unmistakable in the dark, with all my other senses deadened. I avoid talking about my own parents for the same reason, that every time the memories slip out, my voice snags on them.

"I'm sorry you lost them," I say. "I didn't know it's been going on so long."

"I don't talk about it, but I figured you'd understand. Here." He holds out his hand. "The ground is mushy and slippery. There's a spring near here."

It's one thing to meet him alone, after dark, running through town and breaking into a building. But holding his hand is entirely off limits until my foot slips, and I change my mind. When our fingers touch, a chill tickles the back of my neck and runs down my spine. He lets go as soon as we cross the wet earth, and I let out my breath, surprised I didn't lose it entirely. We stick to the edges of the woods and emerge at a long, low and rambling building with windows along the roofline, and rusty old doors at the corner. He scans the walls and the tree line.

The moonlight traces his countenance. He's cautious, eyes narrowed, and his jaw is set. A bit more of my distrust falls away seeing how seriously he takes the mission. I realize his leap of faith in trusting me is as dangerous for him as it is for me.

As if I can see anything in the darkness anyway, I keep my eyes on the distant tree line while he picks the lock. We creep into the building, and he pulls the door closed.

I'm in the black. Not just dark, but the deepest black I've ever known. The walls are close, so I know I'm in a hallway, and the air is damp with oil and rust, thick with the scent of paper and slightly sour ink. It's a comforting mixture, like old books and gigantic machines, strong things I don't understand but trust because they're sturdy.

"I should have left a lantern by the door," Weylan whispers. "I forgot. It's sitting on the press. I'll walk ahead. Stay here."

"No. I'll follow."

His fingers find mine in the murk, sending my heart thumping, and I squeeze his hand back when he tugs me forward into the thick darkness. My skin tingles.

"The press is in the middle of the room," he says.

We inch forward, my feet barely leaving the ground. He lets go of my hand, and I plant my feet against the vertigo of darkness. It seems like a lifetime passes before the glass of a hurricane glass clatters. He strikes a match and a ring of light flares. Flame licks at the wick, and he lowers it, shielding the light with his hand.

My eyes adjust, and I allow myself to breathe.

"Here she is. Isn't she beautiful?" Enchantment lights his eyes, and his fingers trace the metal as we round the machine. "It looks strange, but it works. It's only thirty years old, just left here to rot."

He sets the lantern down. It flickers between us, and he widens his stance, folding his arms, as serious as a man could be, like a battlefield surgeon assessing the odds.

"I should tell you something." I whisper, though I probably don't need to. "The poison that's in the water. It's the same thing that's in the air in Stoke. I'm sure of it, and I think my coal plant boss is bribing your mayor."

He mulls it over long enough for me to wonder if he believes me. When he finally speaks, his voice is angry, but steady. "It had to come from somewhere. Are you sure?"

"Positive. I can't prove it yet, but I will."

He rakes a hand through his hair. "The five-and-dime has ink, but we can't buy it. It would be evidence. It'll take them forever to realize it's gone, though. They have four tins of it underneath a back shelf, and there's so much dust on it, I'd be surprised if they even know what it is anymore."

"Are you talking about stealing?" I have to draw a line somewhere. "No. No way."

"There isn't any other way. The store's empty at night. The family who runs it lives across town. I'm willing to go in and get it. Can you be my lookout?"

I walk to the edge of the lamplight. There's a big difference between breaking into an abandoned building no one cares about and breaking into a store, but it isn't like we can order ink from the *Ladies Home Journal* or walk in and pay for it.

Suspicion creeps in again, and the little voice in my head tells me not to give him enough rope to hang me with. But if I don't jump in now, I'll lose my nerve.

"Now?" I ask. "Are you sure?"

"Why wait?" Weylan asked. "We're already out. Sneaking out a second time will only be twice as risky."

He has a point. Plus, the articles are almost ready to print, and we need to move fast.

"I'll do it," I say.

We lock the door and dodge through town, ducking between houses to avoid being seen. It's almost a game, like hide and seek, but it isn't Emmett who'd find me hiding behind the curtain in our parents' room. It's something sinister. We're breaking and entering, robbing a store, and the crime we're committing will have tangible consequences. I could be kicked out of Leta's, and everything will fall apart.

It's slow going, being careful not to make a noise in the thicket between the shops and the river, and when we emerge behind the five-and-dime, I'm hot and sweaty, and burrs cling to my skirt.

Weylan creeps to the back of the building and pushes up on the rear windows until he finds one unlocked. He winks at me and moves a planter, using the edge to boost himself up.

"I'm coming with you," I say.

"No, you can be a lookout. You don't have to do this," he says.

I shake my head. I don't want to be out here alone.

He pulls me through the open window, and we inch along the creaking floorboards through the stockroom and into the store. It feels nothing like hide and seek, though. It's progress. An exhilarating adventure. But it hurt my heart to take from the owners, so I dig in my pocket, find my satchel of money, and I leave two dollars by the register, on the lap of a wooden doll.

"Did you just pay for the ink?" he whispers.

"Of course."

Weylan smiles and turns away, creeping down the aisle. Patchy clouds that shield the moon part, and the sky grows lighter. Moonlight streams through the windows and glints off pots and pans resting on shelves, limning the floor in pale blue. Rows of perfectly lined-up tea cups and saucers sit on platters, waiting for daylight and shoppers to come. It's as if the world has ended, the rapture has come, and we're the only two left in the world, walking down aisles of all that remains.

"This way," Weylan says. "Over here."

He lowers himself to his knees, looking up at me through heavy-lidded eyes. He reaches beneath the shelf to grasp the tin of ink and hands it up to me just as a clatter of scrambling claws rushes toward us, shaking the floor and sending my heart into my throat. Pans rattle as a beast lunges, snarling, drool flinging from its jowls. It smells like death, like garbage rotting in the sun. In my rush to turn and run, my foot catches on my skirt, and I tumble to my knees.

"Shit. The dog. I thought he went home with them at night." Weylan grabs my arm and pulls, shoving me behind him. Pain shoots like lightning from my wounded shoulder, down my arm and up my neck. I choke back a whimper and grip the tub of ink tight but lose my balance and fall onto my side. I brace myself against the shelf with my bad hand and land hard on the floor, anyway. My broken finger screams in agony, and I recoil, the tub of ink slipping from my grip and rolling across the floor. The dog is on top of me before I can stand, drooling and snarling at my leg, and the ink rolls beneath the shelves. I curl onto my side and draw up my legs, covering my head with my hands.

Weylan snatches the tub before it rolls entirely out of reach, just as the dog nips at my calf, but his teeth catch on my stockings, ripping and tearing them. I bite back the urge to curse.

A sharp, ear-splitting whistle rings out, and the dog turns and runs.

Weylan reaches up and grabs something off a shelf, white and pointy. Deer antler. He throws it underhand beneath the shelves, and I relax at the sound of scrambling claws as the dog turns on a dime and chases it.

Weylan sinks next to me, eyes wide, and grabs my hand. "Are you alright?"

"Fine, I think."

Every sense is heightened, my ears straining for a sound beyond the dog gnawing antler. We wait like this, holding our breath as the moments wear on. It seems an eternity passes before we come to a silent agreement that the coast is clear. I take the pot of ink from him. It's the size of a skillet and five times as deep, more than enough to paper the town twice.

We sneak out the way we came. Weylan lowers the window, moves the planter back where he found it, and we run into the woods where we pause to catch our breath. The creek burbles behind us, through the narrow band of woods. Past the building, moonlight kisses the empty street, and I can't tear my eyes away.

"Who whistled?" I ask. "Someone called off the dog. What if they saw us?"

"Nah. They would have found us. Neighbor? Someone outside thought the dog was making a ruckus? He was awfully loud." Weylan's eyes search the woods. He looks more worried than he sounds.

"You're doing a terrible job of pretending this is fine." I press my back against a tree, watching the moonlight glimmer on the water.

"We just robbed a store. None of this is fine."

I glance back at the street, and movement gets my attention. I tug Weylan's sleeve and point. The shape looks familiar, the curve of a shoulder and the jaunt of a knee. It's a boy from Emmett's group of friends, perhaps. But I can't place them.

"Who is that?" I ask.

Weylan squints. "Where?"

But the figure is gone.

CHAPTER TWENTY-FOUR

Five hours later, I'm wide awake and fending off Bea's questions. She's more ferocious than that dog, begging to know why I showed up close to midnight looking like I dug out of my own grave, but I refuse to tell her a thing. I change the subject and beg her for the last of the stories so I can dig the ink out of the hole in the woods I hid it in and get the printing done.

She wiggles into her shoes. "I'll get the last of them from Hazel and Ruthie tomorrow, but you're not getting out of this so easy. I want every detail."

"It's a large room, mostly empty except for the press. It was dark, but it looked like there were tables and counters along the wall."

I smile to myself as she lobs a pillow my way. "Be serious. This is the most scandalous and exciting thing that's happened in years. You had a fairy tale Rapunzel moment with a prince, and you have nothing to say?"

"He's not a prince. More like Grimm's Fairy Tales."

I'm far too tired to appreciate her enthusiasm. Before Bea plans a wedding, I cut her off, declare Weylan a perfect gentleman, which he was, and insist that we are not and never will be courting. Just because he's easy to look at and threw himself into the path of a snarling dog without hesitation doesn't mean he's wonderful or that I'm interested.

I ignore Bea's pleading, stick to the facts, and swear her to secrecy, omitting the dog and the whistle, because worrying her won't help anything. I feel awful for keeping a secret from Bea of all people, but unless something more comes of it, it can only be a distraction. Besides, the Water Festival isn't that far away, and this'll be over soon.

I grab my netting shuttle out of habit and cinch my books with the leather belt, eat Leta's voluminous breakfast, and rush to the river to meet Emmett before school.

I beat him there, which is just as well, because I haven't had a moment alone to think since the suffragists met in the dining room and Leta found us out. Sitting on a log by the water, I know that whatever poison is killing Stoke is the same thing in the river here.

There are creeks and small rivers, at least three of them by my count, that all lead down to the big river at the park that dumps into the bay. But only one of those small creeks fills up with dead fish. If I'm right—if I were to follow that creek north—I would end up in Stoke.

If evil flows downriver, what I witnessed in Stoke will sicken us all here. It steals a person's body from their soul. And the people doing it on purpose will look you in the eye and tell you it isn't true.

Power changes a man. I always thought that good people can do evil deeds and still find their way back from it, but Pritchard and Whitaker prove the exception. Pritchard, at least, is a devil. Whitaker seems as lost of a cause.

Emmett comes down the hill, swinging the minnow bucket. We haul in the net and capture his herring quarry.

"I'm still mad at you for telling Weylan." My anger has subsided a little. Not enough to let it go. "You promised you wouldn't tell."

"Don't get madder, but someone else knows, too…Max."

He's giving me a headache and enjoying it. I rub at the spot between my eyebrows. "Does the whole damn town know?"

"I don't think so. I told Weylan about the literary society because he said he broke into that newspaper office to see if the press would work, and I figured that might be better than you getting caught at school. Then Weylan told Max 'cause if you two got caught for breaking into that newspaper office, he wanted someone to have his back."

I make a grunting sound from my throat that doesn't register the depth of my disapproval, but if Max was the source of the whistle, perhaps I can let my guard down a little. I'm not sure how I feel about the fact that Weyland didn't trust me entirely, either, but I can't blame him. The least he could have done was tell me it could have been Max.

"It all worked out." That's all I'll say on the matter.

"I didn't tell anyone else."

"Good." I scowl.

"I stumbled on something that might help, though." Emmett drapes the dripping net over a branch. "Max mentioned it. There's a town council. They seem useless, but at least they exist, and they aren't all on Whitaker's side. One of them is a lawyer named Mannix. Jacob, the guy who runs the bait shop, is on it. And the pharmacist. I think his name is Bradshaw or Bradman. Something like that."

"Bradford," I say. "A council. That's good to know." I bet that's what Leta's been working on.

I sit on the fallen log and dig my heels into the dirt, making little horseshoe prints. With luck, there'll be some cracks in that council once the stories come out. One of them may even consider running against Whitaker. That's for Mitchell, Leta, and the women to sort out. I just need to be patient and listen carefully to see if there's a path I can follow that will lead me to the Pritchard connection.

"I didn't just come down here for info, though," I say. "How are things?"

"Nice try. Don't change the topic." He nudges my bad shoulder, sending pain down to my fingers. He still doesn't know about the wound, and I still don't plan to tell him.

"What do you think about Weylan?" he asks. "Do you have feelings for him?"

"Not you, too." I chuck a stone at the creek, but I miss and it rebounds off a tree. It lands in the creek, anyway, with a satisfying plonk. "You're the one who sent him to me."

"You met at night. Alone." Emmett arches an eyebrow. "I didn't send him to you for that."

"What is this, seventeen-fifty? Sorry I didn't have time to coordinate a ball. I barely had time to find an outfit to wear in the dark while breaking and entering. He'd better not tell tales about me." It won't surprise me. Few people around here are what they seem.

"No. I'll punch him if he does."

"How kind of you." I try to roll the tension from my neck, but there's too much of it. "It was all business, and he was a gentleman, but I'm still not sure I can trust him. What's bugging me is having to do something bad for the sake of something good. I keep wondering what Father would do."

"Something worse, I'm sure." Emmett blinks up at the brightening sky. "Mother would be proud of you for even questioning it."

"Father would be proud I did it anyway."

Emmett's shoulders fall as melancholy shades him. "But is this going to make you happy? Fighting with Whitaker and Pritchard?"

"Happy has nothing to do with it. I'll be happy when I see justice." No, it's not justice I want. It's revenge. "I don't even feel like myself sometimes. I worry that I'm in over my head, and that I'm being manipulated, and I just don't know it."

The sun is beginning to blaze through the trees, making a patchwork of bright ripples in the water. Emmett turns to face me, throwing his knee up on the log. "Of course you're in over your head. You're doing something no one's ever done before. If you weren't worried, you'd be stupid, and you're way too smart for that. Maybe no one's manipulating you. The town already hated Whitaker. People were trying to find candidates to replace him. The women were already planning that festival, but *you* connected it to Pritchard. You're thinking of quitting? I thought you wanted to stop him."

"No, I'm not quitting." I take a sharp inhale of damp air and let out a cleansing sigh. "It's just that I don't know who to trust, and you keep bringing people in."

"You don't know your way around this town like they do," he pleads. "If this fails, things will get really ugly for both of us. My neck is on the line, too. Max can help. And Vernon. I want to tell him."

"No." I ball my hands into fists. The dig of my nails in my palms feels good. Everyone always says you'll know something's right when you feel it. If Em's right, why does this feel so awful? "Okay, fine, but they'd better not talk."

"They won't. Calm down."

"Don't tell me to calm down. That never works. And I'm not mad, I'm…" Anxious. Nervous. Terrified.

"A goof." Emmett kicks at the dirt. He almost laughs and for the first time in a while, his words don't sting. "Want some good news? Finn lost a tooth yesterday."

"I wish I were a good enough person to be sad about that. Did you punch him?"

"I wish. It's the poison. It's gotta be. Regina said that because of us, they have more fish than ever. She said he's been coughing a lot and bleeding. You know, like I used to. I don't even feel a little guilty about it."

"It's probably been building up for a while." I grimace. "Just don't eat the damn fish."

He wrinkles his nose. "Ew. I still bury them back in the tree line like you showed me."

"Good. And tell your friends, too." I don't need to warn him that things will get worse before they get better. He's old enough and wise enough to judge the consequences for himself, but I need to say it anyway. "Listen. You cannot say a word of this to anyone. Not a syllable. We're printing the stories soon. Leta's posters go up first, so it looks like an ordinary festival. Then, a week before the festival, we're putting the newspapers in every door in town and papering Main Street with Ruthie's posters. She's been painting like mad for days. Soon, even the people who didn't care about the festival will want to go."

Emmett keeps shredding bark, breaking it into little matchsticks. "I'll help with printing and handing them out."

"You don't have to do that. It could get you in trouble with Finn."

"No, it won't. He's getting sicker, and I'm getting stronger. Besides, I want to help. For Mother."

* * *

At school, I can barely concentrate. While everyone practices sewing buttonholes in scraps of fabric, I write transitions between stories on slips of paper, tucking them in my pocket for later. Vickery's story about being jailed without cause makes the perfect lead-in to Minnie's story of her husband's beating.

When classes change, I find myself looking for Weylan in the halls while telling myself not to, that I don't care where he is. He's never hard to spot, being so tall, and even though I'm looking for him while telling myself I'm not, I feel him before I see him. There's this odd little current that runs through me when he's near. It electrifies me like one of Edison's bulbs.

I can't say for certain when or why I decided we shouldn't speak to each other at school. He's too closed off and mysterious to chat so openly with me, and he probably has some beautiful daughter of a railroad magnate to marry, so talking to me would ruin it. I'm not surprised when he doesn't notice me as I pass on my way to lunch, but I'm disappointed the way you can be when a beautiful sunset falls below the horizon, and it only lives in your memory now. But after Civics, he catches up to me in long strides.

"It takes a while to set type, you know. It gets easier as you practice, but…" He chews his bottom lip. "I'm happy to do it, but it would go a lot faster with two people."

"You want me to help?" Alone? In the print office. Together.

"If you want to. I enjoy your company."

My God, those eyes.

It's not butterflies. No, an entire flock of herons have taken off inside my stomach. They make my knees stop working. I hate the power he has over me.

"When?" I ask.

"Saturday?" I watch as his mouth forms the words. Seven in the morning. I hear myself agree.

"How are the um…" He clears his throat into his fist. "Writing. You know. How's it coming along?"

"Well. We should be finished tomorrow." Girls clutching their books crane their necks as we pass. I don't want to bask in the jealousy, but I indulge a little anyway. He grabs my elbow and steers me into an empty classroom, and I'm certain my heart has stopped.

"You have one more person to talk to."

"Who? What?"

"Finn's brother. He asked to talk to you."

CHAPTER TWENTY-FIVE

Finn's brother's porch bears none of the goose droppings of Finn's. No stray feathers or grit underfoot. One small chair and a little table sit spotless beneath a window. How can these two men have grown up together and be so opposite? I knock and the door opens to reveal a man dressed to the nines in a satin cravat beaming at me with the kind of teeth Finn would have had if he hadn't fought his way clear of them. There's no doubt this is his brother, though. Same chin. Same cheek bones. His dark hair is parted on the side and slicked down to his head as if it might otherwise dare to revolt, and his front room is every bit as tidy as his porch. He tells me to call him Clarence, and I stammer through my introduction as he ushers me inside.

The sitting room is sparse but well-furnished. Two wing-back chairs face a fireplace with a small drum table between them. The rug is aged and worn, belying the path its company takes, but it's immaculate, and the hardwood floors shine in the sun streaming through the open window. A delicate curtain licks at the air.

"Please. Sit." Clarence motions to a chair. "Can I get you a drink?

Tea, perhaps."

I sit with my notepad on my lap. "No. Thank you."

With a chirp, a giant tuxedo cat leaps onto the arm of my chair and paws at my notepad. As soon as I move it, the cat settles and rattles with a high-pitched purr.

"That's Oscar. He's harmless." Clarence shifts in his chair and tugs on the lapels of his jacket.

"You asked to speak to me."

"Indeed." He laces his fingers and tilts his head. He's in his early fifties, perhaps, and he bears the marks of a life spent indoors: pale cheeks and hands unlined by the sun, but with kind eyes that put me at ease. "I want to offer you a different type of story than the ones you've collected thus far. The type of hardship I can describe for you is different from anyone else's here. It's Whitaker's. And it's Finn's."

I snort involuntarily and try to cover it up with a cough. I do a poor job of it.

He smiles down at his hands. "I suppose you think Whitaker doesn't know about hardship."

"Are we speaking frankly, sir?"

"Of course."

"I get the impression the only knowledge Whitaker has of hardship is how best to inflict it."

His lovely half grin says he agrees with me, even if he won't say it out loud. "He does give that impression, but every man who wields a sword learned to do it somewhere."

I've known plenty of people who became the thing they hated most. And I often wonder what Pritchard hated that turned him to stone. "What does it have to do with Finn?"

"Ah. The story begins a generation ago. Whitaker's father and

Finn's mother were quite the item. They were the talk of the town, but they were married to different people. Finn was nine years old when his mother fell out of love with his father and chose Whitaker's instead. Whitaker was eight. Are you following me so far?"

I regret not accepting the offer of tea. My throat is dry and clicks when I swallow. "Finn and Whitaker are related?"

"Only because of me. Whitaker's father had an affair with Finn's mother, and I am the result. I'm their younger half-brother."

I clear my throat. "It seems you couldn't be more different than those two."

"I'm glad you think so. Our similarities are few." Clarence drums his fingers on the arm of his chair. "But I didn't ask you here to talk about me. I wanted you to know why they are the way they are, how they became such bitter men."

"They were both young," I say. "In a town this small, it must have been hard to keep an affair quiet, and it must have been hard on them as boys, but it hardly excuses their behavior."

"Quite right." His eyes widen as if to say I don't know half of it, and judging by what little I do know, I'm sure it's far less than half. "As for the affair, they didn't bother to keep it quiet. They were so overt about it, they nearly tore the town apart. They weren't doing anything new, of course. Everyone has affairs. Humans aren't cats. We mate for life because it's good for security. We make a show of our solemn vows, but the good book also says to be fruitful and multiply, and some people take the scripture literally. I suppose they only think it's a sin if God can see it, so it's not uncommon for a man to marry a woman from *his* church and pick his mistress from the one across the street. When it came to Finn's mother and Whitaker's father, those two were so madly in love, and so stupidly careless…"

He tilts his head and waves a hand, blinking at the ceiling in search of a word. "Careless or carefree, depending on how you see it. The whole town knew. And then I came along."

"And Whitaker and Finn were shamed?"

"Oh my, yes. Finn's mother fell out of love with her husband and in love with a man of the cloth. In a larger town it may not have been such a scandal. But in this town, where the identity of every man, woman and child—even the family pet—is defined by which steeple you worship under, learning that the moral authority isn't worthy of his robes sends the whole place into a tailspin of accusations against the woman. Though Whitaker was an innocent eight-year-old boy, he was branded by pity."

I gaze out the window, seeing nothing at all, trying to piece it all together. "So Whitaker's father, a minister, had an affair with Finn's mother. She became pregnant with you, and the town shunned both families?"

"Yes, and you can imagine what that does to boys of eight and nine. One becomes Finn, the other becomes Whitaker." Clarence runs his hand down his lapel, smoothing his jacket. "But it wasn't just the affair that ruined their lives. Do you ever make a mess and make it worse by trying to clean it up?"

My laugh startles Oscar, who raises his head, his ears back. I apologize and give him a few long pets. "That might just be the story of my life."

"Then you can probably imagine how much worse things got when Finn's mother and Whitaker's father tried to repair the damage. Everyone knew I was a bastard son, and the town that once looked to Whitaker's father as a moral compass now wondered how he'd clean up his immoral act. It ate at his soul. He couldn't abandon me, so he lavished money on my mother, Finn's mother. But her husband—Finn's father—didn't want a penny of it. There was no way he would allow his home to profit off his wife's infidelity. He drowned his sorrows in whiskey and ale, and his pride and ego kept every penny of that money from reaching Finn."

"And it all became yours. She spent it on you instead?" I ask.

"Mother spared no expense. I was raised by my mother as a wealthy child. Finn was raised in the same house by his angry, bitter, impoverished father."

"Forgive me for asking, but where did the money come from? Did it come from the church?"

"Goodness, no." Clarence places a hand to his throat. "He was British. Whitaker's father was the third son of an Earl who had no claim to land, but he was given a small fortune and shipped off to the States. He liked the quiet life and decided the clergy was for him. He was quite miserly but gave a bit of money to my mother, because it was the proper thing to do. Money, you see, was a language where he came from, used for love, revenge, and apologies. And my mother accepted it. She was so out of love with her husband, and her husband was so infuriated at that money, that she raised me apart and spent every penny on me. I went to a boarding school, was raised to become self-sufficient and never wanted for a thing. She vowed to use her money in the best way she could, to compensate me for the shameful skin I was born in and cleanse the town of me. Everyone would win. Or so she thought."

"That must have been awful for both of you. Neither upbringing sounds very welcoming."

"One compensates. I never felt unwanted by anyone I wanted to be around. I learned quite young that happiness, money and morality aren't mutually exclusive." He waved a hand. "But we're not here to talk about me. As for the town, it was all such a scandal that the church split. Many people saw their own sins reflected in the minister. Some gave him the forgiveness they wanted. Others couldn't bear to look their own sin in the eye. But everyone blamed my mother, then they blamed women in general. Temptresses. The town clamped down. They became prisoners in their own homes."

"That's where it all started. And the men went on as if nothing ever happened?"

"Not quite. Not all the men. The minister couldn't go unscathed. His wife's family had been here forever, and they took great pride in their place. Divorce was not an option, and the whole thing was shameful. So her father gave them a strip of land down on the peninsula, and the whole family moved. Poor little Whitaker was ripped from his home and sent to live in exile with his parents. It's the wilderness down there. He was completely isolated from everyone. It was a rough life. By that point, all the money was gone, and his father worked his fingers to the bone to feed his family until the day he died. The only thing he learned of love is that it makes a sharp sword, and he grew intensely jealous and malicious."

"Brutal fate. But it doesn't excuse Whitaker's behavior."

"Of course not. A decade later, Whitaker was back, but he wasn't a well-liked little boy with lots of friends anymore. He was a bully who'd been ripped from his home by his father's sins. He had the voice of a preacher and the heart of a scorned woman, and he sought to control everyone who taunted him. Once he had control over his world, he would never lose it again. That, my dear, is why he twists the screw on anyone who might take the tiniest bit of power from him. Women. Men. Anyone with a heart. He learned early on that love is his enemy."

Oscar flicks its tail.

I haven't written a thing. Not a single note. "I can't believe you stayed."

"Why would I go?" He lifts his hands, palms up. "It's my ground, too. Why should I leave and accept that shame? I wasn't born with it. It isn't a birthmark on my skin or a drop of blood in my veins. Shame is something people give us. It's something we make up in our minds about ourselves. I chose not to accept it. Finn wears it. He tattooed it on his heart."

"He lives like that because he resents his father for keeping the money from him."

"Precisely. He resents his father, his mother, the money, the church, me, Whitaker. He resents anyone who can make a decision that could shift power and change his life. Look at what resentment did to him. And Whitaker."

And look at what it's done to Emmett and me.

My mouth is so dry I have to peel my lips apart. I almost wish I could go backwards and unknow these things. Finn, especially, was easier to stomach when he wasn't so human. I don't want to think of these men as vulnerable, as products of their own misfortune. I don't want to think that thirty years from now, someone could think the same of me.

"Surely you don't want me to put this in print," I say.

"Not the words. Let the sentiments guide your hand."

Am I supposed to show them pity? What a privilege it must be for Finn to drink every penny and deny himself and Regina a comfortable, clean home. All out of spite. All the work Whitaker puts into hatred just because he decided love was wrong or hard or shameful? Why does it have to be one or the other? Why can't they just live their lives and not harm anyone else? Exile isn't the only option, but I can understand why Whitaker might see it that way. I've been exiled from my home by someone else's hatred, too. But I would never be as cruel and heartless as any of those men.

"Why did you tell me this?" I ask.

"Because I support you. It takes strength and blindness like yours—"

"I'm not blind," I say, defiant.

"Oh, you are. You'll understand one day."

CHAPTER TWENTY-SIX

I spend a fitful night tangled in my sheets. For a while I consider rewriting some of my work, incorporating what I've learned about Whitaker's past, but what would it change? Most of the town probably knew the tale already, and any compassion Whitaker was once due had long ago been exhausted. Even so, I can't stop thinking about what Clarence said about resentment and how living with it gives you a hard heart. Is it such a bad thing to want justice? When the other side is so ruthless and conniving, do you just stop fighting because defending yourself causes someone else pain? Am I a terrible person for wanting revenge? Or is it justice? I'm not sure I can tell the difference anymore.

My father and his friends had exhausted the legal means to their peaceful end. The government doesn't care that Pritchard poisons his own town. It may not be illegal, but that doesn't mean it's right or moral. If it takes a hard heart to find justice, then so be it, but what if it poisons me, too? I thought I'd escaped Pritchard's poison by luck and distance from the coal plant, but maybe not. Is this what Finn's brother meant about being blind? Am I so hard-hearted it's obvious to everyone but me?

In the morning, I pack the stories in the bottom of a fruit basket and cover them with apricots in case I'm stopped along the way. I dress in a dark skirt and a shirt I borrow from Bea that will easily hide ink. Bea refuses for the third time to join us at the print office, giving me curious sidelong glances until the moment I'm out the door, making me swear to tell her everything when I return.

With my eyes peeled for anyone who might see me, I traipse through the tree line along the side of the building with my skirt hiked over my shoes to keep the burrs from sticking to my hem. Then I knock on the back door like Weylan told me to. Three quick raps. A pause. Two more.

The door flies open so fast, he must have been standing next to it waiting for me. He pulls me into the darkness, and into a short hall. There are rooms on either side, their doors open at odd angles, and the sunlight streaming in the roofline windows makes triangles on the floor.

He motions for me to follow him down the hall. "Did anyone see you?"

"No." I pull the pages from the bottom of the basket as I follow him down the hall. "How long do you think it will take?"

"No idea."

A room this large should feel emptier than it does. Chairs and stools are scattered around with no rhyme or reason, pushed out of the path of the last people who worked here. Counters run along two walls. All sorts of letter trays and boxes of letters clutter the place. It smells like damp concrete. Like rocks and old wood.

This isn't his first time here in the daylight. I can tell by how easily he moves, pushing letter cases around on the counter. I spread the pages out in order, and he hands me a little metal tray with a locking slide on one end.

"It's a composing stick," he says. "This lever sets the column width. We'll line the letters up in this tray, here. You put them in upside down."

"That's a relief," I say. "Much easier than backwards."

"It still takes time, but at least we can work together. We can work on separate stories and piece them together when we're done."

It's too finicky a task for much talking, and our silence is easy at first, comfortable and warm, but questions worm into the quiet, and I can't resist asking them.

"Do you think Max called off the dog?" I ask. "Emmett told me you let him in on the plan."

"I think so." Weylan runs his wrist across his forehead. "I haven't seen him to ask, but I told him because I wanted someone I trust to know what we were doing."

"You don't trust me?" I ask.

"I do now. Generally, I don't trust anyone."

"I'm honored then."

"Sorry I didn't tell you about Max," he says. "Emmett was adamant that you wanted to control things, and I wouldn't want people knowing either, but I needed to tell him."

"I understand. I do." I add a lead slug to my composing stick and start a new line.

"Is this like what your father did in Stoke?"

"No, not at all. He gave speeches."

"He worked with coal?"

"Not his whole life, but yes." The words fall out of me easily. "When my parents were young, it was a small village. A few houses, mostly farms. A chapel. Then someone found coal, and people sold off their farms in pieces. Their sons started working there, like my father. They liked the company store and all it promised, but they were trading their lives for a pittance. Didn't realize they were selling their souls until it was too late."

"What do you miss the most?" he asks.

"My life," I say with a snort. "The little things, honestly. It was a beautiful place to live, but I miss the tall clock in the sitting room. The sound of people walking on the porch. How the front door slammed. The smell of the kitchen. I miss the woods around us, because I knew every tree. And I miss my father's pen."

"His pen?" Weylan almost laughs.

"It's silly. I know. It wasn't silver or anything fancy. Just carved wood.

"What happened to it?" He lifts a full block of text and places it on the galley tray.

"Lost when we moved. The bank said it all had to be sold, everything but our clothes. It belongs to someone else now. It's my turn. Can I ask you something?"

"Of course," he says.

"Did you ever look into the fish? Were you ever so angry you wanted to know why?"

He raises a shoulder. "The truth belongs to people like Whitaker. It's easier to let them have it."

"You can't honestly believe that." I pluck a comma from a tray and place it at the end of line. It makes a satisfying click as I press it into place. "That doesn't sound like you at all. Besides, that's a reality they're shaping, not the truth."

Weylan says nothing for so long that I think I've offended him.

He works with his head down, finishing a line and topping it with a lead slug. He feels far away.

"All of these people told their stories," I say. "They—"

"I'm not telling mine." His voice isn't rough but it's definitive.

"No, I suspect if you wanted to, you would have by now. I just mean that putting it into words can be good."

"I'm sure that's true," he says. "But once you put it out there, people can do what they want with it. They can twist it. Change it. Call you a liar. I prefer cold facts."

Facts. Another thing we have in common. I would chase them to the end of the earth. "That's fair. Why didn't you hunt down that scientist?"

He chews his bottom lip and inspects the letters in his composite stick. "I don't really want to talk about this, Charlie."

The silence falls on us again, and I'm torn between apologizing and not being sorry at all.

"I didn't mean to push," I say. That much is true. This strange club we belong to doesn't mean we feel the same, and that's okay. We're in different places, pruning different branches of our own shade trees. He doesn't need or want my apology; I can tell by his smile. No offense meant, none taken.

"I'm afraid," he says.

"Afraid of the scientist?

"Of the truth." He places a full block of letters on the galley and starts over. "Because once you know the truth, you might feel even more powerless. I want to build my own life, my own future. Not have it taken from me or dictated. I can't do that if it all feels pointless."

The same tree, indeed. Those same reasons push me to the truth.

"So why did you offer to help us, then?" I ask with a great deal of hesitation. "If you don't want to know the truth—"

He turns to face me, his elbow on the counter, inspecting his thumb. The lead makes our fingers gray and metallic, as if we've been mining for something precious.

"I offered because I met someone who wasn't afraid of it. Someone who went looking for it. And I want to know her more."

My breath catches in my throat. He makes an odd sort of melancholy wince, like he's choking back a disappointment, and I don't know if it's with himself or with me, but I do know this is the best and worst thing I could have heard because every moment I'm with Weylan feels less lonely. It feels like action, like my heart has momentum, and revenge eats at me less since I met him. It's direction and hope, all mashed together, and the lightness I feel with him I can only describe as relief and whatever the opposite of alone is. Since I met Weylan, my life has a purpose even more salient than the acid cloud of vengeance that's hung over me, and not only is it distracting, it's the kind of thing I could get used to. I could come to crave being with him. But that means I'd have something to risk losing, and I'm never going to let myself lose another thing again.

CHAPTER TWENTY-SEVEN

Sunday morning washes the town in a brilliant sunrise, staining everything pink. I sit through church service next to Bea as the minister extols the virtue of patience, and I lace my fingers in my lap to keep from fidgeting and losing my mind. When we've eaten and lunch is cleaned up, Bea and I make our excuses and rush off for the newspaper building. Surely Leta knows what we're up to, but she doesn't stop us from leaving the house.

Even with five of us — the girls and Weylan — it takes a whole day to finish the printing, taking turns at the wheel and setting the pages aside to dry. The building is hotter than the surface of the sun. My finger swells against the splint after several turns at cranking the wheel, and my feet ache from the concrete floor, and by the time evening comes and we're just about finished printing, my stomach is an inferno of fear and anxiety, and I've chewed my nails to nubs.

Every store window in town has been plastered with a poster, and the whole town is buzzing over a festival the mayor won't condone. But tonight, every whispered fear, every little tale told and at risk of being forgotten will be dropped on every doorstep. Those posters will be replaced with new ones. All over town, men and women will wake to the news.

There'll be no denying what Whitaker's done. No brushing it under the rug. No more accepting it. No more whispering down by the river about how hard it is to live by his rules. Every door will open, every neighbor will ask, *did you read this?* And it won't be long before Whitaker finds out who printed it and he turns his wrath on me.

Ruthie and Hazel rush off to dinner. Any later, they'd both be in trouble. That leaves Weylan, Bea and me to clean up.

"That's everything." Weylan checks that the ink is dry on the last of the pages.

I start dismantling the letter blocks, dropping a handful on the floor. We both bend to collect them at the same time. Being so distracted and clumsy isn't like me, and I hate that I feel this way around him.

"I'm so tired," I say, covering up my fumbling.

"I am, too. But still looking forward to tonight."

"Midnight?" Bea asks from behind us where she wipes down the press.

"Yes," Weylan checks the watch attached to his cotton trousers by a chain. "I'll miss this when it's over, strange as it is to say. I've been enjoying it."

"So have we," says Bea with an emphasis on the *we*. I glance over my shoulder and give her a warning scowl.

She abandons the tin of ink and rises to her feet. "I need something to close this with. I'll go out the back and find a rock."

With the door closed behind her, I turn to Weylan. "Can I ask you a favor? I'm worried that if we get caught, Bea and the girls will get snagged up in it. Don't let Bea take the fall. I figured since you know Max, maybe—"

"If such a thing happens, I'll do my best to protect anyone I can." He looks like he means it. Before I can thank him, he reaches into his pocket and extracts a long, thin, wooden pen. "This is for you. A small gift. It's not much, just a thank you."

"For what?" I ask.

"For giving me something to do."

It's a beautifully carved pen with a filigreed C that forms the left side of a cat's face.

"Did you carve this?" I ask.

"I didn't make the pen. I just carved into it. I'm not great at it, but I thought you could use a pen of your own."

It reminds me of my father's pen and his coal animals. Stumbling through my gratitude, the words lodge in my throat, and I barely get them out before Bea returns. I shove the pen in my pocket before she sees it.

Weylan smiles at our shared secret, and it would have made my belly flip this morning. Now it makes me uncomfortable and sad in a way I can't quite grasp.

We close the print office and sneak out the back, parting ways in the woods. Halfway back to the market, Bea nudges me.

"Did Weylan say something to you when I stepped outside?"

"Nothing unusual, why?" I ask.

"You just seem quiet."

"Tired, I guess."

Lucky for us, when we get back, the house is empty. Leta has left a note in the kitchen, saying she went to meet Sarah about festival plans. There's an open letter next to it with a Baltimore postmark.

"It's from the suffragist Mother invited," Bea says. "She must be thrilled. Should I read it?"

"Out loud! I'll start dinner." Before I have the apron around my waist, Bea places a hand at her throat.

"She is. She's coming to speak!" Her energy is enough to make me forget the knot in my stomach about Weylan. Almost.

After the sun goes down, Bea and I climb into our beds fully dressed, curling under our covers. I'm glad she's as antsy as I am, because without her to whisper with, I'm afraid my mind would unspool. Weylan trusts me. It shouldn't matter, but it does. Getting close to the people here is a mistake, because I'll lose every one of them when I leave, and it would be unfair to Weylan to keep up whatever friendship the pen represents.

When the downstairs clock chimes midnight, we creep down the steps, careful not to make a sound, and slip out the back door and into the woods where Weylan and Emmett wait. My feet feel heavy, made of lead.

Emmett shakes a newspaper at me, a hint of playfulness in it. "I've read this."

"All of it?" I ask.

"Enough. Once Whitaker reads it, he'll make these stories look like the good old days."

"That's why we need the festival," Bea says.

"Well, I hope it works," Em says. "Because Charlie has a birthday right after graduation, and she can leave. We're all stuck here."

"Come on," I say. "Let's get these papers delivered before someone spots us."

"Let's split up," Weylan suggests.

"I'll walk with Bea." I sidestep close to her.

But Bea coyly points out that she and Weylan know where all Whitaker's supporters live and which houses to miss, and her convoluted reasoning to pair herself with my brother leaves me standing limply next to Weylan as they cross the street. I fall into step next to him with my internal organs tied in knots.

"Let's start down at the cabins along the river," Weylan says. "Then we can do the houses on our side of the street."

Our pace is swift, and our silence is comfortable which loosens my coil some. We make an unspoken game of it, sneaking stealthily up to doors and mailboxes, rolling up papers and tucking them in crevices where they can't be seen from the road but will be noticed first thing in the morning. Before long, we're halfway done, out of breath, and exhausted.

Weylan eyes the tree line along the river and wipes the back of his hand across his brow.

"I could use a break," he says. "Do you want to sit for a minute?"

"There's a clearing back there. I can show you." I lead him back to the path through the woods and pause at the water's edge. Moonlight filters through the trees there, glittering on the water.

"I never knew this was here. I bet it's nice in the daytime." Weylan washes his hands in the water, scrubbing off the ink and waving them, flinging diamond drops into the air.

"It would make a great place to go fishing if it weren't for all the water and the fish." I settle on the rock. "Found it my first morning staying at Leta's, looking for a way to visit Emmett in the morning. It's a nice place to think."

He sits beside me, resting his forearms on his knees. "Are you really leaving after your birthday?"

I smooth my skirt over my knees. "I wish I could. Haven't anywhere to go."

"I'm glad you're staying."

There's no good way to respond to that, because I'm not sure I'm staying either.

"You were right about the writing," he says. "It did help to put things down. Sometimes it feels like it just happened and other times it's like I'll walk in the door and my mother and brother will be there."

"So that never goes away?" The papers at our feet rustle in the breeze, the top pages curling up around the rock that holds them down.

"Not so far. I can still hear their voices, though. My brother had this sharp crack to his laughter."

Weylan does, too. I wonder if they sounded alike. I don't want to think about it right now, because I'm tired, and we still have work to do, but a heavy weight sinks in my chest, and the melancholy calls to me like the early cicadas. I wish I'd met him earlier. Before all the sadness that seeps into our conversation. But maybe I didn't need to know him back then.

I push to my feet. "We should keep working, before I fall asleep."

I follow him through the trees, along the water, and I'm grateful for the moonlight revealing all the tree roots along the well-worn path. Why couldn't I have had this sorrow in common with Bea or Ruthie. Or even that Max boy. Why Weylan?

The path is slippery where it widens enough for us to walk side-by-side. He looks over his shoulder at me, holds out a hand, but I decline.

"I wish I could move away, too, sometimes. Everything here

reminds me of some memory." The path widens, and he falls back to walk beside me. "I'll be at the general store and something will remind me of Mother, or I'll smell some tree in the summer that reminds me of playing outside with my brother when we were young."

"I feel like I could go home, and they would be on the porch. Like I could get on the train and walk down the street, and there they would be."

He feels it, too. This trudging through quicksand, an ever-growing distance from the life I used to have, getting more entrenched in the one I don't even want. It strikes me how much he loved his family and how much he loves this town because of the memories he has here, and I can't take having one more thing in common with him. But maybe his heart isn't as vengeful as mine.

"Do you think if you left this place, you'd ever want to come back?" I ask.

"Probably. Eventually. It's home."

"Would you do it just to fight Whitaker?" I ask.

My entire identity has been stripped away by coal poison and dead fish, and I can't go back home to get it. It's not like a forgotten hat or a lost pen. I can dream about who I used to be. I can wake up and for a split second smell breakfast and hear chickens outside, and pretend I have homework and a book I can't wait to get back to. For a fleeting second, I can still be a girl who likes the sunshine on my face and running through the woods with my cousin, dreaming about a gauzy, glamorous future. But the instant I open my eyes, I'm not that person anymore, and I do my best to get through the harsh, grating light of day without thinking about it, because if I do, I won't talk about it like Weylan does. He talks about grief as if he's read a thousand books about it in the library and mastered it along with the printing press. If I talk about grief, it will boil and seethe.

I stop at a tree so large I couldn't fit my arms around it if I tried, and I flatten myself against it, pressing my hand against my stomach to make the whirlwind stop.

"Are you all right?" he asks.

It's too late to stop this, and I'm afraid I'm out for vengeance and doing the wrong thing, but I can't say that to Weylan or he might agree with me.

"I'm fine," I say. "I thought I heard something."

He places a hand on the tree, by my shoulder, and stands so still I wonder if either of us is breathing. All I can hear is that one cicada and the voice in my head telling me to run.

"I think the coast is clear," he whispers.

I nod and push off the tree. "We should finish this."

"I'm sorry if I pushed you," he says. "That was insensitive of me, talking about home while you want to go back so badly."

"Think nothing of it. There's something about being in a new place that takes energy. Finding your way and all? Maybe being here will be good for a while. A nice distraction. But I will go home one day."

"I would miss you." His hand finds mine, and he tugs me back, stopping me in the path. He closes the distance. "If you left. I would miss you."

"You would?" I ask.

"Yes." I've never seen earnestness look so pained.

My mouth is unbelievably dry. I could drink down that entire poisoned creek and still be thirsty. "How are you always there? At the train station. At the dance. How?"

"I don't know. Small town. How are *you* always there? In the hall. You're all I see."

Suddenly I wonder if grief draws people to each other as much as it drives everyone else away.

"Please don't go." He squeezes my hand gently. "I think I'm falling for you, Charlie."

"Weylan, I—" I would miss him, too, but I can't say it because it wouldn't be fair when I don't even want to admit it to myself.

He's taller than me by enough that when he dips his head, his hair falls in his eyes, and I can feel a warmth come off him that draws me in. He tilts his head, and there's no mistaking that he wants to kiss me. His fingertips trace down my arm, shooting sparks as they go. I close my eyes and hold my breath because it's all I can do to keep from shivering and falling apart. He squeezes my hand, an invitation, a question. From anyone else, it would feel wrong, but from Weylan, it feels safe. The opposite of alone, whatever that is. And it's lightning and thunder and a roaring river, and the butterflies in my stomach launching into a swarming fury.

Every inch of me begs for it, but it terrifies me with its intensity, and I cannot let it happen.

"Papers." I step back and drop his hand. "We have to deliver them."

I turn on my heel and walk as fast as I can, nearly tumbling over an exposed root that the forest put in my way. Weylan is beside me in what seems like an instant.

"I'm sorry. I didn't mean to make you uncomfortable."

"It isn't you," I say. "I'm not... I can't..."

"It's fine. I would never—"

"I know. It's just that I'm not... I'm raw and I don't—"

"No need to explain." His voice is gentle, and I almost hate the understanding that threads through it. I don't want him to understand me. I don't want to ever rely on him. "We're almost done. What do you say? Finish this up before Bea and Emmett worry?"

"Yes. We should."

We trace the path back to the clearing that runs behind the houses, tucking papers in doorways. With only two left, we split up. I leave mine at a second-floor apartment, and Weylan leaves his at the church parsonage.

Empty-handed, we pause in the middle of the street, at the intersection. The town is empty and silent, but for the distant bark of a fox.

Footsteps send us spinning to find Emmett and Bea emerging from the shadows with their hands empty.

The four of us stand in the crossroads, the weight of what we've done hanging heavy in the air. In the morning, the whole town will know. Everyone will demand justice. Bea gives me the hint of a smile. She has questions I can't answer. No matter what happens from here, the four of us are tied together for eternity, bound by what will come.

Emmett shoves his hands in his pockets, glancing at his feet. "It feels like the end of something, doesn't it? Even though it's just the beginning?"

"There's no going back now." Bea folds her arms, her chin high. She looks like her mother, the way the moonlight glints off her sharp bravado.

Weylan locks eyes with me. "Everything's different now."

I wish it weren't. I wish it were just like yesterday, with hope and promise and a dream of home, but he's right. Everything is different now.

Despite so much weighing on me, sleep finds me the second I settle back in bed. And when morning comes, it isn't a true morning, but a dream state. I know it's a dream because it's absurd and I can't do anything about it. Sun warms my face, and as I take long strides across a meadow carrying a tea tray, rain flows upward from the river, thousands of diamond droplets lifting into the sky, and all I can think is, *who will want tea now?* And when someone hammers away on a tree, I turn to see who would dare interrupt the impending rainbow, but no one is there.

"Charlotte." Bea calls my name. Someone bangs on the front door.

With a rush, I realize I'm late for school. Flinging my feet over the edge of the bed and rubbing my eyes with the heels of my hands, the night stitches itself together. The newspaper. We'd put it in everyone's door and mailbox. School will be absolutely buzzing.

There it is again, the ramming at the door as if the very walls are crashing down. Bea gives me a terrified look, sheet pulled up to her chin.

Leta appears in the doorway in her dressing gown, hands clutched at her chest. "Get up and get dressed quickly, girls."

"Who is it?" I ask.

Leta takes a deep breath, as if she's been asked to explain the birds and bees to a toddler and needs to steel herself against questions. "It's the constable."

CHAPTER TWENTY-EIGHT

Bea gasps. "Is Father…"

"He's in the store." Leta pats her hair. "Get dressed right now and come downstairs. Do as they say."

Bea's as white as her bloomers as she pulls on her skirt. I do my best to keep my wits about me, surprised at how adept my fingers are with buttons, considering how tired and shaky I am.

"They're going to lock us away." Bea's voice wavers.

"Not *us*, Bea. They'll arrest me. Don't say a word. You weren't there. It was only me."

"I thought it would take longer. How do you think they found us out? I hope Minnie didn't give us away. Do you think it was Sarah?"

Ignoring Bea's questions, I finish buttoning my shirt and tuck it in. Loud male voices downstairs rattle both of us. I freeze with my hand on the door knob, taking slow, deep breaths while I wait for Bea's nod.

"It's happening too fast," she says.

My mouth is so dry I can't even swallow. It isn't too fast at all. Not if we were set up.

Weylan. All that talk about what we had in common and him holding my hand. "That son of a bitch."

"What?" Bea asks.

"Never mind."

I pull the door open. It's swollen with humidity and takes an extra tug, but it gives way, and I hold onto the wall as I coil down the stairs. Leta, in her motherly high pitch, apologizes for the state of things in the early hour as she pulls papers together. They'd been playing cards into the night, she says. The dining room table is a mess. Please don't judge. And how is Carla—whoever she is—since she hurt her knee, the poor dear?

Behind me, Bea hisses. "What son of a bitch? Who are you talking about?"

"Shh. Say nothing," I beg.

"Charlotte Morris?" the officer at the bottom of the stairs asks, as if I could be anyone else. "Turn out your pockets."

"They're empty," I say. I pull them out as best I can to prove it.

"We'll do you a courtesy and let you walk into the carriage yourself without shackles," the officer says. "But only out of respect for Mitchell."

"Why am I being arrested?" I want to hear them say it out loud. I want them to tell me that Weylan turned me in because he's a manipulative conman.

Leta stands aside, clutching her hands beneath her chin.

The officer grabs my arm. "We found crates of black blasting powder in the woods behind this house. Label on 'em says it came from Stoke. Damn near enough to level the town, and one of your little *friends* said you put it there." The emphasis he puts on *friends* is how I'd put it, too. I knew I shouldn't have trusted him. "Who else in this town would know a thing about blasting powder, Miss Morris?"

We're a mere three steps from the door when it swings open and Mitchell fills the doorframe. He crumples with a sigh. "I saw them pull the cartons from the tree line back there. Just down that little path that leads to the river."

"It can't be." Leta mutters a quick prayer, and Bea gasps from the bottom of the stairs.

"It wasn't me," I plead. "It isn't true."

"Who would set you up?" Bea's voice quivers.

Weylan. He's the only one who knows. He knows I like to sit on that flat rock. He knows about the printing press, the ink, the houses to avoid, and which route to take. Someone framed me, and he's the only one who would do it. All he had to do was cart the blasting powder back there before going to bed.

The cop shoves me through the door and into an old black carriage across from an officer so young he could be a classmate. His uniform is a size too big, and he gives me an awkward grin and explains he's in training. He seems almost apologetic about it.

The officer who's clearly in charge leans his head in the open door. I've never seen brown eyes so icy. "We got your brother, too."

"Why? He did nothing."

With the slam of the door, they congratulate themselves for a job well done, for saving the town from complete destruction by a girl who wanted to blow them all the smithereens. They call me all kinds of things: a menace, neglectful, insolent, devilish. I'm suddenly glad my mother isn't alive to hear them say such things.

The carriage lurches to a start and leans to the right as the horses turn around. With every rotation of the wheels, the coil around my chest pulls tighter. Other than Bea and Leta, no one here knows me. There's no one coming to save me.

The ride is short, but long enough for my eyes to adjust to the darkness of the carriage, and I'm blinded by sunlight when the door flies open. I follow the recruit onto the sidewalk and into the station. They take my boot laces and march me through a set of iron gates, down a hall walled by bars and more iron gates. The constable steers me into a cell on the left and he wrangles a key into a clanging lock. The slam of the door rattles and peals like a broken bell, and just like that, it's over. My freedom is gone.

There are two other souls already in the room, one of whom is Emmett.

What have I done? I lost myself; I trusted the wrong people. And now my brother's in a jail cell? Father would hang me and Mother would hand him the rope.

His head is in his hands, so I can only see the top of his head, but his whole body trembles. His breaths come in retching gasps. Across from Emmett, a drunk man in a stained shirt, who smells like heat and old cigars soaked in the acid of yesterday's dinner, wobbles his head. Drool darkens his shirt. I swallow hard. How long will this arrangement last?

"Em?"

It's hot and dark. Only one high window covered in bars lets in any sun. Gas lights make up the difference. Counting my breaths, I try not to panic, because if I do, it will make this all the worse on Emmett who is clearly not all right. When he lifts his head, he'll want to know what's coming next, and God's honest truth, I have no answers. Did they lay a hand on him? Will I be able to keep calm while he tells me? And how will I make up for this?

"Em." I'm more urgent this time. "Please look at me."

He lifts his head. It's enough for me to see how red he is, how deep the fear runs.

His head falls back against the wall, and his foot bounces a mile a minute. Terror dilates in his eyes. I know the look.

It takes a few minutes of deep, slow breaths, but the flush leaves his face and his breathing steadies.

"This is all my fault. I ruined everything." I lower myself onto the bench next to him. "Weylan set me up. You're just tangled up in it."

"Weylan? Are you sure? That doesn't seem right."

"Yeah, well, it is. He's the only one who knew I liked that spot by the river. It just makes sense."

My arm throbs against the stitches where the man wrenched my arm. They're more annoying than useful at this point, and outstaying their welcome. Focusing on them makes my skin crawl, and I can't bear one more minute. I pick at the seam where my sleeve meets the blouse until I loosen the stitching, then I peel my sleeve off and toss it on the bench next to me.

My arm gleams alabaster in the gaslight.

"What the hell are you doing?" Emmett's high pitched voice echoes off the walls. The man in the corner jolts and snores, but doesn't wake.

"These stitches are worse than the wound at this point." My nails are long enough to pick at the knots and pull out the threads. "And before you ask, it was one of Pine's friends. Happened at the dance."

Emmett gives me a repulsed wince and goes back to bouncing his foot on the floor. "How'd I miss that?"

I raise my good shoulder. "A man in a barn stitched me up. It should have healed days ago, but I kept breaking it open again. It's just a little sore now. That last one's pretty embedded in there, though." I twist my bicep around to see and go back to plucking at the green thread.

"That's disgusting," Emmett says.

The man on the bench across from us burps, and Emmett scrunches his face like he's been hit with a blast of sandy wind. He shifts and shimmies so he's facing me, and I can't look into his eyes because I know what I'll see there. He'll be full of blame and fear and things I can't quell.

"No, he's worse. He smells like trash set in the sun too long," Emmett says.

"We'll get used to it."

"Charlie, I don't want to get used to any of this." His voice is loud and high. At least it's not like his night terrors.

"I'll figure out a way to get you out of here. In the meantime, there isn't anything *to* do. Just try to relax. Breathe slow. Pace or something."

He grunts. "When are we getting out? How long will we be here? I can't be locked up in here, it reminds me of school."

I tug on the last green knot, picking away at it until it pulls through the scab. "What do you mean it reminds you of school?"

"How they picked on me." His voice is small. "When I was a child. I'd defend myself and get locked in that tiny, dark closet until the end of the day."

"That little walled-in corner where Miss Miller kept books and chalk?"

"Yes. Every day, the boys would follow me home and pelt me with rocks. Miss Miller hated me."

"That's why you did so much schoolwork at home?"

"I couldn't do it in the closet. If I didn't, I'd fail."

I brush little green knots from my skirt to the floor. All this time, and he never said why he panicked when he was locked in a room, why it scared him so bad when the door was closed at night. If he'd said something, Father would have destroyed that teacher.

"What did Mother do when you told her?" I ask.

"I never told anyone."

"Why not? Em, I would have walked you home every day if I'd known."

"I was too ashamed. Who would want to admit to that? I wasn't strong like Father or friendly and loved by everyone like Mother. Not brave like you. I was just useless. Everybody hated me. I figured I deserved it."

"That's not true." Children can be cruel in devious ways but their effect is far from childish. "You weren't like those boys. You wouldn't have to work in the mine, and they owed their whole lives to Pritchard for so little in return."

"Don't defend them," he barks.

"I'm not. I understand them, that's all."

"Who cares why they did it? I couldn't stretch out my legs. I had the worst cramps, stuck in there every day for hours. When the teacher left the room, they'd put frogs in there and really big spiders, and I was scared. I was a child."

His chin quivers, and suddenly he isn't a man anymore. He's my scared little brother, locked in a closet, and I put him there. I give him a side hug that he shrugs away from before leaning in.

"I'm sorry," I say. "I would have boxed their ears, you know that, right?" My nose is running something fierce, and I wipe it on my detached sleeve. Have I been blind for that long? "And you are brave."

"I'm not brave. I'm terrified."

"You can be brave and scared at the same time. Look, there are no frogs, no spiders. Just a really stinky man, and he's not hurting anybody but himself."

Now that Emmett needs softness from me, I feel like all I have is sharp edges. Did this need for revenge actually make me stiff and blind? It certainly hasn't made things better. Neither of us is better off than we were on the day we left Stoke. Finn and Regina didn't help the situation, but I haven't exactly been making the best decisions. Obviously.

"We'll get through this, Em. I haven't given up. I want to go home, to air I can breathe and water I can drink. I want to make a life for myself without owing anything to anyone."

Emmett rises to his feet and paces, giving the fetid man a wide berth.

Sometimes I want revenge on Pritchard so bad I can taste it, but other times I fear if I ever get it, I'll have something to lose. I'll have my home back, but Pritchard will always be after me. He'll always have more power. I thought being in this town and fighting Whitaker would lead me to Pritchard's crimes so that I could take them to someone who cares. But what will I do if Leta casts me away, if I'm no longer welcome here?

Weylan lied and set us up, but I made my own mistakes. I trusted him, and I let vengeance lead me astray. That craving for revenge won't save me. It's just a hatred that spirals and coils, tightening as it goes, choking on itself.

Justice is what I need. I have to figure out how to get it without hurting anyone else, without losing myself, or I could end up like

Pritchard and Whitaker. Angry and hateful, destroying everyone else because I can't bear to live in a world that I can't control. I have a lot to apologize for.

All that anger gave me one small advantage, though. If I'd been even the tiniest bit more prone to swooning, I'd be heartbroken by Weylan's betrayal. Instead, I have a perfectly justifiable anger to sink my teeth into.

Emmett leans his arms on the bars and peers out into the hall.

"You're not alone, Em. We'll get out of here, and I'll take the blame for all of this."

If I ever get out, I have a lot of apologizing to do.

CHAPTER TWENTY-NINE

We eat cold stew for dinner. Emmett chews two bites and swears it's beef, but I'm not so sure. It fills me anyway, and I spend a sleepless night on the hard bench wondering with every strange grumble of my belly if they poisoned the food.

Emmett tosses and turns all night, and we both spend a lot of time staring at the ceiling. I can't get him to talk, so my mind is free to chew over how much of a fool I've been. Trusting Weylan, falling for his charms. Betraying the trust Leta and Mitchell put in me. Disappointing Bea and risking her safety, along with Ruthie and Hazel. I never deserved their friendship.

I picture Weylan and Pine huddled somewhere, rejoicing over their triumph. No, I'm certain it isn't the stew that makes my belly churn. They can't keep me locked in here forever, and when they finally let me out, I will go straight to Whitaker and take the blame for all of this. And then I must find another way to bring down Pritchard. Some judge or a jury or even the President. I don't know who to write to or what to say, but if I have to be stuck in this cell, I will spend every second of my time trying to figure it out.

A slow light builds at our little window, stretching a band of pale blue light across the ceiling. At the end of the hall, constables chatter and shuffle about. Some leave. More arrive. A gruff older woman with her hair in curlers comes in to change the chamber pot and gives us stale bread for breakfast and says to make it last. Just after that, a man with a thousand keys on a ring arrives to take away the drunken man who grew sober and offended by my presence in his cell, as if he had any claim to propriety after peeing on the floor.

Emmett rolls onto his side and faces the wall. He doesn't rouse with hunger when lunch fails to show, and he doesn't flinch when the man with the keys jingles his way down the hall again.

I sit forward, my hands on my knees, praying to a God who left me a long time ago that they'll let us both free, but the man isn't here for us, and he isn't alone.

Women's voices echo off the concrete. Wild-haired and smiling broadly in their stained, disheveled dresses, the women march past in shackles, led by aggressive officers who lock them in cells by twos. There are eight of them. Sarah, the very image of propriety, is among them. I've never heard of such a thing. Eight women arrested at one time? Wide-eyed, all my senses straining to make sense of the sounds in the dim light, I try to make out words between the scuffles and shuffling of feet, the unchaining of hands, the officers giving orders, and doors slamming.

Once the last officer passes, I propel myself at the bars and clutch them with both hands.

"What happened?" I ask.

Their voices rise as one chorus, voices falling away one at a time until a lone woman is left telling the tale.

"We protested here all day. At the station. After every house had a newspaper yesterday morning."

A lightness washes over me tinged with shame. Triumph swirls with the gloom like oil floating on water. I squeeze my eyes shut and beg them not to say more, not to give me away. Not yet. Not until Emmett goes free. The woman isn't as concerned with the papers, however, as she is with the events that came after.

"See, we figured they couldn't arrest the men who spoke out if the cells were full of women. What are they going to do? Beat us all senseless? Good, I say. If we're mistreated, the lazy among the suffragists won't get to sit idly by anymore. Everyone should take a side. We gathered as much from our root cellars as we could."

"Filled our aprons to the brim," comes a small voice from further away.

"Brought them all down here to the station and had a protest. When the police tried to make us leave, we pelted them."

"With tomatoes."

"Good God," I say.

"We heard you'd been arrested," says the smaller voice. "Minnie told me what you done."

"Please," I beg. "Don't speak of it."

"Quiet as a mouse," she says. "People are rallying against the mayor. You should see it. It's beautiful. Wouldn't have happened if not for that paper."

I kick the toe of my boot against the door. Three days ago, I wanted this. Now that it's come to pass, now that people are paying the price, it makes me feel shameful.

The woman in the adjacent cell rests her thick forearms on the bars. "You were set up. Whole town knows they're blaming you for that blasting powder, but it weren't you."

"Does Leta blame me?" I ask.

"She don't know who done it, but she's sure it ain't you."

Something about hearing it come from a stranger's mouth, that the part of the town I care for most knows I'm innocent of the worst charge against me, makes Weylan's setup even more real. Maybe I don't mind being in here after all, if I don't have to be out there where proximity to him will anger me more.

"I know who did it," I say. The sadness in my voice sounds foreign. My heart plummets to my unlaced boots. I've been such a fool. I deserved to be locked away for sheer foolishness alone.

"Who was it? Who set you up?"

"I shouldn't say." Perhaps Weylan pretending to care about me bothers me, after all. I'm furious at myself for trusting him, for letting myself feel those things. Outraged at him for playing with my heart. Hot tears sting my eyes and my throat coats with the salty swell. I turn from the bars, though no one can see me anyway.

The bench creaks and groans beneath me when I settle next to Emmett. The tears won't stop this time. My whole body seems to tense with them. Emmett's dark eyes are pink and sorrowful, full of their own torment, but he leans against my shoulder and whispers something calming, but his words wash right over me.

Big memories arrive in waves, not just the settings but the smells and the sounds. Mother's hand in mine as her soul leaves her body. The texture of Father's sweat-soaked blanket as he shakes beneath it, gasping his pleas to keep Emmett safe. Meeting the banker as he took the house, packing the bag with my clothes and Emmett's. The little coal lion lying in the dry earth beside the porch. Every moment chipped away at my insides, hollowing me out a little more, leaving room for all that vengeance to burrow inside me. It pick-axed my heart until all that was left was one damn tear that I shed while staring at the time on our grandfather clock. It had been there forever, and its hands had stopped because no one wound it since my mother let out that last dying groan.

I thought I couldn't cry any more, but I've been wrong about lots of things.

Down the hall, the women debate a hunger strike, whether to accept dinner if it comes. They choose to keep it as a last resort, to be polite and obedient instead but only until they're released, and then they'll kick up a fuss again, taking turns to keep the cops busy and the jail full so no one's children go neglected. I find their deviance encouraging. Hopeful even. But all the talk about children and families fills me with guilt.

"This is all my fault," I say to Emmett. "I know it would have happened eventually, but I feel awful."

"You're not a martyr." He turns his glazed eyes to me. "And you didn't act alone. You're not the only one who made choices."

"But you blamed me before." I rub at all the tension knotted in the base of my neck.

"That's because I *wanted* someone to blame, not because this is your fault."

The man with the keys comes down the hall. There's only one set of footsteps this time. No protestors. No dinner. Someone asks what time it is. Close to nine, he says.

When the keys jangle together, I know. They're either coming to let someone out, or they're letting themselves in. I roll my neck, and it finally cracks, but relief is short-lived.

The chief of police appears at the door. It isn't just his badge that gives him away. He looks like Max with his ink black hair and eyes so dark the pupils don't contract in the light. He's a thick, solid wall of a man I wouldn't want to cross, and he keeps his eyes locked on mine as he swings the door free. It's unnerving how little emotion there is in his eyes. He could be a shell of a human, an animated corpse, and I wouldn't be surprised.

He fills the door and says, "You're free to go."

CHAPTER THIRTY

I launch to my feet. Emmett looks up at me with terrified questions burning in his eyes. I grab his arm and tug him upright.

"Why? Why are you letting us go?" I ask, but I know. They want to follow me, to see who I run to first, but I want to hear them say it out loud. If they really think I've stashed away enough blasting powder to level the town, they wouldn't be letting me go.

The police chief grips his belt and hoists his pants. "Seems we have to make room for more of these degenerates. First in, first out." He crosses the cell in two strides, his eyes darting between me and Em. "You're to go home and stay there. You step outside and so much as breathe, we will pull you back in here. We're watching you."

The flash of anger, the twitch of his right eye, says he means it.

"Yes, sir," I say.

"Next time, your cell won't be so comfortable."

He steps aside, clearing a path between us and the door. With Emmett on my heels, I slip through the gaping maw in the iron bars, and I march down the hall. Thin purple light of dusk brushes across the desk, across papers and the typewriter, where the woman who has my bootlaces sits.

"Call me Laura." With a sidelong glance at the hallway, she pulls back the edge of her shawl and reveals a little sunflower pin stuck to her blouse. "Leta believes you're innocent. Finn is on his way here."

A wave crashes into me, scraping away the fear of having no place to go as it ebbs. But in its place, a new terror emerges.

"Finn's coming here? Why?" Em asks. His hand is on the doorknob, his thumb on the lever, ready to push his way out.

"Finn's been fishing," Laura says. "Bea told Leta, and Mitchell turned him in. They found the kitchen full of herring." She opens her desk drawer and gives me my bootlaces. "Tax evasion. Theft of town property."

"Regina?" I ask.

"She's fine, far as I know. Take Emmett there."

"Thank you." I fall back with a sigh. Emmett will be all right for now. At least he isn't in Finn's line of fire.

"Heck of a wound you have there." Laura winces and flings open a desk drawer. "You want a pin to put your sleeve back on? I got one in here somewhere."

"No, thanks." I shove the balled-up sleeve in my pocket. "Let 'em talk."

Emmett and I tumble out the heavy double doors and into the sun.

It seems impossible that we'd be allowed to walk out the door and down the street without interference, but we do. Fruit is everywhere. Onions smashed into slivers on the ground. Raw egg slimed down a fence, drying into a congealed mess. My foot lands in the reddish-brown blob of splatted stewed tomato.

"We need to put as much distance between you and Finn as we

can. I'll talk to Leta and see if she can help find a place, but in the meantime, stay put with Regina, okay? And come find me at Bea's if something happens."

"We missed two days of school. However will we catch up?" Emmett squints, turning away from the sun. The disinterest in his voice cracks something inside me, and I laugh.

I try to tame my hair. Strands that came unfurled from my braid whip in the breeze. "I forgot about school."

He half laughs, half grunts and shoves his hands in his pockets. "What are you going to do about Weylan?"

"I have no idea." I rub my eyebrow with my good hand. For the first time since I can remember, my arm doesn't hurt. "Ignore him, I guess. Hope I never see him again?"

I can't believe I was so blind. In a town this small, avoiding him will be impossible.

We pause at the crossroads, and Em pats my good shoulder. "I don't have to worry about you being caught alone with him again, I guess." He gives me a smile and an arched eyebrow and sets off for Regina's.

I cross the bridge over the burbling creek and try to walk down Main Street like nothing happened. Just another day, I tell myself. I could take the back path, but my curiosity itches more than my caution, begging to be scratched. Though I expect to see fruit in the streets and evidence of the protest, I'm surprised to find the road is empty, just the usual shop owners sweeping up porches and closing their windows before evening sets in.

"Good evening, Charlotte. Got the paper. Good work." The man who runs the newsstand gives me a sly smile that I try to return.

The pharmacist taps on the window as I pass. He waves me in, asks about my finger, which swells at times but is healing fine, and he notices my arm. I swear Finn didn't cause the wound and refuse to tell him how it happened, but he clicks his tongue and says *those boys*, and I say nothing as he offers me some ointment.

A dozen people mill about, sweeping their sidewalks and pulling in signs for the night. I wave back at the ones who acknowledge me and avoid the stares from the ones who don't. I must look a sight in a wrinkled skirt with a filthy hem, one sleeve ripped and a bright pink lightning scar down my bicep. Women just don't walk around in such a state. The shame of it burns, and I want to shrink into the shadows, but that's not what warriors do. I'm no Lady Godiva, but if she could do it, so can I.

I wait at the corner of the funeral home as if I can gauge the weather at Bea's house. I thought leaving Stoke felt lonely and confusing, but this is like standing on the edge of a cliff. Whitaker clearly wants my head on a pike, and he's not the only one. Suffragists were already working against him, but now they're tied to the printing by way of having defended it, and the whole town seems full of static, ready to spark. I don't have the complete story yet about how the coal is killing the people and how the town is covering it up, but I will. And I don't know what to do with the information once I have it, but I'll figure it out. In the meantime, I have to make it up to Leta and find out if Ruthie and Hazel are all right.

And then there's Weylan. I don't know how he planned it or who he worked with to frame me, but if I never see him again, it will be too soon.

With a deep breath of mossy, earthy air, I head for Leta and Bea's. It's only about sixty paces away, and I cover half of it before I spot

Weylan pacing the porch, running his hand through his hair. The sight of him makes my blood boil, and I'm tempted to scream at him until my lungs give out, but time spent on him would be wasted, so I turn on my heel to loop around the long way to the back door. I would rather walk to Argentina and back than look at him. How dare he think he can come here to gloat?

I hike my skirt over my shoes and stomp down the alley between the buildings, footsteps closing in behind me. I run, my shoes slipping out of my unlaced boots, and I curse myself for not tying them up.

"Charlie, wait." His hand clamps around my arm, tugging and spinning me around to face him. "Are you all right?"

"Don't you dare call me Charlie. How stupid do you think I am?" I yank free from his grasp, doing my best to keep the fire in me under control, but I'm losing. "*Am I all right?* Drop the act. The only thing you've ever cared about is yourself."

I must be striking a nerve, because he steps back and something like pain and confusion clouds his face.

"Don't you dare play the wounded puppy dog with me," I demand. "I'm over it. I don't have time for your games anymore. Do you honestly think you deserve my time? Look at me."

My tattered sleeve drapes from my pocket, a fringe of loose strings at my shoulder exposes my arm with its scar. My braid only contains a fraction of my hair, and my boots have no laces. If I were the betting type, I'd put my meager life savings on the chance I smelled like vomit and a chamber pot.

"I don't understand," he says.

"Is this what you came to see? It seems awfully petty of you to walk all the way here to take in the sight, but go ahead." I clench my fists in my pockets. "God, I've been such a fool."

"I don't think you're a fool at all. I don't know what I did, or what you *think* I did." Auburn hair tumbles into his eyes with the shake of his head. That soft, pleading look is a lie. His pained expressions and those puppy-dog eyes are just a farce. He steps closer, making me more nauseated with every inch.

"You set me up," I say. "I never should have trusted you."

He flinches. "I didn't set you up. I would never, Charlie. *Charlotte.* Why would you think that? You must believe me."

"Don't tell me what I must do." I shrug him off and step back. "Don't speak to me again. Don't speak of me, to me, about me, near me, or for me. And stay the hell away from my brother."

I make it four steps before he's in front of me again, his face lined with a mix of confusion and anger, his hands on my shoulders, stopping me in my tracks.

"I don't know what you're talking about. Why would I wait for you if I wanted you in jail? I paced out here all evening until Leta ordered me home, and I came back first thing this morning. I haven't been to school, so I could be here when you came home. I ate all my fingernails."

He holds up his hand, and I refuse to look. I walk toward the path that leads to the creek, and I point down toward the water. "I took you back there and showed you a spot with a flat rock where we could sit by the river, and you said you never knew it was there, then all the sudden the cops are dragging a crate of blasting powder out of the woods saying someone tipped them off. Someone told them I was the one who put it there. I'm not wasting any more breath on this." I push him aside. "Go home. I never should have trusted you. I don't owe you an explanation for your own behavior. I'm hungry, and I want a bath."

He overtakes me, blocking my path again. "I didn't do this. Of course, I can see why you would think that, but…"

I ball my hands into fists, and it almost feels good the way my nails dig into my palms. I make it to Leta's backdoor more mixed up and uncertain than I've ever been in my life, but I do know two things for sure. If Leta kicks me out of the house, she'll at least let me take my things. And turning my back on Weylan is the best choice I could make today.

"Give up," I say to him, grasping the doorknob. "Go away. It's over."

CHAPTER THIRTY-ONE

The moment I reach the back door, Leta throws it open, yanks me inside, and slams it shut behind me.

"I have no excuse for what I've done," I say into her shoulder. "It was all my idea to print that paper, but I had nothing to do with that blasting powder. I don't deserve your kindness."

"Hush. This will all work out," Leta says.

"How can it possibly?" I ask. "Do you want me to leave? I can find some other place to go where I won't sabotage your mission." She squeezes me harder and says nothing. "I betrayed you, and I'm so disappointed in myself."

She hushes me and holds me at arm's length. "We'll talk of no such thing."

"But I—"

"You're going nowhere." She draws me into another hug, and I fall to pieces. It isn't the shame or the fear of what will come, nor is it the relief that Emmett is okay and I still have a home to come to. It's comfort. It's not *my* mother, but Leta is a mother, and I didn't think I'd have someone to lean on again.

"Thank you." It's such a small thing to say for such a priceless gift. "I've soiled your blouse."

"Oh, dear," Leta says. "You need a handkerchief."

She puts one of Bea's in my hand and leads me to a chair by the stove. My face feels disgusting, the tears streaking through the grit. I need a bath, and my stomach realizes it needs a meal before I do, growling at the scent of the roasted goose cooking in the sweltering oven. The stove door creaks and groans as Leta bends to jab a spoon in the pan and baste it.

"I'm so tired of being afraid," I admit. "If I hadn't met you, I have no idea where I'd be. Even more lost, I suppose. And I broke your trust. Everything is falling apart. Em is in trouble. School is ending, and I'm no closer to getting home."

Leta squeezes my shoulder and slides a plate of biscuits before me. She sits beside me, smoothing her apron over her lap.

"You needn't worry about any of those things." She levels with me in such a serious manner that I don't question a syllable of her words when she says, "You will always have a home here. Bea is upstairs. She'll be very glad to see you. Now eat up, get a bath, and we'll sort out the rest at dinner."

The dining room table is still covered in the fodder of protest planning. Just the thought of the water festival forms a hard ball of biscuits in my stomach.

"What happens next?" I asked.

"We postponed it in light of the women being arrested. I sent off a letter to the suffragist. I'm sure she'll still come. We can worry about that another day."

At the top of the stairs, I knock gently on Bea's open door. She looks up at me from her bed, where she reads from a book propped on her knees.

"Charlie!" She leaps to her feet. "You're free! What happened?"

"Weylan gave me a pen. That's what happened. I should have known better, but I fell for him. And he set me up."

She uses her finger to mark her place in the book as I tell her how he almost kissed me, and I wanted him to, how he said he wanted to know me better, and how nothing had ever sounded sweeter and scarier at the same time.

"I understand why you'd doubt him, but did they say it was Weylan who turned you in? Do you have any evidence it was him?"

"Other than him knowing about the rock, no," I say.

Bea scans the ceiling with her nose wrinkled and her lips pursed like she does when she's thinking hard. "I'm not convinced yet. He had plenty of chances to unravel you before this. Why say all those marvelous things to you and give you the pen? If he were working with Whitaker, he could have nabbed you when the two of you stole the ink."

"I paid for the ink," I say.

Bea sighs. "You know what I mean. But what about the rock? Mere hours pass between us sitting at that rock and the discovery of the blasting powder there. It can't be a coincidence."

"Why can't it?" She rolls her eyes. "Everyone knows about that rock. I go back there all the time. It's probably flat because humans have been fishing from it since the dawn of time. That powder could have been there for days. Or perhaps someone did bury it that night, and they missed you by minutes."

"It seems far too convenient." I wad my ripped sleeve into a ball.

"Then find evidence."

"No." I toss the sleeve into the wardrobe where it lands with the remains of my old embroidered skirt. But that's a terrible idea because it will make everything smell, so I snatch it back again. "I will not go looking for evidence. I never want to see him again. Ever. He blinks at me with those puppy dog eyes and pretends like he understands me just because he lost people, too, but he's a scoundrel. I see right through him."

Suddenly I'm reminded of his words just two nights ago when he said I could see through him. Now I'm not sure if he was wrong or right.

"What if someone gave you evidence?" Bea asks.

"Of his guilt? I don't care. I don't need it. All of this is his fault."

"Evidence of his innocence?"

A sound escapes me that sits somewhere between a growling coyote and an obstinate toddler.

Bea looks pleased with herself. "You can't blame Weylan for the poison any more than you can blame the coal or the fish. Doesn't Pritchard win if you stop living your life?" She leans forward, snatching my little coal lion from the windowsill, and she shakes it at me. "Your father gave you this and said you were brave. That's the story you told me. I think it's cowardly to blame Weylan without evidence just because you're scared."

"Whose friend are you?" I whisper.

She climbs off the bed, risks entering the cloud of my stench, and puts the lion in my hand. I put it right back on the windowsill again, next to the mermaid's purse.

"And that stupid thing?" I point at it. "It's broken."

"What are you talking about?" she asks with a laugh.

"Mermaid's purse. It's supposed to hold treasure and bring renewal or something like that. This one did a terrible job." My voice is small and tired.

"You didn't think a mermaid's purse would really change your life, did you? That's the kind of thing you have to do yourself." Her bed creaks as she sits on the edge. "What are you so afraid of? Really?"

"Everything. What if I can't get home?" I sit across from her. All the effort of trying to stay strong for Em and being angry at Weylan has me too tired to do anything but cry. My face is tight and gritty. I try to blink the tears back before they make me feel even worse. I want to go home. I want my room and Father's chair and Mother's garden. I want our pigs and our chickens. That was my life, but it died when my parents did, and it isn't fair.

"That place is killing people," Bea says. "It would kill you, too, Charlie."

"Not if I fix it. Make Pritchard pay." I wipe my eyes on my sleeve.

"You have a lot more conviction when you talk about revenge than when you talk about your home. What if you never win? What if he gets away with killing your family? Then what will you do with the rest of your life?"

"Stop." The tears. The wanting. All of it needs to stop. "I can't let that happen, all right? I'm too afraid to find out what will happen if all this anger never goes away. Shoving it into my shoes doesn't work. It's always here."

Bea sits beside me, and in an act of bravery to a fault, she wraps an arm around my shoulder, and we stay like that for a while.

"I can't know for certain," she says. "But I think feelings change. Just the way you arrived at anger, you might not feel that way forever."

"Revenge does feel good," I say with a small smile. "But justice would feel even better."

Now I know how Weylan felt, if he was even honest about his loss. I know why he balled himself up tight and silent, and he hid from the world. Why he ignored Whitaker and the scientist and never indulged in the madness of vengeance. The powerlessness is bound to eat me alive from the inside out, and it has nothing to do with justice or going home. I am Frank Morris' daughter, after all, and I can figure out how to bring Pritchard to justice while making my home wherever I want it to be. If I don't make a home wherever I am, I will always be searching.

"Thank you," I say, resting my head on Bea's shoulder. "Thank you for being like a sister to me."

"I always wanted one," Bea says. "So what comes next for you?"

I pull myself upright. "A bath, I think. If you change your dress, I'll wash yours with mine in the morning. And I have to start making amends with your mother."

I scrub my skin until it's red, and I wash my hair three times.

Too many problems need solving. Too many apologies need to be made. I need to make sure Emmett is alright, that Regina hasn't scolded him too badly, but they told me to stay indoors, and I can't make a new plan if I'm in jail again. I can't make a new plan from here, either, apparently, because I can't untangle my fury at Weylan from my need to get to Whitaker.

Over dinner, I relay the story of all the women arriving at the jail. Mitchell refuses to allow Leta to subject herself to time behind bars.

"I am proud of them, though," Leta says. "And I'm certain that's the only reason they let you out. To follow you and see who you speak to."

I promise to keep out of trouble, and to make up for all I've caused I clean up our dishes and tidy the kitchen. If I sleep at all that night, I don't notice. At some point, the faintest hint of lavender seeps around the edges of the curtain, and I push myself up in bed and lean against the wall, wiggling my toes beneath the sheet. The audacity Weylan had to pretend to be pained when I finally confronted him for lying to me and setting me up. And the nerve he had to show up here and be adamant about his innocence. If he wants to gloat, the least he can do is to be honest about it. And Bea thinks he's innocent?

If only I'd trusted my gut instead of Weylan, I wouldn't be in this mess. He's such a terrible liar and such a terrible schemer that he probably left a million holes in his plan.

If only I could find them.

Weylan had to get that blasting powder from somewhere, and they said it came from Stoke. If that's true, and I can prove Weylan had his hands in it, not only would I feel better and prove Bea wrong, I might have my link between Whitaker and Pritchard.

I throw off the sheet and plant my feet on the floor. I need to get out of the house before Leta wakes and locks us in, find proof he set me up, and be back before breakfast. But where to start?

With my resolve wound tight, I change my clothes and grab my shoes, plopping on the bench outside the kitchen door to tie them up tight. If the whole thing hinges on crates of blasting powder that came from Stoke, they had to get here on a train, and if anyone knows about it, Vernon's father would. He's always there, sorting the mail before the sun comes up, before school starts for the day. Everyone says there isn't a thing in this town he doesn't know about. I hope they're right.

CHAPTER THIRTY-TWO

I follow the creek across town and wait at the woods' edge to be sure the coast is clear, then slip into the train station and tap on the post office window.

"Charlotte. Good morning." Vernon's father is a kind man with a round face, bulging eyes, and a swoosh of hair covering his baldness that runs from ear to ear. He strokes his mustache and scratches at the cleft in his chin. "You'll be wanting a stamp, I suppose. The window isn't open yet, but for you…"

"That's kind, sir, but I have a question." I try to stop him, but he dives beneath the counter, digging out a little wood box.

"I have them here somewhere. They come in books now, you know." He opens the box and rifles through. "All those letters you send, you should get a book of stamps."

"I don't need to mail a letter today, but I was wondering if you saw—"

"I still have some of those Washington stamps from a few years ago, too. Brightest red I ever did see on a stamp."

"Sir?"

"Where did I put those?"

"Sir." I flatten my hands on the counter. "Do you know anything about crates of blasting powder coming in on a train? Say, in the last four or five days?"

He leans back and tucks in his chin, furrowing his brow. He sticks a finger in his ear and wiggles it around. "Yes. Yes, I did see that. Wouldn't have but for the mail being late. Sat here till darn near midnight waiting for it. They said a storm sent a tree on the tracks up north, and it took all day for them to clear it, but I ain't seen no rain."

A lie, I bet. To be sure the train arrived without witnesses.

"And you saw something suspicious? Who was it? Was it Weylan?"

"Weylan?" He shakes his head, brows pinched. "No. It was Whitaker."

"That's not possible." It was possible, though, and it even made sense. More sense than Weylan playing a long con game then pretending to be upset about me finding out about it. I'm such an awful person sometimes. If the train came in at midnight, it couldn't be Weylan.

"How could I be so stupid?"

"I don't know, dear. Train was hauling all the usual things. Coal and crates for the shops. Only noticed 'cause Otto's hinny was here with Whitaker with some of his men. That weren't usual. They came past here on their way off yonder, and I saw the crate had blasting powder stamped on the side." He puts the box back and collects a stack of envelopes, sifting through them, stacking them into piles, and shaking one at me. "Otto could make a living renting that donkey out for hauls, but he'd rather barter. Don't see Whitaker use her, though. They're oil and vinegar, those two, so he must have been enticed." He rubs his fingers together, indicating a hefty profit for Otto.

"Of course." It's like dominoes. All the pieces line up, and Vernon's father has nudged the first one.

A million questions come to mind. Had Whitaker's men followed me? Did Pritchard delay the train on purpose so it arrived under the cover of darkness? He owns the railroad so he can do as he pleases. If so, why go through all that effort to get me into trouble when I'm barely a threat to him? So far.

Then fear chills my spine. Mere minutes must have stood between Weylan and I sitting on that rock and someone placing the blasting powder there. If we'd have crossed paths…

"Didn't it seem odd?" I ask. "Whitaker carrying explosives through town on a hired donkey?"

"Everything he does is odd, Charlotte." He taps the stack of envelopes on the counter. "Figured they must need it down the point, quarrying rocks and such."

Why didn't he tell anyone? "I went to the jailhouse for two days over that."

He winces. "How'd you get mixed up in that?"

"It's not your fault. Even if you did know what was happening, if you'd said something, they'd have ruined you." I push away from the counter. "I have to go. Please don't tell a soul I was here."

Rules be damned. I race up the sidewalk to the intersection. Standing in the middle of the road, out of breath, I soak up the first strong rays of sun that stretch across the packed earth. My God. Whitaker set me up. There's a witness. Possibly two, if Otto will attest to lending him the donkey.

Max is the closest person to law enforcement I know, and he lives between here and school, just down on the left with the barking dogs, but his father is the chief of police, and he told me to stay home. Knocking on his front door would be the dumbest thing I could do. As much as I don't want to trust anyone or need anyone, I can't do this on my own.

Emmett can't help. If he gets caught, I'll never forgive myself.

I can't risk Bea. Leta and Mitchell might be willing, but they're far more likely to stand in my way. And if they helped, Whitaker could destroy their store and their livelihood.

I need to find someone Max talks to all the time, someone the Chief of Police won't suspect.

A dog barks in a distant yard to my left, and when I turn, I face the narrow road that leads to the brickyard and the row of houses where Weylan lives.

He may not be the only choice, but he's the best choice I have. First, I owe him an apology.

With my heart in my throat and my pulse thundering in my ears, I run to his house without stopping to think.

The farmhouse where he lives with his father is tall. Lime-washed brick with a peaked roof and arched attic windows. A porch wraps all the way around, the paint wearing off. A vast lawn swaddles the house, and a vegetable garden has outgrown the fence that sways in its failure to hold it all in. It's so tangled and unplanned that it must be the result of years of neglect.

I stand in the street, breathless, with Weylan's words ringing in my ears. His mother and brother are gone, and they'd taken with them the spirit of the house. It had been grand once, I can tell, the kind of home that raises good sons, but it's a shell now.

The front door cracks open, and a woman emerges, shaking a rug off the porch rail. A bonnet covers her dark hair and a crisp, white apron covers her dress. I introduce myself and ask if Weylan is awake yet. She looks over her shoulder and shakes her head, stretching the rug along the rail.

"I just got here," she says. "Haven't seen either of them yet. You're Miss Charlotte, right?"

"Yes, ma'am."

"He talks about you all the time. Damn near broke his heart, you did. Had to bake him a pie. Come, girl." She waves me onto the porch. "Can't stand out there all day. Take a seat up here. I'll go wake him."

I test the weight of an old ladder-back chair sitting against the wall. A carpenter bee slaps into the porch roof, looking for home. I wad handfuls of my skirt into my fists, having no idea what to say when he steps outside, and pretty sure he won't even bother to emerge at all. He has every right to be furious, to kick me off his porch, to demand I never talk to him again. I'd deserve it.

It seems like a hundred years go by before the door opens. I fly to my feet before he even steps outside and don't give him a chance to take in a breath.

"I stayed up all night. I couldn't stop wondering why you'd do it. Bea made me realize your motivation was lacking, and if you did do it, you probably made a mistake, so I figured if I found the mistake, I'd know you did it for sure."

He folds his arms, his jaw set. "Oh, I'm the one who made a mistake?"

"I deserve that. I made a huge mistake, but I figured it out, and I know it wasn't you. It was Whitaker." I stand and pace. "I need someone to tell the police so they can talk to Vernon's father, because…"

"Sit down." He puts his hands on my shoulders, backs me up to the chair, and pushes me onto it. "You could be seen."

"That's what I mean. I can't walk up to Max's front door or march into the police station and turn Whitaker into a police force that does his bidding. They'd put me in jail and hurt Vernon's father. And he won't turn Whitaker in on his own. I need help. I need someone in authority to talk to Vernon's father and Otto and investigate the truth."

He sighs and leans on the porch rail, shoulders hunched as he gazes down into the overgrown shrubs. I can't tell what he's feeling.

"Look at me. Please," I beg. "How can I fix this? I'm sorry I didn't believe you. I'm so sorry. Surely you understand why I thought —"

"I do." He turns to face me. Understanding and forgiving are two different things, and I can tell by his look, he's only arrived at one of them.

"Hate me. That's fine, but please tell someone what happened. Do it to get back at Whitaker."

I want to touch him, to grab his hands and beg him to forgive me, but the world is beginning to rouse and stir, and I'll only get us all into trouble if I'm seen standing on his porch. I sit with my hands on my knees wishing he'd just look me in the eye.

He takes a deep breath and closes his eyes, and whatever happens inside his head is sad and painful. No matter how delicious, that poor woman's pie couldn't budge this much despair. "It took me all night, but I understand why you suspected me. It hurts that you went straight to betrayal."

"It was too easy," I chew on my bottom lip and watch the bee creep into a hole in the rail.

"What was too easy?" he asks. "Blaming me?"

All of it. Finding him, his easy solutions. Sneaking around with him. Talking. The way he made me feel like I was still human and not some hollowed out rind, dried out and discarded.

Damn the rules. I'm on my feet again, next to him at the railing. He smells faintly of woodsmoke, and I remember meeting him that first day while walking home from school, and how he always seemed to be there to stick up for me with Pine. I didn't need him to, but I liked it.

"Everything was too easy with you," I admit, finally. "You terrify me. But this is serious. The right person must investigate so it isn't ignored, and I don't know who that person could be. Maybe Max does? I don't even know Max."

A puffy white cloud passes between us and the sun, throwing the house into shadows.

I might if I'd listened to Emmett. Now I have to rely on Weylan after having been so horrible to him. My conscience strains against my willpower. I ought to tell him the truth, how I really feel about him, and I know how to put words together. I've written them just fine many times before. Why can't I just speak to him?

"I'm sorry." I resist the urge to touch his arm, though I feel like if I did, I could make him believe how sorry I am. "A million times over. I don't want to lose anyone else. I don't want to like this place because it isn't home, but Whitaker is connected to Pritchard and I need this town because it's the link."

"You need people, too." He turns to face me. The morning is crisp, and I can see his breath in the air. He folds his arms and looks down at the porch floor, and a slow realization lifts the corners of his eyes, but it's the kind that masks a sadness. "Oh, you don't want to need me, but you do."

"People leave." I mean it as an explanation but it comes out like a plea.

"No, they don't. Not all of them. I can't believe that anymore, and it's too exhausting trying to pretend I don't have feelings. Emmett is here. Bea and Leta. And me. I'm still here."

"Are you?" I ask. "I didn't break this?"

"You tried hard enough, but I am still here."

My throat closes, trapping all the words. He unfolds his arms. His hands find mine. There's so little space between us that I swear I can feel his heartbeat.

"Every time I saw you, I counted the steps between us," he says. "Nine hundred and ninety-seven steps between here and Leta's."

He wants me to pry the lid off Pandora's box and tell him I can feel him in a room, that an invisible string connects us, but I can't meet his eyes because he should look disgusted with me even though he doesn't.

It's like all the pieces of my brain are scattered on the floor, mixed up like a jigsaw puzzle, and half of them are upside down, a quarter are missing, and there's no way to put it together again.

"But you don't trust me." He backs up a step, and I grip the railing before the porch consumes me.

"I'll talk to Max. Go back to Leta's and wait. If you're lucky, I'll still be here when you're done trying to push me away."

* * *

How dare he?

At least he believed me about Vernon's father and Otto. I slog back to Leta's in a disembodied fugue, wondering if I need a doctor to bring me back to earth. One minute I wish I'd kissed him, the next I wish I'd kicked him. How can so many emotions fit in one person?

No one even noticed I was gone, but I dive elbow deep into an act of atonement for sneaking out, doing Bea's laundry with mine. Once our clothes are on the line, I scrub Leta's copper pots. All day, I mull over Weylan's words and the fit of my hand in his. Hours pass, and I hear nothing. Not a peep from him, for which I'm mildly grateful. I don't hear anything from Max either.

When Bea gets home from school, she dives in with me. We scrub and scour every copper pot in the kitchen and several from the market as well, and I try to convince myself Weylan was lying about how he felt. That he's mistaken. That he doesn't know me well enough to feel those things. By the time I reach for Leta's favorite stock pot, I've nearly fooled myself into thinking I never felt anything for Weylan, either. That I don't want him to wait around for me or still be there when I realize what I could be missing. I already know what I need. Justice.

The pot shines after I rinse away the baking soda and vinegar.

Wiping sweat from my brow to my sleeve, I hang the pot from its peg on the wall and catch motion at the door. I dry my hands and open it before Max has a chance to knock.

"It's done," he says. "A messenger sent for the county police this morning. They rode down to take all the statements. Vernon's father saw Whitaker and two other men take the crates off the train."

So it was Whitaker. I should have known all along. Weylan didn't do it. And I could have trusted Max all along. I could be so stupid sometimes.

"Thank God," I say. "Do they know about Otto lending him the donkey?"

Max nods and plants his feet. His posture seems oddly familiar. "They brought Otto in to give a statement."

"It's not going to come back on Otto, is it? They believed him? He's safe?"

"Yeah. Look, I just want to be clear that I have to be very careful. We're on the same side, you and me. But you know who my father is. I have access to people and information, and I don't want to risk that."

"I would never tell a soul. And thank you for calling off that dog."

With a flick of his neck, his hair flies from his eyes. "I followed Weylan because I didn't trust you the way he did. I was suspicious and wanted to know who he was tangling with. There are divisions here. Pine's inner circle is thick as thieves. It's almost like he and his father have been ramping up for a war. Then you showed up. I had my eye on Emmett, but I heard what your father did, that you wrote his speeches."

"I didn't trust you either, to be fair. But Emmett never had anything to do with Father's work, and I never meant to do anything here," I say. "How did you hear about Stoke?"

"My Father." He glances out the window. "I should go, but Mannix asked me to tell you he's down with Emmett right now."

"Who's Mannix? Where?"

"He's a lawyer. They're at the Ryans' house."

"Why does Emmett need a lawyer?"

"I don't know. Just passing on the message."

My fingers can't loosen the knot in my apron fast enough. It flutters to the table, I thank Max, and rush out the door. It seems to take all of ten seconds to reach Regina's. I'm still lightheaded when I sit between Regina and Emmett and beg to know what it's all about.

Mannix cleans his glasses with a blue handkerchief. "Emmett could sue."

"Sue who?" I ask.

"Whitaker. You can't sue for damages for being falsely arrested. That's not a woman's place, but Emmett can. I've been trying to get men in this town to press charges against Whitaker for quite some time, but most see it as a losing proposition. I've been working piecemeal, following rumors until that newspaper. It's a city directory of atrocities."

If he knows about my involvement, I don't need him to mention it in front of Regina, so I sidestep. "Why would it be different for Emmett? He'll never win. It'll cost him a fortune he could never repay. And if he does win, the money would end up in Finn's hands. What's the good in that?"

Mannix pushes papers around. "Emmett won't pay a thing unless he wins. No risk, except for fear. With Finn away, Regina would have to sign off on it as his legal guardian. Odd little twist of the law that she can sign off on this, but women can't bring a case. Ridiculous. I can hold the funds on Emmett's behalf. Please ask around. I'm not a charlatan."

I turn to Emmett. "Is this what you want?"

"I think so." He seems surprised. "I think I want him to suffer."

"I can understand that," I agree.

"It would force the evidence into the court records," Mannix explains.

Emmett turns in his chair to face me. "It could be good for you, too, Charlie. Do you see?"

"I do see, but not in the way you think." There's a lawyer. An honest-to-God man who knows about atrocities, sitting right across from me. "Em, this isn't about me. You need this money. It could buy you some freedom."

"Just write what happened. It's that easy." Mannix clears his throat. "We need to move fast because Whitaker's men will destroy evidence. He's being arrested by the county police at seven tomorrow morning. They like to do this bright and early to keep the perpetrators from sneaking away."

"What?" I sit up straight.

"Why?" Regina asks. "How do you know that?"

"I heard about an hour ago from a constable. I kindly ask you to keep that to yourself, of course."

Regina looks as pleased as I've ever seen her. She probably loved Finn once, and I realize now that Whitaker took things from her too.

"I'll do it." Emmett picks up a pen, pulling a blank piece of paper closer.

"It's Emmett's money, right?" I ask. "If he wins? Finn won't get his hands on it?"

Regina reaches across the table to me. "If Mannix will hold it for Emmett, in a trust perhaps, that would be best."

I'm not ready to forgive her yet or let her in, but I thank her all the same. I realize for the first time since I walked in the door that she's sitting up straighter. She looks happier. Lighter. Perhaps without Finn around, she feels a little hope. And Whitaker finally seeing the consequences of his ways, perhaps she feels a little justice has been served.

"Wait." I turn back to Mannix. "You said Whitaker's being arrested?"

"Indeed."

"When?"

Mannix slips the signed papers into his briefcase. "At seven tomorrow morning."

CHAPTER THIRTY-THREE

The moon scrapes across the ceiling as the clock downstairs chimes midnight, but the only thing I see is the mix of certainty and fear in Weylan's eyes as he said he'd still be there when I'm finished trying to push him away. Instead of counting sheep, I've counted all the ways that he could be wrong, all the reasons he shouldn't love me, but none of it makes a difference because they aren't his reasons.

Why is it so hard for me to accept that he cares? Why do I stay awake all night looking for signs that he's lying or wrong? Why does it make me so sick to my stomach?

Maybe it's because solving the mystery of Weylan's true feelings for me seems easier than following the breadcrumbs to my own. Every time I try, all I see is Stoke and the porch I should be sitting on as I tell my family about him.

Ever since I stood on his porch, I've felt a melancholy akin to grief teasing at my edges, and I don't know why. It's almost as if I'm not allowed to explore my own feelings. I haven't been granted permission to even feel my own. Of course, I know I don't need permission to feel affection for anyone, but there's some greater invisible force that holds me back. It's me. I'm terrified to lose anyone, and I don't know how to fit anyone else into my future because I don't know what it looks like. Losing Bea or Leta, Ruthie or Hazel, would be nothing like losing Weylan. Yet the loss of him seems so complete already that I mourn him as much as I mourn my own parents.

Mother would have loved him. She should have had the chance to know him. Father should be here to approve.

That's what it comes down to, isn't it? If I can push Weylan away, I never have to accept that my past and my future will never intersect. I will never have one big melded family. His will be ever-present, and mine will be in the past. There will never be a home I can return to once I make a new one, but as long as I stay in this purgatory, I can hang onto the feeling of home being out there somewhere, waiting.

I relished the idea that Weylan had set me up. Strange as it is to realize, I did enjoy the rush of being furious at him. It didn't feel good to lose trust in him, but it felt better than being abandoned. And Bea is right. All this focus on revenge and anger and pushing Weylan away is because I'd rather keep life from happening, painful parts and all, than accept that it can go on.

The clock chimed six some time ago, and the faintest blue oozes around the curtain. Bea's watch on the windowsill says it's after six-thirty. Whitaker will be arrested soon. It isn't the end of my fight, by any means, but it's a step.

With only fifteen minutes to set it right, I jump out of bed, pulling a shirt and blouse from the hangers.

"What's happening? What time is it?" Bea mumbles and rubs her eyes.

"It's six forty-five. I have to go."

"Go where?" Bea sits up, resting on her elbows.

"The park. I have to watch Whitaker be arrested, and I have to find Weylan."

Bea puts her feet on the floor. "But what if Whitaker fights back or something awful happens?"

"It doesn't matter," I say. "Bea. Weylan has feelings for me."

"I know he does. Hazel said the same thing yesterday."

"I need to find him before it's too late."

"Do you want me to come with you?" she asks through a yawn. "It'll only take me ten minutes."

I wiggle my toes into my shoes and tie them tight. "No, I have to go."

I fix my hair, clean my teeth, tuck in my blouse and run down the stairs. The morning air is heavy and humid, and every breath is like forcing my lungs to work underwater, but I run down Main Street, right down the middle of it, so hard and fast that my legs are giving out by the time I reach the street that leads to the park where Whitaker's house sits. I brace myself against a rough oak tree, lungs heaving as I double over.

Weylan will be here. I don't know how I know, I just do. Word will have reached him, and he'll want to see this.

A shiny black carriage approaches from the direction of Whitaker's house. It has an ominous, official sort of emblem on the side. It's the kind of carriage I wouldn't want to be pushed into if I were under arrest. I missed it. I was too late. My heart sinks, but I step into the street and wave my arms as it grows close.

"Stop," I beg. "Please."

The horses slow, and the driver leans down. "Miss, is there

trouble? Do you need help?"

"No." Lord, the morning is sweltering already. "I want to talk to Whitaker."

"To me?" He turns his shoulders as best he can to face me, but I can tell they have him secured in the back of the carriage.

I approach the side, raking my hand along my brow. I finally have a chance to ask everything I want, and questions spill out of me. "How do you know Pritchard? Why didn't you tell people there's poison in the water? Why are you protecting an evil man instead of your own town?"

His nostrils flare. Red as a beet, he either put up a fight or they caught him unawares. His clothes are disheveled, his cravat a knotted mess.

"Young lady, for most of us, there's a difference between what we want and what we really need. You, however, will get what you deserve."

The driver, who clearly cares little for any of this, snaps the reins, and the horses lunge forward, throwing Whitaker back in his seat. I watch them turn the corner. I still have to turn mine.

The street of little houses and tidy yards opens to the park. Whitaker's home sits in the distance, facing the water. A quarter of the way between me and it, a small pack of men stands. Some I recognize, others I don't. Max is there, next to Vernon, who has his hands in his pockets. And Weylan, four inches taller than any of them, lingers at the edges.

My breath steadies, no longer coming in gasps and gulps. With my heart on the line, I walk up to the crowd. They make room for me in their circle, but it's Weylan I need to see.

"You missed it," Max says. "You're late."

"I hope not."

Weylan bristles beside me, his hackles up like a wary cat.

"Weylan?" I don't mean it as a question, but his name turns up on the end all the same.

"I figured you'd be here if you knew," he says.

"Could we…" All that rushing to get dressed and running to get here, and I haven't yet put my feelings into words. Not the kind that makes sense, anyway. "Can we talk?"

He tears his eyes from mine and glances at the gazebo. "We could sit there, if you want."

I try to read his expression, but he turns away. It's only been a day, but maybe I am too late. I can't blame him if he's set his mind to hating me already. I have to take cautious steps on the slippery grass, and my long slow breaths aren't preparing me at all for the possibility that I've already driven him away with my stubbornness.

The gazebo floor is covered in a thin layer of pollen, but I sit anyway, and as he lowers himself across from me, it feels for a second like nothing ever happened. Like the same comfort could still draw us to each other and the same electricity could spark. Just being near him is like the excitement of a summer storm barreling down the horizon, even though he could, and might, hate me forever. Every time I see him, I feel just like this. I know it will always be grand, with thunderbolts and a few broken branches that leave me breathless in the end. But this storm is a little different. I might break before it's over.

"Me first." I called him here, after all. "It might take me a second."

His eyes are fixed on his hands. He plucks at a hangnail. "Will it help if I tell you I meant what I said?"

"Which part?" I ask. "When you said I'd be lucky if you were still here when I finally stop pushing you away? Because I'm ready."

These stupid tears. They show up for all the right reasons at all the wrong times. I lower my head, but that's the worst thing I can do, because one of them spills out and makes a dark spot on my skirt. And then another. It's getting harder to see with my vision all blurry, and I'm so bad at crying.

"I know my home is gone," I say. "I might get justice and still never get my home back. I may never hear feet on the porch or someone climb the stairs or slam the front door. But that was a house. Home is a feeling. I don't have everything figured out yet — bringing Pritchard to justice or what home is — but I don't want to stop living until I figure it out."

He inches closer, his shuffling echoing off the domed ceiling. He takes one of my hands in his, leaving the other free to wipe at my eyes.

"I think living is how we figure it out," he says.

"I understand that now."

"My turn? Avoiding people and feelings was a habit for a while, then it became who I am. I don't know any other way to be. You are the first person I've met who's reminded me what I could lose if I start trusting someone and talking about feelings. And you're the only person I've ever known who makes me want to do it anyway, Charlie."

"I believe you. And I feel the same way. But more than anything I need you to know that I believe you. I trust you." I peer between the gazebo railings to watch the small crowd depart, off to breakfast and school. "This thing with Pritchard isn't over. Not even close, but…" The path to Pritchard is a million miles long. Breaking it down into little steps will just be returning to old habits and keep me from living in this moment, though. "But there's room for other things to begin. I want to find them with you."

He threads his fingers with mine. His hands are warm. "Are you sure?"

"I am. I'm positive." I wipe my cheek on my shoulder. "I do finally see a future for myself. The hint of one, anyway. You asked me that once. Do you remember that?"

"I do. I remember," he says.

"It didn't come easy, because I'm stubborn."

"You don't say."

I playfully lift a shoulder. "The picture is still fuzzy, but there are some vivid parts of it. I want one of them to be you."

My cheeks burn and look down at our hands, our fingers entwined. There's a timeless sort of rightness to it.

He leans in. "There's nothing wrong with that. It's all right if you let me in. It's not like I haven't been asking."

"I'm not done, you know. Whitaker didn't act alone. Pritchard was in on it, too. It was his blasting powder; he's sending a message to us that this will get explosive. I don't know what to do next, but there's a lawyer here I need to talk to, because the air and water are still poisoned, and I think he might be able to help."

He puts a finger to my lips and inches closer. Our knees touch. A jolt of lightning laces through my bones and sparks a fire in my gut. I could melt right here on the gazebo floor.

His eyes find mine. A million things swirl there, things he wants to say. I can feel them in his touch as he brushes my cheek with his thumb. He traces my cheekbone, his fingers strong on the back of my neck, his palm brushes my jaw. I tilt my head into his hand and warm all over at the pure comfort.

"I'll help," he whispers. "We'll do it together."

I lean in and brush his lips with mine. His breath is warm on my cheek. I didn't know it would be like this, like jumping off a cliff and freefalling into blissful nothingness, that I would be reduced to sparks and smoldering embers.

* * *

With strict orders from Mannix not to taint our memories by discussing anything related to Whitaker, it would make sense for Emmett and me to go in separate directions, but we don't. I get the feeling Emmett doesn't want to be trapped in the gloom at Regina's. Neither of us have been back to school yet, and we both have work to catch up on, so Leta makes room at the dining room table for us. Bea fills us in on what we missed at school over the last four days, gracefully skirting reactions to Whitaker's arrest so we don't accidentally say something we shouldn't. Then Ruthie and Hazel come over with a thousand questions. We can't answer any about Whitaker, and I won't answer any about Weylan. I can describe my feelings for him perfectly, but for now, I'd rather not. I much prefer to simply feel them.

Instead, I smile to myself a lot while we play cards, and Emmett shoots me curious glances. I watch him carefully for traces that he's clearer, steadier than he was at the jailhouse. He brushes off my questions about it and teases me for being concerned. In my mind, it isn't settled, but it's satisfactory for now.

Mannix arrives at four. Leta brings out lemonade, and we sit in the dining room while Emmett and I tell him everything, only holding back the parts about what a dunce I was about Weylan. When it's all written out, we use Mannix's fancy fountain pen to sign our names at the bottom of our pages, and when the signatures are dry, he seals them away in his clunky briefcase.

"You can leave the house now," Mannix says. "You're free."

"Didn't even get a whole week off school," Emmett says.

"How long will Whitaker be in jail?" I ask. "The reality, not the law. When will he be back?"

Mannix rakes his fingers through his wiry, protruding beard and adjusts his glasses. "He will be there for quite some time on the criminal charges. He won't do time on Emmett's civil case, but there may be compensation."

"At least two weeks?" Leta asks. She leans in the doorway to the kitchen, wiping her hands dry on her apron.

Mannix bobs his head, counting up some invisible sum. "At least."

"Good. We've put off the festival," Leta says. "Just long enough to secure a candidate who can speak."

"What about the suffragist?" I ask.

"She'll still speak. With Whitaker's arrest, the festival is more than a protest. It's a chance to put forth a strong candidate and let him speak his mind."

Mannix gives Leta a nod and gathers his beard in his hand. "I'm sorry that I can't do anything to redress your wounds, Charlotte. Women, as you know—"

I wave a hand. "Not your fault, sir. Someday."

"Indeed. What's important is holding Whitaker accountable, getting it on file with the courts. No other man in town has been willing to do it, even though it wouldn't cost them a penny."

"Yet." Emmett says, gently slapping the table. "If anything comes of it, I'll share it with you, Charlie."

"Don't you dare," I say.

Mannix lifts the briefcase. It dangles at his side. "Do you have any other questions before I go?"

"I have one." I sit up straight, tucking my feet beneath the chair. "If someone were to poison the air or the water, would that be a crime?"

He thinks for a moment, and his internal debate plays out in his eyebrows. "Not that I'm aware of, but that's not my expertise."

So it's not a definitive no, then.

CHAPTER THIRTY-FOUR

June breeze sails up the Chesapeake Bay, pushes up the river, and sweeps across the park. Weylan loops my hand through the crook of his arm. He's been tied in knots for days, wound tight by uncertainty over the festival, though I prefer to call it a protest. He says he has a bad feeling he can't brush off, but I think it's just paranoia.

We follow the flittering red, white, and blue pennants down Water Street, and wave at Minnie as she passes. She looks a bit green, and I can't blame her. I'd be nervous, too, speaking such truths as hers in front of the whole town.

"She's been practicing her speech at Leta's," I say.

"Is it..." He searches for the right word.

"Incendiary? Yes. She's supposed to introduce Harrison as a candidate for mayor." I've never met the man, but I hear good things. Mitchell seems hesitant but says people will warm up to him. "Do you know him?"

He shakes his head as if he can't quite place him, which is worrying for a town this small. "I've seen him around, but I've never met him."

The street widens where the houses grow further apart. They give way to the expanse of lawn that sits within the horseshoe of the river. Weylan pats my hand when the gazebo comes into view, and I know he thinks of it as our space. We've taken to sitting there to talk sometimes, but today, it belongs to the speakers. A crowd has already grown.

We stroll past pens of goats and ponies, where Otto guides a boy around on a young brown horse. Down the path, by the water, the air is electric. Table after table of local wares edge the green. There are duck decoys and painted fishing lures, pottery and carved wood toys. Little boats for children and big ones for adults are perched at the water's edge, their noses jutting into the river, hulls slapping against the tide. Mitchell sells baked goods and candies, jars of honey, canned preserves and fruits at their table. Behind the displays, women sew and lounge in chairs and on blankets. Men gather, smoking pipes and talking taxes. Several of them had shared their stories in our paper, and they tip their hats as we pass.

"I can't believe we never got caught for breaking into the print office," I say.

"It was abandoned," Weylan says. "I suppose no one was left to care."

Sarah and Anne are spread out on the grass, sunflower pins fixed to their dresses, teaching a group of young girls to tie nets. Their little fingers fumble with the needle, and I yearn for my own and the comfort it once gave me. It was once a symbol of moving on, learning new things, finding myself in a new place. I stopped carrying it after I moved into Leta's and started leaving it on the windowsill next to that mermaid's purse. I'm beyond those false comforts now, anyway. I squeeze Weylan's hand. He is a true comfort.

"What if something goes wrong today?" he asks.

"Whitaker's in jail." I bite back my sigh. "There are too many children. Too many innocent people. Even if he has supporters who are that vengeful, they'd be crazy to do anything here." I lace my fingers in his. "I forgot to tell you. Leta invited me to stay with them after graduation."

"I was hoping she would. I wouldn't let you get away, anyhow."

Though I try to make light of his words, offer up a witty retort, I can't. In the few short weeks we've been courting, if that's what you could call it, we've observed the rules of polite society, but the look in Weylan's eyes only grows more wanting, and I occasionally worry that he might propose. I'd be thrown into a whole new conundrum. I would like to think he'll spare me discomfort until life is more stable, and we can be afforded some security. The fact I even think about such things as finances makes me immeasurably uncomfortable at times. It feels like giving up on Stoke and abandoning a part of myself. Home still calls to me, and I can't yet bear to tell him.

We make our way toward the gazebo. Someone shouts my name, and I spin, looking for the culprit. Weylan tilts his chin in the crowd's direction.

"It's Vernon," he says.

The postman's son takes long strides across the lawn, waving a bundle of envelopes tied with string. "These have been… It's a long story. Anyway, they're yours."

"Sophie!" All this time. "I thought she gave up on me. And letters from our aunt. She must be mortified."

I fan them out, a disorganized hand of cards, and pluck at them.

I peel back an open flap, and the loops and curls of Sophie's handwriting seize my heart. Every envelope was opened. Every single one. I unfold a letter from three weeks ago.

The whole town is talking about you, saying your father was into more than they knew and they think you might know...

"The mayor read my letters." What did that mean? They think I might know what? I scan for a place to sit with them.

"He intercepted all your mail," Vernon says. "It was returned to us when his office was emptied, and we sent all your outgoing letters this morning."

"Isn't that some kind of mail fraud?" Weylan asks.

Vernon shrugs. "Just another of Whitaker's crimes. I know you probably want to catch up on news from home, but..." Vernon motions toward a group of people beyond the gazebo. Bea is there. Ruthie. Emmett. "They're looking for you. Bea seemed frantic."

Behind Vernon, the crowd applauds the suffragist. Her voice booms over the park, and she leans into her audience, tipping her wide-brimmed yellow hat. Her yellow striped dress is the color of a sunflower, a bright contrast to the purple quilts strung up in the gazebo as a backdrop, and a cheery polar opposite to her stern words.

Yes, men. You may be surprised, but women are human beings too.

There's commotion, though, among our friends behind the gazebo, and Bea peers around, waving us over. The letters would have to wait.

"Minnie's a mess," she says when we reach her.

"But she was so excited last night. Is she ill? She looked a bit green around the gills when we saw her earlier."

"Stage fright, I'm afraid." Hazel points over her shoulder, and I realize Minnie's been there the whole time, sitting on the ground, hugging her knees.

"I can't do it," she says. "All those people."

"She's supposed to introduce Harrison," a woman says. "Her story is the biggest one."

I notice, then, the group of men standing just off to the side. Mr. Bradford, the pharmacist, is among them. Mannix. And Jacob, who runs the bait and tackle shop. A fourth man hangs back, shrinking and timid.

"Town council," Weylan whispers.

Mr. Bradford asks about my finger. The splint is gone. It's stiff and sore, and I swear it can predict the rain. He declares himself proud of his work. Jacob huffs at our pleasantries, hoisting his pants over his gut. He's dressed in high waders held up with wide suspenders, a black shirt with white buttons, and an ancient painter's beret with a frayed brim. His ears stick out beneath his short-cut hair, and his trim mustache frames a twisted, impatient smile. The fishing tax has hit his business hard.

"We got to get Harrison up there," he says.

"Have you met Charlotte?" Mannix draws the mystery man into the circle. "Her brother brought the suit I told you about."

The man who clearly is Harrison sticks out his hand and lowers his head. He's tall and lean with thick glasses, a quaff of dark hair and a hint of stoic wisdom to his eyes, but he flinches when Weylan shakes his hand, as if he's afraid he'll be bitten.

"Wallace. Harrison Wallace," he says.

Dear God, if this is the best the town could put forward to challenge Whitaker, it will take an army to shore him up.

Mannix clears his throat. "Harrison has bold ideas and smart plans for loosening restrictions and getting the town on track financially without extra taxes."

Jacob agrees. "I like what he has to say."

"The speaker is winding down, Bea. Where's your mother?" Ruthie asks Bea. "Will she take Minnie's place?"

"She can't." A hint of panic threads through Bea's voice, lifting it up at the end. "She's not here. She went to get something from home."

"What did she run to fetch?" Hazel asks.

"I don't know?" Bea is nearly panicked now. "What does it matter? Minnie needs to go out now or people will leave."

"One of us will have to do it," says Hazel.

"Not me." Ruthie blanches. "I don't have the voice for it. Bea?"

"Have you lost your mind? All those people?"

Hazel deflates with a sigh. "Mother would kill me. It has to be Charlie. You spoke to Minnie. You wrote the story. Don't look at me like I've sprouted a third arm. All you have to do is read what you wrote in the paper, then introduce Harrison."

I wonder if he could introduce himself, but he has the charisma of a raw potato and can barely introduce himself to me.

Father spoke in front of people under far worse circumstances. How hard could it be to say a few words? I know them. I wrote them, after all.

Bea is right, the crowd will leave if no one speaks, and there isn't time to waffle. I squeeze Weylan's hand, take a copy of the newspaper from Ruthie, and climb the gazebo stairs.

There are a few mumbles and murmurs as I reach the edge of the stage, and a strange sort of silence settles over our end of the park.

Maybe I imagine it, or they really are paying attention to me, but I realize most of these people don't know me at all.

"I'm Charlotte Morris," I say, not as loud as I need to, judging by the straining to hear from the back of the assemblage. "You're expecting to hear Minnie's story. I suspect a good number of you know it already."

I fold the paper so Minnie's story is all I can see, running my nail along the folds.

"I don't want to read this. Not today. It hurts to hear it. We know Whitaker's time in office was brutal, that a man lost his home and all he owns, and he nearly lost his life. Whitaker was an awful man, and he's not truly gone. Men like him are just a patchwork of malicious ideas, and malicious ideas never really go away. But I'm having a good day today, and I just don't want to be reminded of what that man endured and all that Minnie's lost."

A few people make sounds of agreement. I look down to see Weylan standing with Max and Emmett. The girls are with them, and Bea nods, wide-eyed, with the hint of an encouraging smile.

It's not often I'm in a place where I feel I ought to be. The last few months have been a disorienting swirl of new places I never should have seen and people I never should have met. Even at Leta's, where I feel safe, there's a layer of wrongness, like if I grab the edge of a piece of wallpaper and pull, the life I should live would be underneath it all. Father always told his friends to be in the right places to do the most good. Maybe the universe thinks this is the right place, but it isn't home.

"The fish aren't poisoned," I say. "It's the water. It's poisoned, and I'm pretty sure I know who's doing it because my parents had the same symptoms as Weylan's family, and they all died the same way, with their teeth falling out and spitting up blood until their internal organs failed. I bet a lot of you have seen it too. But people don't talk about illness. And there's a reason Whitaker wants to keep the truth from you, and I think I know what that reason is."

A different type of mumbling burbles in the crowd, like ripples from an underwater disturbance. Sunnies scattering in the waters as a bass swoops in.

"But like I said, things won't always be like they are right now," I say. "They can't be, because you don't… we don't want them to be. Suffragists have spoken today, asking you to vote for people who will do something different. Progressive. Even if you don't agree with them, now's the time to take a chance on something better."

I see Bradford first, walking around the gazebo on my left. He has kind eyes, and I wish Stoke had someone like him, someone who would tell you the truth when you needed to hear it, someone who would tell you it's okay to be afraid of men like Finn instead of pretending it's all okay and bad things will fix themselves, because they won't. They never do.

Harrison fills his chest with air and places a trembling hand on his stomach. He inflates so much his chin dips down and when he looks back at me, he's a few inches taller. But he's still nervous and jittery, his eyes darting around. I remember what Mitchell said about him, how he studied medicine before coming home to care for his dying parents, and how he's a good listener and a man of discernment. I think of my father, who wasn't exactly designed for the role he stepped into, but he was great at it. That might be true for Harrison, too.

"I was thinking not that long ago about what my mother once said about the Devil, that he never looks like a dangerous man. Being so attractive helps him lure you to your doom. And I think that means the opposite might be true, too. That the right man for a task might not look like you expect him to. He might be a quiet man who listens and does the right thing. We don't need a lion-hearted ruler of regiments. Or a dreamer of dreams. We need a man who leads from the humble seat he's granted, not a man with his sights set on a glittering horizon. I think I'd like to hear what Harrison has to say."

I walk down the gazebo steps just like I have so many times recently, but without Weylan at my side this time. I see him and the girls beam at me and walk around the back of the gazebo, waving for me to follow. Now that I've finished, my knees are wobbly, and I could go for some refreshment, but just as I turn the corner, I step right into the path of a tall, thin man in a thick, dark suit. My eyes travel up from the glossy silver buttons on his black vest to the short dark hair and long straight nose that belong to Nels Pritchard.

CHAPTER THIRTY-FIVE

Instinct tells me to run, but I'm as stiff and numb as if a blizzard came along and turned me into a block of ice. My heart throbs in my ears.

"What do you want?" I ask. "What could you possibly want that you haven't already taken?"

"Not even a hello?" He strokes his thin mustache, eyes sparkling.

"Did you come for lunch? The town is famous for its herring. I'd love to serve you some. Fresh. Straight from the water."

He doesn't flinch. "Do you remember the day your father died, when I came to the house?"

"How could I forget?" I ask. "You said I look just like him. I told you the similarities don't stop there. Is that what you came for? To talk about my father's death? I'm ready if you are."

Behind him Emmett has his hands up, stalling our friends. He whispers to Weylan.

"I'm as like my father as you are like yours, I suspect." He looks wistful, but it's an act. He's never been any such thing. "We all are, deep down. We don't know any other way of being. You learned to make bad decisions, and I learned to protect myself."

I huff. "I haven't made a bad decision."

Despite my need to appear stoic and confident, the last syllable trails off, because I've made a billion bad decisions, including, perhaps, telling the whole town that I know who's poisoning the fish while the culprit is in the audience.

Oh, no.

"Miss Morris, the world is made up of people who have and people who don't. If you have money, power and control, like I do, you'll do anything to keep it, to invest it, to make it bigger. It's just that simple. That's what successful people do. People like you and your father, however, claw and scrape."

He leans in, pressing into my space. I step back to keep my balance, but I clench my jaw in defiance.

"You cling to power at the expense of everyone else," I say. "It's not really power if you have to kill to keep it." It dawns on me that maybe he doesn't have so much power after all. "Is it really power if you have to go sixty miles to intimidate a schoolgirl?"

Behind him, Emmett stifles a laugh.

"Take my advice, Miss Morris." His eyes are cold. "People are only as good as what they can do for you. If they can't do anything for you, they can be manipulated. And if they refuse, you can take them captive, like I did with your grandfather. I wanted his land. He wouldn't sell. So I squeezed him until he caved. And then I took his son. It wasn't my intention, but it worked out in the end."

"My father was never yours. That's the problem, isn't it? You can't have me, and you'll never have Emmett."

He reaches into his jacket and extracts something from its inner pocket. Sun glints off metal. I flinch, but it's just a pen. He pulls out folded papers, holds them both out, and shakes them at me.

"What is that?" I'm not touching anything he hands me.

"It's the deed to the house where you grew up and an acre of land it sits on. Take it. It's what you wanted, right? Take Emmett and Weylan and all the people you manipulate and make a pig farm. Then leave Whitaker alone."

I snatch the paper from his hand. Old ink bleeds through yellowed paper, boundary lines and corner markers laid out in paces and feet. "You bought this from the bank?"

"It was pennies to me."

I throw it at him. It bounces off his vest and lands in the dirt. "I won't live under your poisoned sky, and I'll never live at your mercy."

"How will Leta and Mitchell feel when they suffer and starve because *you* chose cruelty?"

A hot, sour taste floods my mouth. "You're the cruel one for threatening people in a town you can't control."

"And Weylan?" He folds his arms, his eyes widening. Behind him, Weylan looks furious, and Max stills him with a stern gaze. "Working in that brickyard for the rest of his life? The boy is milquetoast. I know more about your friends than you ever will. He'll ride the coattails of a strong speech or a pretty face, but when it comes to substance, he's an empty shell. He'll run when something better comes along. It's inevitable, isn't it?"

He looks me up and down. My skin crawls, but I'll never let him know. I laugh, and it doesn't sound genuine to me, but it gives me a little bravery. "You judged this entire town wrong. You only see the world through your shattered, distorted lens."

"I know this town better than you. I already own it." He waves a hand.

"You think you own this town because you bribed its mayor?" I fold my arms. "If you truly believe no one is on my side, then why come here at all? Why try to bribe me into silence by giving me the one thing you think I want? Why not punish my friends and family already?"

"I don't have to punish them. You'll do it for me. They're bait, child. This whole town will turn on you for destroying them." He bends and picks up the deed, putting it back in my hand. "It would be a mistake to turn this down. I won't offer it again. And you won't be welcome here forever. Where will you go when you're all alone?"

Pritchard puts the pen on the deed, and I catch it before it falls to the ground.

"Tick tock," he says.

The deed to my childhood home. In my hand, for the taking.

If I go to Stoke, I can fight Pritchard from the inside. I won't need to waste my time with North East. I can cook eggs in my own kitchen and raise pigs in my own yard. My grandfather clock would measure my days, and I'd wind it with my own hands. I'd reclaim the home that had been ours for generations. I'd have everything I wanted. But now that it's so close that I can picture myself carrying my suitcase onto the train, I'm not sure it's worth the price.

Weylan would never come with me. He belongs here. I would only be dragging Emmett away from the promise of life far from mining. The same maliciousness would still hurt Bea and Leta, Ruthie and Hazel.

"Sign it," Pritchard growls. "You get the house, I get my peace."

The crowd gives Harrison a surprising round of applause. He's more energetic than I expected, and it wakes me.

"No." I place the deed and the pen in his hand. "I won't take it."

"You're making a mistake," Pritchard hisses.

"I'm not. This is the best thing I've ever done."

I love this place and the people in it, and I finally understand why I couldn't see the future for so long, why it was always so blurry when I tried to imagine it. I'd been looking backwards.

If I ever get that house back, it won't be on Pritchard's terms. I don't need that house, anyway. I certainly don't want that sky or those hills with those veins of coal. I want my own home wherever that might be. Not because it's an instrument of revenge or a reclaiming of what's been taken from me. I'll go back to Stoke one day. For justice, though. And I'll do it on my own terms.

Pritchard puts the deed back into his pocket.

"You're like a stray thread, Pritchard. All I have to do is pull. The whole thing will unravel. All those people… they'll be voting for Harrison. It's that simple. They had the power all along. It isn't a mutiny or a revolt. It's not a revolution. It's democracy. And once Stoke wakes up and realizes they have it, too, you'll be done."

CHAPTER THIRTY-SIX

Late June in North East is like living under a cloche in a kitchen garden. It's hot and sticky, and soil clings to my feet. I tie up my plain brown skirt and wade into the river. Emmett's already out there, two paces ahead. He throws a stone, skipping it along the water's surface. It's not *that* creek, of course. That one's full of poison, and Regina refuses to eat from it now. This one's crystal clear.

"I have a new letter from Sophie," I tell him. "There's a note in it for you from Cousin Edward. He's learning to carve. I'll show it to you later."

"Hmm. I have news. We settled." He pulls another rock from his pocket and tests its weight. "Three hundred buckaroos. I'm rich."

"That's wonderful!" I wiggle my toes in the water, finding my footing on the slippery rocks. "That's a lot of money."

"Half of it's yours." He lets the rock fly, and it skips across the water seven times before falling in with a plunk.

"No. I told you before, I don't want it. You suffered, and that money's yours."

He shrugs.

"If we push hard enough, I bet Regina would vouch for you. Lie to the state or whatever she had to do. You could move into your own apartment, get out of that house, and have your own key, Em."

"I did consider that." He digs into his pocket for another stone.

"You could get away from Regina. You wouldn't have to stay in that room anymore. I know she doesn't lock the door but…"

He squeezes the rock in his fist, his knuckles whiten. "I still get nightmares."

"You deserve your own keys. I'll help you find a place."

"You would?"

"Of course. You still have to finish school, though." Mother would be mortified, Emmett living on his own before he graduates. Or maybe not. Perhaps she'd think we've made the best of things. We're healthy, safe, and warm. We're well fed and looking out for each other.

"Charlie!"

Emmett looks past me and his eyes cloud over. "Weylan."

"You two used to be friends."

"Before he started defiling my sister."

"No such thing has happened, and you know it. Stop being mean. Someday you'll meet a girl, and you'll want me to be nice to her."

I reach down and cup my hand, skimming it along the water. I don't splash him, but I threaten to, which makes him step aside and wobble on the rocks, arms pinwheeling for balance.

He snorts with a laugh. "You? Be nice? Never."

By the time I finish chiding Em for the hypothetical choosing of an unreasonable girl for the sole purpose of making my life a living hell, Weylan reaches the creek. He looks dapper for a Saturday afternoon in a gray suit, dark blue tie, and shoes that shine.

"I have a surprise for you." He looks proud of himself. "Come with me?"

I slog through the water and flop on the log to tie up my boots. "Where are we going?"

"If I told you, it would significantly shorten my enjoyment of the surprise."

"Fine," I say with a laugh. "I'll be right back, Em."

"It might be a while," Weylan says.

"Tomorrow morning then?" Emmett agrees with a hint of disdain.

Weylan holds out a hand and I take it, launching off the log and up the hill.

We stroll all the way up Main Street and turn left before we reach the church.

"Are we going to the old newspaper building?" I ask.

He says nothing, but gives me a sly little smile, the kind that lifts the corners of his heavy-lidded eyes and goes straight to my knees.

"What's the surprise? Just tell me," I plead. We don't walk around the back the way we did before. Instead, he walks me up to the big wood door set into the chamfered corner, and he leans against the frame. He pauses and smiles like he's savoring a moment, and something new flashes in his eyes. It's playful and childlike, tinged with a bit of worry, and for a moment that old urge to run flares within me again. I know it for what it is, though. My old fear. My old enemy. But I still decide I don't like surprises.

He pulls a key from his pocket and slips it into the lock. With a turn and a push, the door opens, and he grabs both my hands and pulls me inside, kicking the door shut behind us.

"You have a key. What is this?" Laughter arcs in my voice, and I glance around the room. Mid-day sun splashes across the floor through the small windows that rest along the roofline. It's just as we left it, the tin of ink on the counter, lanterns scattered about. The machine is there like an old friend, and it smells like wonderful memories.

"What did you do?" I ask, though I'm fairly certain I know the answer.

"I bought it," he exclaims. "Well, my father did. Bricks aren't what they used to be, and he had the money. God knows I'd be terrible at running that place. This is more to my liking. Mannix hunted down the old owner, and now it's mine."

I place a hand on his cheek. "Of course it is."

"It's everything I want. Almost."

The word *almost* echoes in the empty room. "When did this happen? When did you buy it?"

He pulls me deep into the room and leads me to the printing press.

"Today. This morning. Father signed the paperwork. It's my inheritance and his new business all rolled into one, but I get to run it. It's mine. Well, ours, if you'll let it be."

There it is again, that smile full of mischievous plans and adventurous dreams he wants to share with me. It fades, but only a little, as his own old fear sets in. It's the same look he gave me on his porch just before he realized I loved him but wished I didn't. But that's well behind us, and he's wrong this time. I drag him down for a kiss to prove it, and it shifts my worries a little but not entirely.

What will I do if he gets down on one knee? Run first and cry later? Everything is fine just the way it is, and I don't want it to change. I'm barely used to this new life, and sure, I think about forever every time fireworks go off between us, but I'm not ready for more yet. What if being married and starting a family leaves no more time for justice?

"I don't know anyone smarter than you," he says. "I can't think of anyone I'd rather run a newspaper with. You'll be brilliant at it. What do you say?"

He creeps closer, inching me back against the press in the most delightful way. I draw in a deep breath of him. Leather and wood and ink.

He traces my jaw and tips my chin, and he draws me in for a kiss that spirals down deep until it curls my toes and makes my knees crumble. One hand on my lower back holds me up, thankfully, and the other traces my ribs in a way that makes me arch into him, and there it is again, that free-falling feeling of diving off a cliff and landing in a pool of sweet honey. He returns me to earth gently, leaving me breathless.

"We can take down Pritchard from here," he says.

I stroke the lapel of his wool jacket. He looks handsome in anything, but he looks years older in a suit.

"We can influence Harrison's campaign," he says. "Find the evidence that links Pritchard and Whitaker, find proof they're poisoning the people downriver. We can print all their crimes and sins and distribute them to the people. And we can help the suffragists at the same time."

"That sounds delicious," I say.

"I want to go on this caper with you. What do you say, Charlie? It might not be easy." He lets me go, and walks to the far wall, leaning against it like a man assessing his new empire. I grab the edge of the press for support. A newspaper. A whole newspaper that we can run together.

"Who needs easy?"

"It will be a lot of hard work," he says.

I nod and cross the concrete floor that leads from the press to him. I lean next to him against the wall, looking out at the future we could make together, and he leans to the side until his shoulder rests against mine.

"We could make a lot of memories here. A lot of change," he says.

I like the way the sun traces his profile. It makes him look ethereal. Both of us have aged over the last few months, and I feel closer to eighty than eighteen some days, but there are many more years ahead of us than behind. The feeling of being settled is new to me, and I think I could get used to it.

"I agree. We'll make a lot of memories, but more importantly," I say, "we can make a home."

This book is entirely a work of fiction. It's true that coal processing has sickened people and caused death. Anyone who's seen the teal-green waters in Northeastern Pennsylvania knows there are places where fish can't live, but the details are fictionalized for the story. The locations, however, are inspired by real places. The inspiration for Stoke can be found at Eckley Miners' Village in Luzerne County, PA. The inspiration for North East is a town by the same name located in Maryland, at the top of the Chesapeake Bay.

Maryland was one of three states that had public orphanages in 1900, but in the states where there weren't such facilities, wards would be placed in private institutions, mostly funded by individuals and communities that lacked taxpayer funds. These systems were financed and administered by wealthy patrons with educators or religious leaders who were paid to run them. But orphanages of any type were overcrowded, and some in Maryland were restricted to only full and half-orphan children. Older children like Charlotte and Emmett were often treated like indentured servants in a private home or business, working at a trade to earn their keep. Though Charlotte and Emmett's situation is fictionalized for our dystopian purposes, that is the fate they would have faced if the opportunity to live at Finn and Regina's hadn't come along.

It isn't uncommon for historical fiction to take some liberties for the sake of making things work, and that is true here as well. Geographic distances, in this case, were shortened or stretched, and waterways were altered. The poisoned creek and river here are not directly linked to a coal village. They start just north, in Pennsylvania, but far from coal country. The school is real, as was the general store. Leta's house is fictional, though the market exists. Finn and Regina's house is fictionalized. The house that inspired

Weylan's exists, but on a different street. And the newspaper office is located where the fire hall sits. There's never been a printing press there, as far as I know, but to soothe any curiosity, Weylan operated a Hoe's rotary press.

The high school is also real. Some surrounding towns already had high schools prior to 1898, when North East's school was established. It opened in 1900, was rebuilt, and reopened in 1906. Younger students studied on the first floor, high school on the second.

And, yes, there are herring in the waterways. The habitats for Alewife and Blueback Herring span the east coast of North America, and both are most abundant in the area of the Chesapeake Bay. During spawning season, they travel north up the bay and settle in the rivers and tributaries like those in North East. They spawn and leave their juveniles behind to feed on zooplankton through the summer. Herring are protected now, thankfully, as their spawning areas are diminished by destruction of habitat, dams, and fishing, but they were once a primary part of life there. The people of North East were once called Herring Snatchers.

I'm glad you made it this far, and if you'd like to know more and you find yourself on I-95 in northern Maryland, it isn't hard to visit. After you stop for lunch and shopping, follow the road south to the town park. The gazebo is there, though it didn't exist until nearly a century later. And there is a museum, as well, where you can discover a lovely collection of net-tying shuttles. The net tying implement is more often known as a netting needle, but I changed the name to shuttle to aid readers in visualizing it and to distinguish it from the needle Charlie sews with.

Thank you for going on this journey. Charlie can't wait to see you again in book two.

ACKNOWLEDGMENTS

I would like to acknowledge the extraordinary impact on my writing made by the wise words of Cheryl Murphy Lowrance and the friendship of Shelly Campbell and Al Hess. Not only do they cheer me on, but they wince and laugh with me as I fumble along, trying to make solid things from ether. Fumbling is where the magic happens, and I'm so honored you've been there to experience it with me. I've learned more from you than I can express.

Extra special thanks to Jennifer Babineau, whose skill made this shine. To Shelly Campbell, who took my vague idea for a cover and turned it into stunning art. To Donna Sullivan, whose kindness is a light. And to Barbara Schneider, who is eternally encouraging.

Thanks to Alicia Anderson, Sage Baird, Michéle Callart, Cassie Greutman, and Daniel Roberts for their insights. Charlotte owes much to all of you. And thanks to that middle school writing teacher who taught me that spite is a marvelous motivator. And I am eternally grateful for the spirit and kindness of my local writing group for the friendship and encouragement.

Special thanks to my parents who raised me in one of the most beautiful places the world has to offer.

Above all, thank you to Matthew. He doesn't read books but knows all of mine by heart, because he hears me talk about them endlessly. And every day he proves that he's been listening.

ABOUT THE AUTHOR

A Maryland native and Pennsylvanian at heart, Jennifer M. Lane holds a bachelor's degree in philosophy from Barton College and a master's in liberal arts with a focus on museum studies from the University of Delaware, where she wrote her thesis on the material culture of roadside memorials. She resides with her partner Matt and a tuxedo cat named Penny.

Receive free prequel stories, news about upcoming releases and more by signing up for the author newsletter at

jennifermlanewrites.com

OTHER WORKS BY THE AUTHOR INCLUDE

Of Metal and Earth
Stick Figures from Rockport
and
the six-book series
The Collected Stories of Ramsbolt